Murder
in York

ALSO BY J. R. ELLIS

Murder in York

Prologue

The ancient City of York was founded in 71 C.E. by the Romans, under the name Eboracum. Emperor Severus declared it the capital of the province of Britannia Inferior. Emperor Constantius I died in York in 306 C.E., and his son Constantine the Great was proclaimed emperor by the troops in the fortress. The original wooden walls of Eboracum were rebuilt in stone, and the fortress grew to cover an area of 50 acres, accommodating 6000 soldiers. The site of the stone principia of the fortress lies underneath the foundations of York Minster. Excavations there have revealed Roman structures and columns.

It was a December afternoon not long before Christmas in the city of York. The day was dark with an overcast sky, the feeble daylight of the winter solstice season already fading. This gloom was counterbalanced by the bright lights and decorations of Christmas celebrations. There was a sense of excitement in the narrow medieval streets, in the warm, brightly lit shops, cafés and pubs, and in the busy Christmas market in Parliament Street and St Sampson's Square, where a large illuminated Christmas tree rose up into the early evening sky.

There was no such excitement for Henry Marlow, though. He was largely indifferent to his surroundings, having little appreciation of beauty or sense of place. Instead, he glanced out of the window of his office, which overlooked the River Ouse. It had been raining very heavily over the past few days, and the water was dangerously high. Properties by the river which regularly flooded, such as the famous Kings Arms pub, were already inundated at their lower levels. The river was devoid of boats due to the fast currents and low clearance of bridge arches.

Marlow turned back to his work and gazed at the figures on his screen. For him, life was about acquisition and money. He ran a development company, Marlow Holdings, which owned a large portfolio of properties – from offices to terraced houses and flats rented out to the people of York and beyond.

Marlow was a thin man with a pinched, hatchet face and cold eyes. He had fought his way up from a poor background, starting as an estate agent's clerk before he began to first rent and later buy run-down clubs and semi-derelict houses that no one else wanted. He had a reputation for being ruthless and miserly. He had considered moving to a bigger city, but he was York born and bred. On top of that, he preferred to be a big fish in his familiar small pool. His headquarters remained in York although his business interests ranged much wider than the ancient city.

There was a knock at his door and his PA Anthea Marston came in. She was a tough woman in her early forties with a conservative style of dress – mainly dark blue trouser suits and crisp white shirts. She knew how to deal with her boss, who could be quite abrupt and had little sense of humour. Their interaction was always concise. Marlow had no time for chat.

'Three messages, Mr Marlow.'

'Go on.' Marlow didn't look up from the screen.

'The first is from Crisis Help at Christmas. They came to the door asking for a donation. I took a leaflet and said I would ask you about it.'

'No, thank you. I'm already paying enough in tax, a lot of which is wasted helping feckless people who've got themselves into a mess. Next.'

'Mr and Mrs Braithwaite of twelve Rowntree Mansions in Deepwood. The husband rang to say that as you have refused to do anything about the damp and mould in the flat, they are reporting you to the council.'

Marlow laughed derisively. 'They're not capable of doing that. They must have been helped by that Roof thing – that housing organisation. They're a bunch of interfering do-gooders. Anyway, the best of luck with it. It'll take the council months to even send anybody to have a look at the flat. And then maybe a few years while they mess around trying to make me spend money on the place and threaten to take me to court. What do they expect anyway for the rent they're paying? A palace?'

'They have a little girl who has asthma, don't they?'

Marlow waved this away. 'Last message.'

Anthea glared at her boss, and for a moment there was something that looked like a deep contempt and revulsion in her eyes, but her voice remained very controlled.

'A Mr Donald Hutchinson rang, about that property in Butcher Lane off Stonegate. He's very interested in buying and wants to meet you there tonight at six o'clock. He said his phone had given out and he was in a call box with not much cash, so I said you would be probably there at six. He said he would turn up and wait for a while, and if you couldn't make it that was fine.'

Marlow raised his eyebrows. Now this was something that interested him. The property in question was not much more than a glorified outhouse that had once been part of a larger dwelling going back to Tudor times. It was sited in one of the narrow snickelways in the ancient city centre – the warren of narrow alleys and backstreets. Because it was in a conservation area, there were restrictions on what modifications could be done to the structure. Marlow hated regulations like this. He'd been sitting on the property for years, as with many of his acquisitions, waiting for someone to make an offer that would enable him to make a big profit. He smiled at the news someone wanted to view the property; there was always some gullible idiot who would part with their money if you waited long enough. But not that many for properties like this, so he knew he'd better follow this up.

'Fine, I'll be there.'

'And so the future of policing will belong to those who are prepared to question the paradigms – people who I will call the paradigm pioneers – those who are willing and courageous enough to think outside the box and soar into the blue sky of new ideas.' The speaker's tone was preacher-like in its sombreness and intensity. He opened his arms and smiled beatifically at the audience. 'I'm sure that will be all of you people here today,' he finished, as if expecting some kind of mass conversion after such inspiring words. The applause was, however, perfunctory as he reached the end of his so-called motivational talk and sat down.

Detective Chief Inspector Jim Oldroyd closed his eyes and took a deep breath. Next to him, Detective Chief Superintendent Tom Walker had an intensely sour expression on his face, as if he was chewing on an underripe lemon. Further down the row, Oldroyd could see heads drooping and some people definitely asleep.

'Good God!' whispered Walker.

The two senior detectives, from West Riding Police in Harrogate, were in a hotel in York where they were attending a residential conference entitled, 'The Future of Policing: Developing a New Paradigm'. This was the second and final day, and the end could not come quickly enough for either of them.

The conference had been organised by Matthew Watkins, the trendy and ambitious chief constable of West Riding Police, and he had required Oldroyd and Walker to attend. They were there with senior officers from other police forces around the country. It was a huge feather in Watkins' cap to have organised this and he was strutting around and beaming at everyone. He clearly hoped that the current home secretary would be taking note. Oldroyd noticed Walker's grinding jaw; the man clearly would have done anything to wipe the smile from Watkins' face.

The content of the conference had been predictable: motivational speakers bouncing around the stage and making tired jokes; presentations laced with management jargon, some delivered by people who had never been in a police force; 'break-out' groups where people were asked to discuss topics such as: 'How Do You Respond to Change?' and 'What Are Your Limiting Beliefs?' It was a lot of sloganised cod psychology and philosophy, all of which bored Oldroyd and infuriated Walker. The only consolation was that the food in the hotel turned out to be quite good. That evening, as they ate dinner together, Walker was unusually quiet, occasionally shaking his head; it was as if his outrage had gone beyond words.

'What's happening tonight then, Tom? Do you fancy anything on the evening's agenda?' asked Oldroyd. In private, Oldroyd and his boss were on first-name terms. They'd worked with each other for many years, and shared a pride in their Yorkshire identity. They both had a no-nonsense, practical attitude to policing, which they felt was very much at odds with the content of this conference.

Each evening there were voluntary sessions on diet, exercise and meditation, dubbed 'self-improvement groups'. Oldroyd admittedly had found some of these quite interesting, if a little oversimplified. His partner Deborah, a psychotherapist, had persuaded him over the years that the maintenance of his health and well-being was a top priority. On the other hand, Walker was still contemptuous of the whole affair.

'I think it's yoga and tai chi or something?' Walker said. 'Not for me, Jim. If I got down on the floor I'd never be able to get up again.'

'That's the point, isn't it, Tom? Once you do something like yoga, you *will* be able to get up and down because your joints will be supple.'

'Aye, maybe,' replied Walker, eating a piece of steak and kidney pie, but he didn't sound very convinced.

Oldroyd smiled and looked out of the window. The sky was dark but there were Christmassy, coloured lights everywhere, and people walking up and down. It was very inviting and he wanted to go out and explore the old centre.

'I'll tell you what, Tom,' Oldroyd said. 'Why don't we go on one of those ghost tours? There are lots of them here in York. I know you don't believe in such stuff, but it'll be fun, you know. What an atmosphere there'll be in those medieval streets!' Oldroyd had always been fascinated to learn esoteric information about wherever he was; something that also came in useful during a number of his more unusual cases. 'We could have a look at the Christmas market too. I'm told it's very lively.'

Walker shook his head. 'Nice idea, Jim, but I'm tired out after all we've had to endure today. I'm going to go and sit in that lounge and have a whisky. Then I'll get to bed early. One more damn session tomorrow morning and then we're off home, thank goodness.' He shook his head again. 'You know, sometimes I don't know how much more of this I can take. Maybe I should retire.'

'Don't do that, Tom – we need you to protect us from all the daft stuff that people like Watkins come up with.'

Walker liked this and his mood improved. 'Aye, maybe,' he laughed. 'I'll certainly do my best. Anyway, you get off on your ghost tour, if you fancy it.'

'OK,' Oldroyd said. 'There's one that starts at eight o'clock down by the river. I think I've just got time to get there . . . if I leave soon and don't have any pudding.'

'Well, you'll be missing a treat. I notice that there's blackberry and apple crumble tonight – my favourite.'

Oldroyd laughed. 'Oh dear, never mind. I've eaten too much already in the last few days. It won't do me any harm to miss one dessert.'

∼

It was turning cold when Henry Marlow finally left his office. He walked through the festive streets, past the lively bars and restaurants. Inside, people were laughing, eating and drinking. Some of the bars were full and people were spilling out on to the streets. It was quite a raucous scene in places, but Marlow passed by with complete indifference.

As he walked past Riverstone's bookshop, he saw a display of festive fiction, including *A Christmas Carol* by Charles Dickens. This caused his normally grim expression to crack into a twisted smile – he'd always thought of himself as a Scrooge-like character. Despite what people said, the man actually had the right idea. Money was reliable and useful, unlike most people, in Marlow's experience. And so Marlow lived alone, like Scrooge, and his main aim in life was to make money. Christmas was 'humbug' to him too:

he had no family, and was estranged from his wife. He had actually been very fond of her, even if he never admitted it. The fact was that Janice reminded him of the first woman he had loved, a long time ago – a woman whom he'd lost, so the break-up had made him even more curmudgeonly and cynical about people. Nowadays, he lived comparatively frugally and eschewed fun of all types. He felt little empathy for people generally, but especially for those who wouldn't pay their rent or who complained about things; they were mostly malingerers or people who had squandered their money.

As he passed through the narrow, winding streets, there were – sadly, as in all British cities – distinctly Dickensian scenes of wealth and poverty side by side. In contrast to the revellers enjoying themselves in the warm glow inside the bars and restaurants, homeless people were laid in cold shop doorways, clad in dirty clothes, some with small boxes asking for donations.

But Marlow walked past them all and gave nothing. His family had been poor when he was young, but his father had always worked while his mother kept a decent home. In Marlow's view, people were lazy now and expected handouts. They needed to get a job and stop begging. The Victorians had it right; he would actually be in favour of reintroducing the workhouse to get these people off the streets. In fact, he had the very property ideal for the purpose, and York Council, that incompetent bunch of spendthrifts, could rent it from him. His thin face formed into an even nastier smile at the prospect of this scheme.

On one street corner, a bunch of dogged people were braving the cold to fundraise for a homeless charity.

'Help the homeless at Christmas!' called out one of them as he rattled his donation can. Marlow sneered as he walked past. People were always trying to get your money from you.

He reached the network of narrow medieval streets near the minster and headed down the wide, pedestrianised Stonegate, and then off down a dark alleyway towards the property he had for sale. He looked at his watch. Those damn ghost tour people would be around before too long on one of their dreadful pantomime-like displays. He'd have to get this meeting completed as soon as possible before they put the client off the purchase altogether. He approached the door, and realised there was no one there yet. He fumbled with his keys and switched on a torch. An evening like this wasn't the best time to view a property, but at least the darkness would cover the many deficiencies of this building. A barely visible cat brushed against his legs. He kicked it out; it meowed and ran off.

He waited by the door for Mr Hutchinson to arrive.

Sometime later, a dark figure flitted spectre-like down the snickelway and back out into busy Stonegate, where it disappeared among the groups of people on their way to the Christmas market.

~

Oldroyd, dressed in an overcoat and scarf, walked through the streets with a spring in his step. He was glad to escape from Walker for a while. He had a lot of respect for his boss, but his persistent moroseness in the last couple of days had become very wearing. He had never heard Walker talk about retiring before. It made him think a bit – none of them were getting any younger, and he knew things couldn't stay the same forever. One day, he knew, the younger generation would have to take the reins.

He reached Precentor's Court and Minster Yard, trying to turn his mind to more positive thoughts. The magnificent, illuminated medieval minster rose up into the dark sky. Oldroyd always felt tremendous pride when he saw this building, especially the Great West Window with its fourteenth-century curvilinear tracery, affectionately known as the Heart of Yorkshire. It was all quiet now, but Oldroyd remembered some wonderful Christmas Eves when he and his family had attended the carol service, which rivalled the one at King's College Chapel in Cambridge. Maybe this year he would attend again.

He turned down Minster Gates, on to Stonegate, Coney Street, then down to the meeting place by the river for the start of the ghost tour. There was a slight mist over the water – it had been a dry day but the water was still creeping slowly up over the stone embankment. It would often last for a while – the wide and deep River Ouse took all the water down from the hilly, wet areas of the Dales, from the rivers Swale, Nidd and Ure.

There were already a number of people gathered by a lamp-post, and he assumed they were others waiting for the tour to start. After a short while, a tall figure appeared as though from nowhere, wearing a long black cape and hat on top of long hair. He immediately launched into a melodramatic delivery, which Oldroyd suspected he would keep up throughout the tour.

'Ladies and gentlemen, prepare to walk through the most ghost-ridden city in Britain, if not the world. We're going to see some of the most haunted buildings in the country and hear about some of the most terrifying ghosts.' He wafted his cloak around, and shot piercing looks at the group, some of whom laughed as he did so. 'Be warned! This is not for the faint hearted!' he declaimed – and so on. Oldroyd loved the melodrama, as – judging by their reactions – the others in the group did too. 'We will be going down a number of narrow alleyways – also called snickets or ginnels. Sometimes in York we call them snickelways. So, stay together and make sure no one is pulled by ghostly arms from one of these dark snickelways into a creepy house!' There was some grim laughter at this.

The guide then led them away from the riverside and up a road to the first stopping point at one of the many old pubs in the city. This particular tavern, he informed them, had associations with the outlaw Dick Turpin, who was hanged in York. His body was later taken to the cellar of this pub, where it was stolen by body snatchers and later re-buried in quicklime. The ghost of Turpin and the sound of his horse, so the guide claimed, could often be heard nearby. Oldroyd looked around the dimly lit street and back down towards the black water of the river and could actually imagine that happening. There was no doubt that the darkness of December was the most potent time for ghost stories.

The guide moved the group on to more eerie sites, including Coppergate – where Jorvik, the Viking city of York, was excavated in the late 1970s. He claimed that when Viking remains were dug up, spirits were disturbed and there had been hauntings reported in local shops ever since.

In Bedern, an area near the minster, a man called Pimm had run a school and workhouse for poor and orphaned children. He neglected them so badly that many died. Pimm buried a few but stored others in cupboards in his school. It is thought that the spirits of the children haunted Pimm, and drove him to drink and madness. He was eventually taken to an asylum. 'The children can still be seen and heard today,' said the guide in hushed tones. 'There are little faces at the windows. Sometimes a shadow is seen, an invisible hand felt on the shoulder, or a giggle heard from just behind.'

Oldroyd and the rest of the group were very engaged, and entered into the spirit of the evening. The tour was great fun but also rather chilling. After hearing those stories, no one wanted to be in the narrow streets or behind the old churches by themselves at night!

Oldroyd was thoroughly enjoying himself as they went past a pub that the guide claimed was the most haunted in York, with as many as fifteen spectres seen at different times. At this point, another ghost tour passed by with a similarly dressed guide.

Oldroyd wondered if they'd been told that a different pub was the most haunted in the city!

The guide led Oldroyd's group down a curving snickelway off Stonegate with tall, rickety buildings on either side. Oldroyd saw an ancient sign: 'Butcher Lane'. The guide stopped, gathered them together and began his next story.

'As we left the main street, you probably noticed the sign for this one. It was here that butchers slaughtered animals in their dozens every day. Sometimes this snickelway ran with blood and . . .' His voice trailed off uncertainly. He stopped and looked hard at a doorway behind the group. 'Sorry, ladies and gentlemen, I'm just surprised to see that door over there open. It's always been closed in all the years I've been coming to this spot. I'm sure the building is unoccupied. Maybe a ghost is coming to join us—'

'Just a moment, please,' said Oldroyd tersely. He'd seen a pool by the door, which was starting to trickle on to the path, and his instincts told him that things were not right. He went through the doorway, and immediately found a body in a dark room. The man was sprawled on the cold floor, surrounded by another dark pool of what was surely blood. One of the ghost tour participants who had followed Oldroyd through the doorway also saw the body – and screamed.

Whether or not the man's ghost would haunt this place in the future, and his story become part of a ghost tour, was impossible to say. But he certainly was dead.

One

After the Romans left, York became an Anglian settlement and the first minster was built of wood. The city was known as Eoforwic and became an important royal centre for the Northumbrian kings. In 866 C.E., York was conquered by a large force of Danish Vikings who established the Kingdom of Jorvik, which lasted nearly a century until the last Viking, Eric Bloodaxe, was expelled and the kingdom became part of an Anglo-Saxon state. Wulfstan, a famous scholar in this period, became Archbishop of York.

As the evening passed, it became chillier in Butcher Lane – the snickelway where Oldroyd had discovered the body – and a cold drizzle started to fall. After the gruesome discovery, he had quickly contacted the emergency services, then brought the ghost tour to a conclusion, announcing that he was a police officer and producing his warrant card. He asked the tour party and their stunned guide – a local man called Gary Owen – if they had seen anything or anyone suspicious as they entered the snickelway, but none of them had, other than the pool of blood. Once Oldroyd was satisfied with their statements, they dispersed looking grim-faced. The thrills and fun had evaporated; real murder was a different proposition from interesting and thrilling stories.

Now, a couple of hours later, the streets were much quieter. The snickelway had been cordoned off and police constables were guarding the entrances. It appeared that the building where the body had been found was once a small dwelling place at some point and also, ironically, a slaughterhouse. The interior had been empty, though now was illuminated by the portable floodlights that allowed the SOCOs in protective clothing to do their work.

As a forensic pathologist was examining the body, Inspector Anne Hopkins – from the York force – sheltered under the arch at the entrance to the alleyway as she spoke to Oldroyd. She was a tall, keen-eyed blond woman in her mid-forties who seemed like an older version of Detective Sergeant Stephanie Johnson, from the Harrogate force, who regularly worked with Oldroyd alongside her partner – sometimes professionally, but also romantically – DS Andy Carter.

'What brings you to York then, sir?' asked Anne. 'You didn't come all this way just for a ghost tour, did you?' She flashed him a mischievous smile that reminded him very much of what Steph might do in a similar situation.

Oldroyd explained that he was attending the conference for senior officers and had left the hotel for a walk and some light relief. Anne pulled a face. 'Right, I don't blame you, sir. Rather you than me at a conference like that. But then you go and find a body. Isn't that just like a detective?'

Oldroyd laughed. 'Indeed it is, and it's happened to me before. Do you have any idea who the victim is?'

'Yes, it's a man called Henry Marlow. He's quite notorious around here as a rogue landlord and property developer – treats his tenants really badly, won't do any maintenance in his crumbling flats and houses. He's sailed very close to the wind more than once

14

on his property deals; you know, things like concealing faults with buildings, stuff like that. But he's very clever, gets good legal advice. The council authorities are desperate to be able to call us in to arrest him but there's never sufficient grounds.'

'Sounds like it's not really a surprise that he's been done in, then?' Oldroyd said.

'No. I would think the problem might be which of the many people with a motive actually did it.'

'I see.' Oldroyd looked around the scene. This murder had the makings of a very interesting case and he couldn't resist thinking about how he could become involved in the investigation himself. As he had discovered the body, maybe it was meant to be. He felt a duty to be involved.

One of the SOCOs came to speak to Anne. 'We've bagged up all his belongings, ma'am – standard stuff: wallet, keys, coins. A torch was lying near the body. If he was going to look round the property, he would have needed it – there's no electricity.'

'OK, thanks.'

Oldroyd turned to Anne. 'You know, having found the body I already feel a part of this case and I would love to be able to help you investigate it. How would the senior people here in York feel about that? And how would you feel?'

Anne looked surprised and pleased. 'I'd be delighted, sir. We're perpetually short staffed here in York, so I'm sure my superintendent would welcome it too. It's more a question of whether Harrogate would release you.'

Oldroyd knew that Walker was always eager for his officers to assist other forces, provided that he could spare them. It gave kudos to the Harrogate station and showed Matthew Watkins that Walker had a good team of detectives which was the envy of other forces.

'Well, I'll speak to my superintendent – he's here in York too for the conference – but I'm sure he'll be agreeable. He might also release one of the two detective sergeants who work with me regularly. Would you be happy with that? Of course, you would remain in charge of the investigation.'

'It's all fine with me, sir. I'm not territorial – the more help we get the better. It will leave me with less work to do.' Her eyes twinkled again. Oldroyd liked her sense of humour.

A forensic pathologist, Dr Eve Redgrave, came over to speak to the inspector. Anne introduced her to Oldroyd. They shook hands.

'Oh, you're famous, aren't you?' Dr Redgrave said. 'I've seen you on television.'

Oldroyd laughed. 'Yes, but I must say that my appearances on television are not as enjoyable as those of an actor in some popular drama. I've usually got some grim news to impart, and I'm generally under great stress.'

'Yes, I can imagine,' said Dr Redgrave. 'Anyway, this case seems fairly straightforward from my point of view – cause of death was most likely a stab wound to the back with a knife which went through the ribs and penetrated the heart. He's been dead about three hours. I'll be able to confirm everything when I get him back to the lab. No sign of the weapon, but it was unusual.'

'Unusual, how?' asked Oldroyd.

'Well, it was wider than something like a kitchen knife and I would say probably heavier – a thicker blade. Not a weapon easy to conceal.'

'Right.'

'OK, thanks, Eve,' said Anne as Dr Redgrave packed up her bags and left.

'You two have obviously worked together before,' observed Oldroyd.

'Yes, she's always very helpful.'

'It's good to get on well with the regular forensic person,' said Oldroyd, thinking about his own long association with Tim Groves, the forensic pathologist with whom he often worked back in Harrogate. 'They can provide interesting detail about a crime, which can be a great help.'

'I agree.'

'OK, well, I'll talk to DCS Walker tomorrow morning and get back to you. I'll try to get some sleep first – it's gone midnight.'

'Good idea, sir.'

~

Early next morning, Oldroyd rang his partner Deborah to tell her about the body he'd discovered on the ghost tour. Deborah worked mainly from their home in New Bridge, a village near Harrogate.

'Good Lord, Jim! Can't say I'm surprised, though. Things like this are always happening to you, aren't they? There's never a dull moment,' she said, in her typical bantering.

'Well, as I always say, I did warn you about what you were taking on when we got together,' joked Oldroyd.

'I suppose so,' replied Deborah, with a teasing sigh. 'So, I take it you'll be working in York for a while?'

'Yes, I'm going to be part of the investigation and I'm getting Andy Carter to come over too.'

'It sounds exciting. And I assume it got you out of the final bit of the conference. I'm sure you were devastated.'

Oldroyd laughed.

'But don't forget,' Deborah continued, 'Louise and Patrick are coming up tonight, so don't be too late back.' Louise was Oldroyd's daughter, who worked in London, and Patrick was her Irish boyfriend.

'I won't, don't worry. I'm looking forward to seeing them. Bye for now. I'll have to go and tell Tom Walker what's happened. He won't believe it either.'

～

The chief superintendent was just tucking into his bacon and eggs when Oldroyd joined him at the table.

'Have you packed up then, Jim? One more stupid presentation and then we're off. Oh, how was it last night?' He glanced at Oldroyd. 'You look tired. Did you go on to a nightclub after the ghost thing?'

Oldroyd laughed at that prospect, and then told Walker what had happened. His boss put down his knife and fork, shaking his head.

'And you found the body? Are you sure it wasn't a stunt by the people who do these ghost tours? You know, to add to the drama?'

'I'm afraid not, Tom. It was real blood, alright.' A waiter came over, and Oldroyd ordered some scrambled eggs on sourdough. Once the waiter was out of earshot, he continued. 'Now the thing is, the inspector who attended the scene told me that they're a little short staffed here in York. So, I was wondering if you'd be agreeable to me helping out a bit.'

As he expected, Walker liked the idea. 'Well, why not? Miss all the rubbish this morning and get on with it. Do you want Carter or Johnson to come over? I like it when Harrogate shows how damned good we are. It shows that twerp, Watkins, what a great staff he has that he doesn't appreciate. That we're better at solving crimes than sitting around all day at these stupid conferences.' He was full of indignation and stabbed the air with his knife.

Oldroyd smiled. Walker's response was exactly as he had predicted; his enthusiasm returning as soon as he was talking about the practicalities of real policing.

Walker continued cutting up his bacon for a moment, before chewing on a piece. Then he laughed and put his knife and fork down. 'Imagine, he organises this stupid carry on in York . . . but while we're here, we actually thumb our noses at him by doing some proper work and solving a murder. I like it! I'll get on to Malcolm Hainsworth – he's the chief super at York, good bloke – he'll welcome some help in these days of cuts. He's not here wasting his time at this farce, of course. More bloody sense. I hear the chief constable of East Yorkshire Police has a lot more about him than Watkins, probably told all his staff to steer clear.' He laughed again. 'I don't think there's anybody here from East Yorkshire. Watkins won't like being snubbed like that.'

Oldroyd listened to this, and a little more. He usually found a way of excusing himself when Walker began one of his rants against Watkins. But this morning he felt he owed it to the old boy to hear him out. And, as usual, he agreed with most of what Walker had to say.

∿

It was a quiet morning at Harrogate police station. Detective Sergeant Andy Carter sat back in his chair, put his arms behind his head and looked across the room to where his partner Detective Sergeant Stephanie Johnson was working. Andy grimaced. It was getting near to Christmas and he was facing the usual problem: he'd done no shopping and still had no idea what to buy Steph. She helped him choose things for his mother, his sister and her kids, but he was on his own with Steph herself. Maybe he should just ask her what she wanted, but somehow that felt like a cop out. It would be much better if he could think of something. Maybe an experience of some kind. He'd recently been on a stag do that involved axe throwing, but Steph had said that would remind her of one of the gruesome cases they'd encountered.

Still thinking about what he could do, he rummaged in the desk drawer until he found his secret stash of chocolate digestives. As he enjoyed his second biscuit, an idea came to him . . . Didn't she once say that she'd like to try paddleboarding?

His phone rang, breaking his train of thought. It was his boss, Detective Chief Inspector Oldroyd.

'Good morning, Andy. Are you busy today?' It was an unexpected question delivered in Oldroyd's typically jaunty tone.

'Oh, good morning, sir.' He put the third biscuit back in the packet, making sure that Steph didn't see him. Both he and Oldroyd were banned from eating biscuits because of their weight issues. 'Er . . . no, not particularly. How's the conference going?'

'Just about over, thank goodness. But something else has happened over here.' He told Andy about the discovery of Marlow's body, and explained that he was going to take part in the investigation. 'And to do that properly, I will need the help of one of my trusty lieutenants. I assume Steph is still working on that arson case with Inspector Wood, so I'd like you to get over here as soon as you can.'

His boss sounded quite excited, and Andy was delighted that he'd been asked to join the investigation in York. There was nothing he liked better than working with DCI Oldroyd. The inspector's cases were always interesting, usually with a mystery to solve. When Andy finally put the phone down, he saw Steph looking at him.

'You lucky sod,' she said. 'That was the boss, wasn't it? And you're going over to help him in York.'

Andy smiled. 'That's right.'

'Well, spare a thought for us back here. This case I'm working on is going nowhere.' She looked around and then whispered, 'Inspector Wood is OK but he's so dull! He has a model railway in his attic. I'm sick of hearing about it. Yesterday we were in the car and I got a full description of this new engine his wife is going to get him for Christmas – I pity her. A Coronation Scot, or something with streamlining on, whatever that is. I wouldn't mind, but he never bothers to find out what I'm into.'

'So-*rry*,' replied Andy, in a taunting sing-song voice.

Grinning, Steph stuck out her tongue. 'OK, well, seeing as the shops are good in York, you could do some Christmas shopping while you're over there. I'll make you a list.'

Andy's face fell. He believed that domestic chores should be shared equally, but he often found Steph's lists of shopping or jobs a bit too demanding.

'I don't know whether I'll have the time,' he said, trying to nip the idea in the bud.

Steph cocked her head to one side. 'Oh, really? The boss is never as demanding as all that. I'm sure you'll get a bit of time off – especially if I tell him how important it is because I'm so busy here.'

'You wouldn't do that – it's unprofessional. You can't ask him to let me go shopping.'

'Oh, can't I? You forget that I've known him for a long time – ever since I came to work here straight from school. I'm one of his protégés. He's proud of me and the progress I've made over the years. He wouldn't refuse me a little request like that.'

Andy frowned. 'Fine, but don't say anything. It'll be too embarrassing. I'll do the shopping, no problem.'

'Very good, that's more like it. Anyway, it will be very helpful to you. The list will include something you can think about getting me for Christmas. I know you'll be struggling to think of anything. As usual.' She gave him a sarcastic smile.

'Right,' said Andy, feeling completely outwitted.

∿

Wycombe Road in the Deepwood area, just out of the centre of York and away from the picturesque old city centre beloved by tourists, contained many neglected blocks of flats. Some of these were owned by Henry Marlow, including the ironically named Rowntree Mansions. This was a 1960s flat-roofed block of small dwellings. It was very shabby on the outside, the old wooden window frames were rotting and the plaster rendering was peeling off. It was unworthy of being named after the great York family of philanthropists.

Terry and Ailsa Braithwaite lived at number twelve, with their six-year-old son Sam and two-year-old daughter Rosie. Terry worked as a taxi driver, while Ailsa had a part-time job in a supermarket. They found it very difficult to make ends meet – made harder by the fact that Rosie suffered from bad asthma, and their flat was constantly damp, with mould on the walls.

It was a dark, cold morning. Ailsa had taken Sam to school and was wheeling Rosie back in her pushchair. The little girl sometimes lacked the energy to walk. As they arrived home, Ailsa was surprised to see Terry's car pull up. He'd gone out to work at six o'clock that morning. He was a stocky man of medium height and always wore a baseball cap. He got out of the car, waved, and called to her with a smile on his face.

'He's dead!'

'Who?'

'Marlow! Pete's just rung me. They found him dead in one of his manky old properties. Pete thinks he was stabbed. Do you wonder? There will be a lot of people celebrating tonight. I wouldn't like to be the police trying to find who killed that bastard.'

'Dead? Oh God! But what will happen to us and the flat now?'

Terry shrugged. 'There'll be a lot of legal stuff to get through, but hopefully we'll get a better landlord. They could hardly be worse, could they?'

'No,' agreed Ailsa.

'Anyway, I have to get back to work. I just had to tell you. See you later. Things will get better, you'll see.' He gave her a kiss, got back into his car and drove off.

Ailsa entered the flat and got Rosie out of the pushchair. The little girl had a bit of a coughing fit and Ailsa went to get the inhaler. She looked around the walls and the ceiling, at the damp marks and the places where water sometimes streamed down in the cold weather. They'd had to get rid of a carpet on which fungi had started to grow. She knew that it was having an effect on Rosie's health, and it was a terrible worry. It would be wonderful if whoever took over the flats would put some money into renovating them. They'd thought about leaving, but there was nothing available they could afford that was suitable for a family with young children.

As Rosie watched some cartoons, her mother made a cup of coffee. She felt uncomfortable at being glad that somebody had died, but they'd felt like prisoners of that terrible man. Terry had absolutely detested Marlow, and he could be quite short tempered. When they'd first got together, he'd been prone to getting into fights and had been cautioned by the police. She'd made it a condition of their relationship that he wouldn't express his anger in this way any more, and as far as she knew the fights had stopped and he'd started slamming his fist into furniture instead. As she drank her coffee, there was something nagging at her mind. Last night Terry had been out working. Had he also been involved in something else?

~

In another of the narrow snickelways in the centre of York, known as Ouse Passage, was an old building – the Roman Hall, the origins of which dated back to very early times. It was shabby and rickety now but it had been a wealthy merchant's house in the eighteenth century and was clearly marked on maps of the time. Since then it had gone into decline, and some alterations over the centuries had not been sympathetic to its age. It now presented a mishmash of styles, and lacked any kind of architectural integrity.

Roman Hall housed a small museum about Roman York. Coins, fragments of statues and other artifacts from the period sat alongside detailed, illustrated information boards on how the Romans came to York, how they lived, what structures they built, and the importance of Eboracum as a strategic fortress. There were displays about Roman soldiers and what their lives had been like, and yet more about the generals and emperors who visited. The centrepiece of the collection was a large and detailed diorama of Roman York, which was contained in a glass case. It had been constructed by a wealthy local historian over many years before being donated to the museum.

Philip Storey – a thin, balding, bespectacled man in his fifties – had been curator of the Roman Hall Museum for many years. The museum represented his life's work. He was a History graduate from the University of York, specialising in the history of Roman Britain. He had never married and had spent much of his work life in the sometimes dusty and arid world of museums and their collections, though he had a social life through the arts – in particular music

24

and theatre. Sometimes he took part in amateur dramatics. The Roman Hall Museum was his pride and joy. It had been financed by some small legacies, and was run by a board of three trustees. Despite not being a major tourist attraction, it managed to keep going, partly because Philip was only paid a small salary, and he had only one part-time voluntary assistant who helped with some of the admin.

Winter was not the best time for the museum, both in terms of business and in terms of working there. The building was difficult to keep warm with its antiquated and inefficient heating system. The number of tourists in the city was smaller, and during the darker months fewer penetrated the maze of streets and snickelways to find Ouse Passage and the museum, especially when the more famous tourist attractions were easier to find. On this dark December morning, no visitors had yet arrived. Philip was walking up and down the ground floor, trying to get warm, when Brian Lacey – his volunteer assistant, and a retired History teacher – arrived.

'Good morning, Brian,' Philip said, coughing into his gloved hand. Maybe he had the beginnings of a cold.

Brian looked rather animated. 'Morning, Philip. Have you heard the local news?'

Philip didn't listen to local radio. 'No, I haven't. What's happened?'

'It's Marlow.'

'Marlow, our landlord?' The museum didn't own the building in which it was housed. It was leased from Marlow's company.

'Yes.'

'What about him?'

'He's been found dead in an alley off Stonegate – murdered, I think, though they didn't give much detail.'

'Really? Good grief!'

25

'Yes . . . Mind you, are you really surprised? He wasn't the most popular man around here. I've heard some awful stories about how he treats his poor housing tenants.'

Philip sat down in his seat behind the ticket counter at the entrance. He took a deep breath. 'Yes, I've heard the like too.'

'Do you think it will affect us?' asked Brian.

Philip shrugged. 'I don't know. It's bound to in some way. It depends on who inherits his properties. He was married but separated from his wife, I think. I don't know what will happen.'

'Didn't he come here to talk to you recently?'

'Yes, he did. Nothing important, though. I wouldn't worry. I'm absolutely committed to keeping this museum going, and one way or another we will.'

'Good, I know how much it means to you, Philip. I'm certainly with you and I'm sure the board will be fully supportive, even if we have to move. Surely the city couldn't allow this place to close? It might be small, but it's part of the tourism offer.'

'Absolutely! And an important part of the city's heritage. So, let's not be too pessimistic. There may not be a problem.' He looked at the door and saw that there was someone waiting. 'Anyway, it seems we have a punter so I'd better open up.' As Brian went into the tiny office behind the reception area, Philip glanced after him before he unlocked the door and frowned. The death of Marlow was of greater significance than he'd implied.

Another person who heard the news of Henry Marlow's death on the local media that morning was Janice Marlow, his estranged wife. She was in her apartment in a converted warehouse, overlooking the city of York. She was wearing expensive second-hand casual clothes that she'd picked up in charity shops and online: a cashmere jumper from the Oxfam shop in Ilkley, and a pair of retro Sweaty Betty jogging pants from Vinted. Gone were the days when she'd thought nothing of shopping in Hobbs and Jigsaw. She already knew her husband was dead, having been visited by a police officer in the early morning.

She was sitting by the window in the dark of the early morning, smoking a cigarette and feeling rather depressed. She didn't have a job. She'd always survived on the earnings of whoever she was married to. She was old school, and thought a man should support his wife. However, she could barely manage on the meagre allowance that her husband had given her, which was a situation that she could not have tolerated for much longer. Unfortunately, very much against his character, Henry retained a fondness for her and didn't want to get a divorce. She would have had to wait until they'd been separated for five years.

Her marriage to Henry had been very unsatisfactory although she had, admittedly, not had high expectations. It was her third marriage and she was over forty. She had a son and daughter from her first marriage who seemed to constantly need her support, and bailing them out meant that she was perpetually short of cash.

She had thought that marrying the wealthy property owner – somewhat older than her – would be a shrewd move, but hadn't considered just how suffocatingly tedious it would be to live with a man who did nothing and went nowhere. Henry just stayed at home in his crumbling house on the outskirts of York and worked on his accounts. He may as well have sat in a Victorian counting house, piling up his gold sovereigns. Every Christmas he would joke that Scrooge had the right idea, but Janice was never quite sure it really was a joke. She enjoyed a comfortable life but she also liked a good time and had hoped for more than what Henry offered. In the end, she had decided to leave him before she went mad with boredom. She stubbed out her cigarette and sighed. What was wrong with her? She had recently begun to examine herself and her behaviour. Three failed marriages, now . . . But what did she expect if money was always her motive?

She lit another cigarette and switched on the radio for the local news just in time to hear the announcement of her husband's death. The cigarette nearly dropped from her fingers. It was a shock to hear Henry's death stated on the radio. 'Good God!' she exclaimed. She switched the radio off, sat for a moment and then reached for the phone. It was time she told someone before they found out from the media.

'Justin . . . I'm glad you're up – have you heard the news? It's Henry, he's bloody dead . . . Yes, I can't believe it! I was told early this morning, a police officer came round. He was very nice. They want to search everywhere, of course, so I gave him my key to Bishopthorpe Manor. They'll have fun going through that rabbit warren of a place. Anthea will see them in the office. But, Justin, it's just been on the radio. The police are saying he was murdered . . . I know, murdered! Well, to be frank it could have been lots of people, he wasn't very popular in this city – too much of a grasping skinflint. I don't know what I ever saw in him— What do you mean, money? Oh, yes, very funny. Well, I suppose I should be due some now— Yes, tonight . . . I still want to come. OK, see you there at half six.'

The call ended. She leaned back in the chair and closed her eyes as she tried to absorb the shock of her husband's death and work out what she felt about it. She had, despite the things she'd said, been quite fond of Henry but her feelings for him were really no deeper than that. And not a basis for marriage.

She could see the sun coming up over the river from out of her window. It could herald the dawn of a new phase of her life, with her new partner. She'd met Justin, a divorced local businessman, just before she left Henry, and they would now be able to get married.

She liked the married status as it gave you greater rights over money and property should the relationship break down. She was very pragmatic about such things and, in her experience, relationships didn't last forever. Maybe this time it would be different because now she should be a wealthy woman in her own right, with what she would inherit from Henry, so not dependent on Justin. Then she shook her head. There she was again, thinking about money and financial security. No wonder her relationships didn't last. She was glad that she was meeting Justin tonight. She needed to talk to him. She was determined that this time it was going to be different.

Her mind went back to Henry's murder. The detectives investigating would want to interview her, and she knew that she would be a suspect. She would be ready for them.

The police station in York was just out of the old city centre. Inspector Anne Hopkins set up an incident room there. It was a pleasant space with views over York, including the minster in the distance. There were comfortable chairs, a table and a whiteboard where photographs and diagrams could be attached and drawn. Anne found visual material helpful and she had already placed a photograph of Henry Marlow in the centre, then drawn a line from him to his estranged wife. This was as far as she had got when she was joined by Oldroyd and Andy. Oldroyd introduced his detective sergeant, and Anne looked appreciatively at the handsome young detective as they shook hands. The two Harrogate detectives sat down and were joined by two detective constables who were going to work on the case: Kate Warren and Liam Jefferson.

'Well, sir, everything's clear at this end,' she said. 'Chief Superintendent Hainsworth nearly bit my hand off when I offered him the possibility of help from yourself and an officer from Harrogate.'

'Good!' Oldroyd beamed. 'DCS Walker was also pleased with the idea. He likes it when we help out other forces. He thinks it makes us look good especially when we solve the case!'

Anne laughed. 'Great, then we're all set to go. There have been things in the media about the discovery of the body.' She looked cheekily at Oldroyd. 'Maybe someone on that ghost tour has spoken to journalists.'

Oldroyd laughed. 'Well, I can assure you it wasn't me, Anne. Anyway, tell us what we know so far then.'

Anne sat at her computer and turned to the whiteboard. 'Well, we haven't got much on this board yet. The only person we have clearly identified so far who had a motive to kill Marlow is his estranged wife, Janice. It seems that she was his only family – there's no record of siblings or children, and his parents are long dead. As I said to you, Marlow was notorious in the city. There will be a long list of angry tenants, people who think they have been cheated by Marlow in property deals, maybe campaigners on housing issues, and so on. I think it's true to say he was a hate figure for anyone concerned with housing. So, it would be sensible for us to start with people he's encountered recently. It's more likely that one of them has finally had enough, rather than someone from the past suddenly deciding to bump him off now. Though, of course, that is not impossible.'

'I agree,' said Oldroyd. 'I assume you're getting your team to identify these people. It could be a long process. In cases like this, the suspects can even broaden out into the relatives of tenants – parents who think their sons and daughters were badly treated. We're not sure yet, are we, that this murder was planned? It could be someone who came to confront Marlow about something, then a fight developed. Just because someone was carrying a knife doesn't mean that they necessarily meant to use it.'

'You're right, sir,' said Anne, 'but the fact that Doctor Redgrave thought the knife was rather unusual in shape and size suggests some purpose in carrying it. We're contacting the local authority and housing charities to see what's been happening, see if we can pick up anything about recent conflicts or threats. There is a person we need to speak to urgently who might possess some valuable information: his PA.' Anne looked at her screen. 'A woman called Anthea Marston. How do you feel about going to interview her while I speak to his wife?' She turned to Andy. 'I want you to go with some of my team out to Marlow's house in Bishopthorpe, see what you can find there.'

'Ma'am,' said Andy.

'Sounds like a good plan to me,' said Oldroyd.

'OK, here's the address of his office – it's quite near to the river. Of course, Ms Marston may have already heard about his death and won't turn up today. I don't know whether anyone else works there at the moment.'

'I'll go and see what I can find.' He nodded at the whiteboard. 'I suspect it won't be long before that's covered with pictures of suspects and lines leading to Henry Marlow.' He turned to Andy. 'It's a bit of a TBWDI.'

Andy laughed. 'A what, sir?' Oldroyd was famous for his tongue-in-cheek murder case acronyms, although some of them were easier to guess at than others; Andy suspected that he made some of them up on the spot.

'They Bloody Well Deserved It – applied to cases where we don't have much sympathy with the victim.' Oldroyd smiled archly.

'I think you're right, sir,' said Anne. 'It's just that his unpopularity makes our job harder.'

◇

The Deepwood district of York was a very different place to the medieval centre and the streets of large Georgian and Victorian houses just outside it. There was considerable deprivation and some poor-quality housing. An organisation called Roof maintained an office there, in a small room attached to the community centre. The office had three work stations crammed into the main space. There was another tiny room, which had once been a store cupboard, where they could talk privately to clients.

Three people worked there, led by Saskia Middleton – a dark-haired woman of about thirty, who had studied Housing and Social Welfare at university, then gained experience in various housing projects around the country until she was selected to lead Roof. Saskia was an energetic, determined woman who would stand up for the clients and knew no fear when tackling powerful landlords.

She sat at a desk in a thick woolly jumper as well as a scarf and cord trousers; the building was rather cold in winter. She was dealing with the enormous number of requests for help coming through. December was a difficult time for struggling families who had housing issues; the dark and cold of the winter season were setting in, which made conditions in damp, badly heated homes more severe. And Christmas, which should be a happy time of celebration, could be a nightmare for struggling families with young children, especially those who were unhoused and living in hostels or cheap hotels. Saskia found the situation very challenging, especially as Roof's resources were limited. They had some money from the government and from the council and they accepted some private donations. Despite their best efforts, they were often unable to help people as much as they would like.

Linda Black – another member of the team – entered, brandishing her phone, and looking animated. 'Have you heard the news? I've just had a call from a mate of mine. That bastard's dead!'

Saskia looked up; she found listening to the news too depressing. 'Who?' she asked.

'Marlow, the demon landlord! Someone's done the world a favour and bumped him off. He's been found dead in one of his run-down properties. Do you wonder? That miser must have acquired more enemies than Ivan the Terrible.'

Saskia sat back in her chair. 'Bloody hell! Where did it happen?'

'In the city centre, down one of those snickelways. Angus said he heard that someone on a ghost tour found the body.' Linda laughed. 'Maybe he was done in by the ghost of one of his victims. And I'll tell you what, I'll bet he'll never rest. His evil spirit will be haunting the place and a terrible ghost it'll be too. Good news for the ghost tour people.'

Saskia shook her head. She found Linda's triumphal attitude a bit hard to take in the context of murder, but there was no doubt that Marlow's removal would make things much easier for many of their clients. There had been a constant stream of complaints from people about him – his hard, unfeeling attitude, his neglect and refusal to pay for repairs. Whoever inherited his properties could scarcely be a worse landlord, although Saskia knew there could be other consequences in the short term.

'I expect we'll get a visit from the police at some point,' she said.

'Why? What've we got to do with it?'

'They'll be following up all the leads on people who might have had a grudge against Marlow. We're a good source of information about people who had conflicts with him and reasons to wish him harm.'

This seemed to deflate Linda, who spoke more quietly when she asked, 'You don't think they'll suspect us, do you? We've had few run-ins with him ourselves.'

'Us?' Saskia laughed. 'I don't think so. People who work for organisations like this don't usually go around murdering people, do they, even if they make enemies. There are lots of people around who have much more personal reasons to want him out of the way.'

'Yes,' replied Linda. 'You're right, the police will want to speak to us.' She frowned. 'The old bugger's still going to cause us problems from beyond the grave.'

Oldroyd walked through the streets of the old city to the riverside address, accompanied by DC Evans from the York station. The route took them past the hotel where the conference had taken place. It was now clearly coming to an end as he recognised people leaving the hotel with bags – unless they were skiving off the final sessions. He certainly wasn't sad that he'd missed the last part, and knew Walker would be delighted that it was over, and perhaps jealous that Oldroyd had got himself involved in a real investigation.

When they arrived at Marlow's office, Anthea Marston welcomed them and explained that she'd been expecting a visit from the police – she'd heard about the death of Marlow on the local news. She offered Oldroyd and Evans coffee, which they accepted. They sat down in a couple of easy chairs, while Anthea remained behind her desk. Oldroyd looked around at the shabby space with its battered office furniture and worn carpets. It didn't seem like the office of a well-to-do property owner.

'I see that your employer wasn't too bothered about having a smart office. I understand he was a wealthy man?'

'He was, but you would scarcely have known it. "Tight-fisted" is what people would say, I think.'

'I don't know exactly what they said on the radio, but Mr Marlow was found dead in one of his properties in Butcher Lane, off Stonegate. He was killed sometime between six and seven in the evening. Do you know anything about his movements yesterday?'

'Yes, I do. A man calling himself Donald Hutchinson rang in the afternoon – said he was interested in buying that property, and asked to meet Mr Marlow there at six o'clock.'

Oldroyd sat up. This meant that the murder was very likely to have been premeditated.

'I see,' he said. 'Did he say anything else about himself? How old would you say he was? Did he have any kind of accent?'

'He didn't give any details. I would say he sounded middle-aged – difficult to be more precise. His accent was Scottish.'

DC Evans was making notes on the key points of the interview and he wrote this down.

'Scottish? OK, well, it would seem that it's very likely that was the murderer you spoke to, or at least someone involved in killing your employer.'

'Yes,' replied Anthea laconically.

Oldroyd looked at her. She seemed to be reacting to Marlow's death with a certain equanimity. Neither her words nor her facial expression conveyed anything about how she was feeling. 'How would you describe your relationship with your employer?' he asked.

She frowned. '"Transactional" is the word I would use. Henry Marlow was not a pleasant man, Chief Inspector, but he paid a decent wage and didn't micromanage me. A job is a job, isn't it? My husband is disabled and can't work, so money isn't plentiful – we take what we can get.'

'So, you admit that you didn't like him?'

'I didn't have to like him. It wasn't necessary for me to do my job.'

'But what was it about him that you didn't like?' pursued Oldroyd.

Anthea shrugged. 'Personally, I didn't care what he did with his money – that was his own affair. But I didn't approve of the way he treated some of his tenants who were often very poor and in bad health, including children.'

'Did you argue about it with him?'

'No. Sometimes I gently reminded him about something if I felt it was his legal responsibility, but it wasn't really my business and I didn't want to lose my job. Actually, there was an example yesterday afternoon. There's a Mr and Mrs Braithwaite – they live in Rowntree Mansions and they have a little girl with asthma. Mr Marlow refused to do anything about the fact that their flat has mould. Mr Marlow was out when the husband rang, who sounded very angry and said he was going to report it to the council. I told Mr Marlow but he just scoffed at it.' She shrugged her shoulders, implying that there was nothing more she could do.

Oldroyd looked at her very closely. 'You say you need the job . . . but nevertheless, it must have been difficult to work for a man whose behaviour you found irksome.'

Anthea returned Oldroyd's look. 'We all make our accommodations when needs must, don't we?'

She's a cool customer, thought Oldroyd.

'We understand that Marlow had a number of conflicts with his clients and tenants,' said Oldroyd, changing tack. 'Do you know of any threats made against him?'

'I saw some angry letters that people had written, and I heard Mr Marlow arguing with people on the phone, but I'm not aware of any physical threats being made. People said they would report him to the council or take him to court, and he had a lot of verbal abuse, but I don't remember any threats to his life or anything like that.'

'OK, so what I'm going to need you to do is provide a list of all Marlow's clients and tenants. I want you to highlight the ones who you know had serious conflicts with your employer. This includes anyone he had dealings with – house or flat tenants, people who leased commercial properties. Could you also list people who you were aware of who opposed Marlow or argued with him – you know, maybe campaigners on housing issues, or anybody else? Please send the list to this email address. The card also contains my number.'

Anthea nodded but didn't say anything as she accepted his card.

'And please try to do this as soon as you can. This is clearly a case that is going to have numerous suspects, and we need to get on with investigating them and narrowing the field down.'

Anthea nodded again. 'I'll get on with it straight away.' She looked around the office. 'I don't really know what else I'm supposed to do here now. Mr Marlow ran the business entirely by himself apart from me. He had no business partners. I've no idea who's going to take over things now he's gone. I suspect it may go to his estranged wife, but I don't think she will be interested in running it. I expect she'll sell it.'

'Maybe,' said Oldroyd. 'I'm afraid I can't help you with that one. You'll have to wait to see what's in the will. You mentioned his wife – what do you know about their relationship?'

She shrugged. 'Nothing. Mr Marlow rarely talked about his private life. But he did tell me they were separated. I got the impression he was sad about it, even if he would never admit to such a thing.'

'I see.' Oldroyd stood up. 'I'll leave you to get on with that list, but I must just lastly ask you where you were yesterday between five-thirty and seven-thirty.'

Anthea raised her eyebrows. 'Am I a suspect, Chief Inspector?'

'Not a serious one at the moment. But you have expressed some animosity towards your employer, so we have to eliminate you from the investigation.'

'I left here at five o'clock and went straight home. I arrived at about five-thirty and remained there for the rest of the evening. My husband can confirm this.'

'Did anyone else see you?'

'No.'

'OK, well, an officer will come round to your house to speak to your husband, and to take a statement from you about the phone call from Donald Hutchinson. Thank you. If you can just give me the address of the man who rang about mould in the flat, I'll be on my way.'

When Anthea had given him the address and showed the two detectives out, she returned to her desk. For the first time that morning, she smiled. She was sure that the police didn't really suspect her. That might be different had she revealed her true feelings about Marlow, and told them about other things – which she had no intention of doing. She went over to Marlow's desk, opened a drawer and pulled out a bottle of brandy and a glass. He had kept this for an occasional drink with a business associate. It was a cold morning and there was cause for celebration: two good reasons for pouring herself a generous measure. She took a drink of the deep amber liquid; it was warm and satisfying.

Anne Hopkins drove with a young DC, Kate Warren, over the Ouse Bridge and glanced over at the regularly flooded Kings Arms pub, which stood very near the water's edge. As the river rose, could it be threatened yet again? Hopefully not in the Christmas season. She turned left on to Skeldergate, which went behind the blocks of apartments that overlooked the Ouse, and parked up.

'Wow, it's posh here, ma'am!' said Kate, who had grown up in one of the poorer parts of York.

'Yes, it shows how well you do even when you're separated from a big property owner.' She rang the buzzer of Janice Marlow's residence and explained who she was.

'Come in, I've been expecting you,' was the reply and the lock buzzed as it opened.

The communal areas of the apartment block were very plush and well maintained. Anne and DC Warren took the lift to the fourth floor and Anne knocked on the door.

'Come in,' Janice called. 'It's open.'

The detectives entered a rather dimly lit corridor.

'In here,' came a call. Anne went through a door into an expensively furnished sitting room with thick pile carpets. Janice was sitting in an armchair by a window overlooking the river. She had a wan expression. 'Please sit down,' she said. 'Can I offer you a drink?'

Anne and Kate sat down as Anne expressed their condolences. Both detectives declined a drink. 'This has obviously come as a terrible shock to you,' began Anne in a kindly voice.

'It has,' said Janice, shaking her head. 'Even though we were separated, I retained some affection for my husband. I hoped that one day we could be reconciled. Hearing about his death has been a blow.'

'I have to ask you, what caused the breakdown in your relationship with your husband?'

Janice sighed as she considered how to answer the question. After a few moments, she finally spoke. 'It wasn't anything to do with infidelity, Inspector. Henry and I had too much respect for each other. It was just that we discovered that we didn't really have the same interests in life. Henry wasn't what you might call a socially active person, although he was always very fond of me. I longed for a bit of excitement – so I left him.' She took a deep breath. 'I felt it was time for us both to move on. We stayed on good terms.'

'When did you last see your husband?' asked Anne.

'It was several weeks ago. We occasionally met for dinner . . . you know, to keep in touch? He didn't seem to be in a very good mood, as if he was worried about something.'

'Do you have any idea about what that might have been?'

'No, I don't, but Henry did have a lot of enemies. He used to talk to me about difficult people that he had to deal with.'

'Were there any in particular? Maybe someone who threatened him?'

Janice waved her hand. 'Oh, I don't remember any details. I never got involved in Henry's business, but I know he wasn't popular for some reason.'

'So, he never spoke to you about fearing for his life or anything like that?'

'No, I would have been worried. And I would have remembered that.'

'I presume your husband amassed a great deal of wealth through his property dealings. He must have done to have been able to purchase Bishopthorpe Manor.'

'Yes, but as I said, I never had anything to do with that part of his life. I must tell you, Inspector, Bishopthorpe Manor is one of the dullest places imaginable. It's not exactly stuffed with exotic and expensive treasures, and it's hardly appointed to the highest levels of comfort. Living there was one of the things about our marriage that I found . . . difficult.' Anne sensed she had paused before the end, carefully choosing a word which did not create the impression that she had clearly been at the end of her tether.

Anne was careful not to look at Janice with the suspicion she felt.

'I understand that you have two children from a previous marriage?' she continued.

'Yes. Alex and Penny. They're both in London.'

'And what do they do?'

Janice looked at Anne. 'Is this relevant, Inspector? I can't see that my children have got anything to do with this.'

Anne was firm. 'I need to get the whole picture of you and your relationships, as you are the wife of the victim.'

Janice frowned. 'Well, Penny works for a publisher, and Alex is in the City doing something in finance.'

'And are they doing well?'

'They're still quite young, so they struggle a bit with the cost of living and housing down there, but they survive.'

And I'll bet they come to you as the wife of a wealthy man for help, thought Anne.

'Another thing I have to ask you – have you entered another relationship since you left Henry?'

Janice became quite angry. 'Really, Inspector, I think that's my own business.'

'All this is relevant to the case, so just answer the question, please.'

For a moment it looked as if Janice might refuse to say anything more. She looked down at the plush carpet and was tight lipped. Then she said, 'I'm friendly with a man called Justin Hayward. He runs a business selling upmarket kitchens.'

'Has he met your husband? How do they feel about each other?'

'No, he's never met Henry . . . and we never talk about him. I don't think that will come as a surprise,' Janice replied with some sarcasm.

Anne paused for a moment. 'I take it that you expect to inherit the business, the house and other assets from your husband, unless he had other relatives to whom he might have left something?'

'I'll spare you the effort of finding out for yourself,' said Janice, again in a rather hostile tone. 'Henry had no family other than me and I don't think he had any close friends, so, yes, I expect that I will inherit his estate.'

Anne returned the cold stare with one of her own. 'Did your husband threaten to change his will after you left him?'

'No, Inspector. Who would he have left his estate to? I didn't kill him for it. Which is what I think you are driving at with this line of questioning.'

'Everyone connected with your husband is a suspect until we have eliminated them, including you, I'm afraid,' Anne said. 'So, finally, where were you between five-thirty and eight o'clock last night?'

Janice looked at her triumphantly. 'I was here all evening. Daphne, a friend of mine, came round and we watched a film.'

'OK. You'll need to provide us with her details so that she can verify your alibi. Please give the details to DC Warren and also the contact details for Mr Hayward. Thank you.'

Janice frowned at Anne but gave the DC the details.

'OK,' said Anne as she got up. 'We'll leave it there. I'll send an officer round to take a statement from you, so I must ask you stay here in York during the investigation.'

'That's no problem,' replied Janice. 'There's going to be a lot to do. I will have to arrange the funeral and everything, so I'm going to be around.'

Once they got outside the building, Anne turned to DC Warren. 'What did you make of her?'

'I wasn't sure what she really thought about her husband, ma'am.'

'No, it was hard to tell. But as she's going to inherit all the money and the business, she's definitely a suspect – and so is that new boyfriend of hers.'

As Anne drove back, she reflected that the encounter with Janice Marlow had not revealed very much, except that, for now, she remained a suspect. Just how many suspects might they end up with?

The case was also bothering her on a personal level. Christmas was rapidly approaching, but the investigation was intense, and the work was piling up. How would she ever have any time to undertake her own preparations for the festive period?

∼

Andy sat in the back seat of a police car driven by DC Liam Jefferson, along with DC Fletcher – also from the York station – sitting in the passenger's seat, to the old village of Bishopthorpe on the outskirts of York. The roads were wet and some of the dull fields near to the river were flooded. It was only lunchtime, but the heavy sky and low light made it feel as if the day was about to end.

As they were driving through the village, Andy caught a glimpse of a Gothic revival gatehouse entrance to an elaborate palace by the River Ouse. He turned to DC Jefferson.

'Wow, that's some pile! Who lives there?'

'It's where the archbishops of York live, sarge – Bishopthorpe Palace.'

'Palace! Bloody hell! Well, they say the church has plenty of money, and it must have. They knew how to live when they built those places, didn't they?'

'They did, sarge, but it wasn't the same for everybody, was it?'

'No. I suppose they built it out here so that they were some distance from the poor in York.'

Passing through the pretty village, they saw the sign for Bishopthorpe Manor and turned up a short gravel drive. The home of Henry Marlow was not in the same league as the palace of the same name, but it was a sizeable mid-nineteenth-century brick country house in a couple of acres of ground. They parked outside the front door and got out. The place was quiet and deserted. Andy looked around. The shrubbery and lawns of the gardens were maintained in a functional manner and not by someone with a love of gardening. The house itself was faded and shabby; there were old wooden sash windows from which paint was peeling and some of the walls needed pointing. The flagstones on the paths were broken and uneven.

Andy was carrying some bags in which to place evidence, pairs of plastic gloves, and the key Janice had given to the officer who came to tell her about Marlow's death. He opened the door and they entered a cold, echoing reception hall. There was a musty smell in the room, which was constructed in the Victorian faux-medieval style with dark wooden panelling and a large open fireplace. The walls were covered with famous but clichéd paintings of nineteenth-century British landscape art: *The Monarch of the Glen*, *The Haywain*, *Salisbury Cathedral from Lower Marsh Close*. Light came only from high up in the stairwell of the heavy staircase, leading to the first floor.

Andy screwed up his eyes. 'Bloody hell, this is a gloomy old place!' he exclaimed. 'Who would want to live here? It reminds me of something in a Dickens novel we read at school. Are there any lights?'

Liam went to a panel of ancient metal switches. Some bulbs imitating candles came on in two medieval-style metal chandeliers. They didn't make much difference. The DC shivered, and not just from the cold.

'God, sarge, this is a classic haunted house, isn't it? I wouldn't want to stay here overnight.'

Andy laughed. 'Well, who would have thought the tough detective would be frightened of ghosts?'

'It was my gran, sarge. She lived out in the countryside north of Ripon. She and my grandad had worked a farm and then retired to this isolated cottage, and I used to go and stay with her in the school holidays. She was superstitious and told stories about ghosts and stuff like that. I used to lie in bed in the dark, scared to death of any noise outside – the wind moving twigs against the windows or owls hooting.'

Andy laughed again. 'Well, I'll hold your hand when we go up the stairs, just in case something leaps out to get you. I've got experience with this. DCI Oldroyd and I were once snowed in at Knaresborough. We had to spend all night in a supposedly haunted medieval church. We actually saw something – but it turned out to be somebody pretending to be a spectre.'

'God, that was brave of you, sarge. I'd tackle some dangerous criminals any day rather than stay the night in a haunted place.'

They were discussing where to start their examination of the house when they heard the sound of a car coming up the drive. Footsteps sounded across the stone flagstones by the door, then stopped abruptly – presumably when the person found that the door was unlocked. The door was slowly pushed open.

'Hello?' called a tentative voice.

'Come in, we're police officers,' called Liam.

'Oh.' A woman with her hair tied back walked in cautiously, holding yellow gloves and carrying a bucket. She looked around.

The detectives presented their warrant cards. 'I presume you are Mr Marlow's cleaner?'

'Yes. Melanie Jackson.' She looked at the detectives. 'What's going on? Is everything OK?'

Andy and Jefferson exchanged glances.

'You've obviously not heard,' said Andy, and he explained how Marlow had been found murdered.

Melanie put her hand to her mouth. 'No! That's terrible. I didn't know. I don't listen to the news and . . . Oh my God! That's what Josie must have been calling me about. My phone was on silent and she left a message for me to ring her back. It must have been about this.' She shook her head.

'Not to worry,' continued Andy. 'I'm sorry it's come as such a shock. We're here to have a look round and see if there is any evidence concerning who might have murdered Mr Marlow. Just take a seat, will you?'

Melanie put down the bucket and sat on a large oak chair in the hall.

'How well did you know him?'

'I've been his cleaner for three years. I come in once a week for half a day. It's just the kitchen, living room, bathroom, his bedroom and a general vac round in the hall. I never touch the other rooms upstairs or his office.' She pointed to a door which led off the entrance hall.

'Was he a good employer?'

'He was always polite and paid a good wage, but he wasn't chatty. I don't feel I got to know him very well. But I didn't see him very much. He was usually either at his office in the city, or working in the one here.'

'You were around before he and his wife separated?'

'Yes.'

'How did you get on with her?'

Melanie frowned. 'I found her a bit snooty. It seemed like she enjoyed being lady of the manor and didn't talk to me much, just let me get on with things. I couldn't imagine her doing any cleaning. She'd think it was beneath her.'

'And what was their relationship like?'

She thought for a moment. 'To be honest, I got the impression that he was fonder of her than she was of him. He said nice things about her occasionally, but she never mentioned him.'

'Did you witness any rows?'

'I heard them arguing once or twice.'

46

'Any violence or threats?'

'No. They weren't getting on very well but I was still surprised when she left. I thought she enjoyed the lifestyle too much to give it up, though I don't think Mr Marlow did a lot, and I can see that she might have been bored.'

'Were you aware of any enemies he had? Did anyone ever come here to make threats against him?'

She shook her head. 'No. I know he had a bad reputation as a landlord but he was always fine with me. I felt quite sorry for him. I think he was lonely after his wife left.'

'When was the last time you saw him?'

'A week ago, here in the house.' Her expression was sad and suddenly she burst into tears.

'OK,' said Andy gently. 'We're going to look round and it won't be possible for you to do any cleaning. You could disturb some evidence.'

'Oh, right.' She dabbed her eyes with a tissue, then gazed around forlornly before picking up her bucket.

'You say that was his office?' said Andy, pointing to the door.

'Yes, he was in there most of the time.' She took a deep breath. 'I'll be off then. Bye.' Melanie, still carrying her bucket, walked back to the front door and left.

The three detectives put on gloves and entered the office, which was not much more than a gloomy little cubbyhole. It looked as if, once upon a time, it could have been a storeroom or something similar. Andy switched on the light. Everything was arranged very tidily. There were filing cabinets and a solid oak table with a desktop computer and screen all crushed together in the small space. The desk was clear.

DC Jefferson looked at the computer. 'This is a pretty old model, sarge. It was probably doing what he wanted it to do, and he didn't want to pay for an upgrade.'

'That's consistent with what we know so far about his character. Anyway, we'll need to take it all back to the tech team.'

As Liam unplugged the old computer and took it out to the car, Andy began to look in the desk drawers and the filing cabinets. There were reams of documents and sheets of figures relating to properties, sales and rents, and Andy bagged some of the more recent ones. If they didn't yield anything, he would send a team out to look around in more detail.

A quick search of the other rooms produced little of interest. There didn't appear to be anything personal – no diaries, keepsakes or mementos. Unless they were hidden somewhere. The only notable thing they found was a picture of Marlow's wife Janice – a framed photo on his bedside table.

Andy looked at the picture. Did this mean that he was still fond of her? What kind of a man was he? Just a miser sitting in his counting house, poring over his accounts like Scrooge in *A Christmas Carol*? Maybe this picture showed there was another side to him. But Andy could understand why Marlow's wife had left him if she had to spend most of her time in this unpleasant place. It would send him mad.

This visit had not yielded very much so far, but it had added a little to their knowledge of the relationship between Marlow and his wife. Andy looked forward to discussing this with Oldroyd and Inspector Hopkins.

∽

At Harrogate police station, Steph sat back in her chair, yawned, stretched her arms behind her head and sighed. She was looking at forensic reports concerning the serious fire at a local country pub near Harrogate, which she was investigating with the worthy

Inspector Wood. They already had a significant amount of evidence to suggest that the fire had been started deliberately by a disgruntled chef who had been sacked for stealing money, but Inspector Wood was extremely meticulous in pursuing other somewhat unlikely scenarios in order to make sure that they had the right person. It was all very correct but also somehow very tedious. Steph didn't like it when either Andy or DCI Oldroyd were working away. With both of them absent, it could get dull in the office.

Steph grimaced. She felt tired and lethargic. Maybe it was because she was bored, or maybe it was due to the lack of sunlight at this time of year. Was she starting to suffer from SAD? She'd never had the disorder before, so it seemed unlikely. But a number of people in the office were down with colds – she could have caught something from them, perhaps?

She took a short break and started jotting a few things down on her Christmas list. If she did get unwell, Andy would have to take more responsibility for the preparations. They were having Andy's mum up for Christmas and her mum and sister Lisa over on Boxing Day. December was passing quickly. Why was Christmas something for which you never felt properly prepared?

As if someone had read her thoughts, she heard a voice say, 'Hi, sarge. Are you writing your Christmas list? There's not long to go now, is there?'

Steph looked up into the smiling face of Sharon Warner, a young detective constable who Steph had mentored since she had joined the force a few years ago. Sharon had already gained a reputation as an outstanding researcher.

'Hi, Sharon. I was just thinking that myself. I—' She broke off and sneezed quite loudly.

'Bless you, sarge! I hope you haven't caught the cold that's going round.'

Steph shook her head. 'I don't feel all that good, if I'm honest. The trouble is a lot of people do get things at this time of year. I think it's the stress of getting ready for Christmas.'

'Yes, it's a lot of work – but I love Christmas though, don't you? It's such a nice time with all the family together.'

'Yes, though a lot of people seem to fall out over the festive period. And I don't think it's necessarily such a good time if you're single.' Realising what she'd said, Steph shook her head. She wasn't usually negative about things like this. 'Sorry, of course I didn't mean you. I'm a miserable so and so today, I just don't feel well.'

'That's OK, sarge. Take it easy. Don't make yourself ill for Christmas.' She smiled knowingly at Steph. 'You'll be missing Sergeant Carter. How's it going over in York?'

'I haven't heard anything yet, but he's not going to have all the fun and leave me with the work. He's going to get a big shopping list from me.'

'Good on you, sarge!' They both laughed and Sharon went back to work. Steph carried on with her list, which was actually more interesting than the reports from the arson case. Sharon was right: she was missing Andy, maybe because she was feeling run-down. She was looking forward to his report tonight of what was happening in the investigation in York, and she would take pleasure in handing over the Christmas shopping list. You had to delegate things and not try to do it all yourself.

'So, we've made a good start, and, as expected, there are a number of suspects.'

Anne Hopkins stood and looked at the board in the incident room where she had placed names and some pictures around a photograph of Henry Marlow. Board-marker lines and brief notes showed the connections.

'And that's only what we know so far on day one,' observed Oldroyd, who was sitting opposite Anne and next to Andy. DCs Warren and Jefferson were also in attendance. 'I suspect that once we start to look in more detail at all his properties and clients, more will surface. We've got the material that his PA Anthea Marston provided, and the stuff that was brought back from Marlow's house.'

'Yes, I've got a team working on all that. What did we make of the people we've interviewed?'

Oldroyd continued. 'Anthea Marston made no secret of her dislike for her employer, but I don't think that amounted to a motive to murder him. She has an alibi for last night which will need to be checked. She remains important because she knew more about Marlow's business than anyone other than Marlow himself. She admitted to seeing angry letters threatening to report him to the council, but denied being aware of any threats of violence. She gave the address of one family who have a dispute with him about mould in their flat.'

'If she was involved in his murder, sir, wouldn't she have talked up threats from other people in order to distract us from her?' asked Andy.

'Possibly,' replied Oldroyd. 'But that has to be done very subtly in order not to appear suspicious. She could be playing the role of a truthful and honest witness. She also took the call from the person who we assume was the murderer. She said it was a middle-aged man with a Scottish accent who called himself Donald Hutchinson. He expressed an interest in that property where Marlow was found dead. It was obviously a set up and I don't think the details of the caller take us very far. She could have invented it all, of course, or be in league with whoever it was.' He turned to Anne. 'What about the wife?'

She shrugged. 'She didn't seem to be heartbroken by her husband's death. She claimed they were still on good terms, and I couldn't see her going round to that snickelway in the dark by herself to stab Marlow. But she has a boyfriend, who we need to follow up on. He could have been pretending to be the mysterious Donald Hutchinson, I suppose. If Marlow had no other family, she will probably inherit his business and properties and they'll be very rich. They must have the strongest motive to get rid of Marlow. Whether they could be working together or by themselves, we don't know.'

Oldroyd turned to Andy. 'How did you get on at Marlow's house?'

'Well, sir, it's a crumbling old place – a bit spooky at this time of year. DC Jefferson here was a bit scared.'

'Oh dear,' said Oldroyd, as Jefferson laughed a little sheepishly.

'As you mentioned, we brought back a mass of documents and Marlow's computer, but there's more to come. It's going to take a while to work through it all. It seems like he's been a landlord for a long time.'

'If we focus on people involved with any recent conflicts,' said Anne, 'like the family with mould in their flat, hopefully we'll get a breakthrough without having to plough through the whole lot.'

Andy continued. 'While we were there, the cleaner arrived. She was able to tell us quite a bit about Marlow's habits and his relationship with his wife. Apparently they could be quite stormy at times but never violent. Interestingly, on Marlow's bedside table I found a photograph of Janice Marlow. I know the general view of him seems to be of a cold-hearted miser who only cared about money, but I wonder if he really was fond of his wife and missed her. If that was the case, and his wife knew it, she may have been confident that he hadn't changed his will to benefit anybody else, maybe as a way of luring her back to him.'

'She told us that she was going to be the beneficiary. I suppose this meant that she could go ahead and get rid of him, secure in the knowledge that she would inherit everything,' added Anne. 'I asked her if her husband had told her that he was intending to change his will following their separation, but she denied it.'

Anne paused to consider their progress so far. 'Well, we've made a good start, I think. And it's only day one.'

'Hear, hear,' said Oldroyd. He looked out of the window. It was only quarter past four but it was already dark. 'I think it's over to your team to analyse all that material and we'll follow some more leads tomorrow. I think we're going to find there are a lot of potential suspects when we have the full picture of his property dealings.' He turned to Anne. 'By the way, you seem to have successfully avoided the press so far.'

She smiled. 'You've spoken too soon, sir. I'm going to speak to them first thing tomorrow. It might be useful in bringing some more people forward who knew things about Marlow. But don't worry, I know how to handle the press.'

Oldroyd nodded and smiled to himself. I bet you do, he thought.

Two

In 1068, two years after the Norman conquest, the people of York rebelled against William the Conqueror. After putting down the rebellion, William built two castles on either side of the River Ouse. A Norman cathedral was completed by 1100 and this was later redesigned and expanded over the course of more than two hundred years into today's magnificent Gothic building. The original Roman walls were partly incorporated into the medieval walls that surrounded the entire city and survive today. In 1190, York Castle was the site of a terrible massacre of the local Jewish inhabitants when at least 150 died. King John granted the city its first charter in 1212 and it became a major trading centre with many countries in Europe.

When Oldroyd arrived home at his cottage in New Bridge, he found that his daughter Louise and her boyfriend Patrick had already arrived. They were staying up to and over Christmas, and then returning to London the day after Boxing Day. Patrick was a tall, soft-spoken Irishman with dark hair and a beard who worked for a publishing house in London. Louise now split her time between lecturing at university where she taught units in

Women and Gender Studies, and working at the women's refuge she'd helped to establish several years before.

Louise gave her father a big hug. 'Dad, it's great to see you. I couldn't wait to get up here and see the fells again. We're going straight out tomorrow to walk over to Almscliffe Crag. I miss Yorkshire so much.'

'Don't we all when we're away from it!' declared Oldroyd with a laugh. 'I suspect this man feels the same about Ireland.'

Patrick grinned. 'Well, I'm a city man, Jim, so it's not so much the countryside . . . but I do miss Dublin. It's really beautiful round here, though.'

'You have to say that to a Yorkshireman like me,' laughed Oldroyd, and he clapped Patrick on the back. He liked him and was glad that Louise had found such a nice partner. 'I'd love to come with you on the walk, but I'm working on a case in York at the moment.'

Deborah appeared from the kitchen wearing an apron. She gave him a hug. 'Ah, the wanderer returns. Just in time to eat – and wouldn't you just expect it?' She turned to Louise and Patrick with her hand on her hip. 'Can you believe it? He's supposed to be having time off from his detective work, goes to York to a conference, then an entertaining ghost tour, and suddenly – *bang*! He finds a body! It's amazing, isn't it?' She gave Oldroyd a playful punch. 'You seem to be a magnet for this stuff!'

'Maybe I am. We'd just got to this old snickelway, as they call them in York, and I noticed that a door into one of the old buildings was open and what looked like blood was trickling out.'

'Ugh!' exclaimed Louise.

'My first thought would have been that it was a prop for the ghost tour,' said Patrick.

'Well, that did cross my mind fleetingly,' replied Oldroyd. 'But it was a genuine corpse, alright, and he'd been murdered.'

'I can tell you, Patrick,' said Deborah, 'if it was Jim who was walking past, it would definitely be real blood. He can encounter murders and dead bodies without even trying.'

'Who was the victim?' asked Louise.

'A local rogue landlord and property speculator – not a popular man, by all accounts, so I don't think we're going to be short of suspects. There's an excellent DI from York in charge of the case, and Andy Carter is working with me, so I hope that we can get it all sorted out before Christmas.' He looked to Deborah. 'If we can't, don't worry, I will definitely take some time off.' Deborah gave him a mock frown, and he held up his hands. 'I promise,' he said, as she returned to the kitchen.

Louise shook her head and turned to Patrick. 'This is what it was like when I was growing up. Working over weekends, cancelled holidays, late to birthday parties.'

Oldroyd gave a rueful smile. 'I know. It was hard on your mum, especially when you and Robert were little. I'm not really surprised that she got tired of the marriage.'

Oldroyd had been separated from his wife Julia since Louise and her brother Robert were teenagers. They had divorced and she was now remarried to a colleague who worked with her at a sixth-form college in Leeds. 'There must have been some benefits of having a detective as your father,' he suggested.

'Oh, yes. We got a lot of status at school from you being famous and on the television and so on, and things were never boring. I think, looking back, that Robert felt the fact that often you were missing from our lives more than I did.'

Oldroyd looked thoughtful and rather sad. 'Yes, I think you're right.' Robert was an engineer and lived in Birmingham with his wife and two children. He'd never come back to his home area after being a student there. There were visits – he and Deborah were going down for the New Year – but he'd never been as close to Robert as he was to Louise, and didn't see as much of his grandchildren as he would have liked.

Patrick nodded. 'My dad was an executive in a graphic design company and he was away a lot when I was little. It was difficult and I missed him, but I always knew he cared about me because he always made time for us when he was at home. I think that's the thing: the quality of the time you do spend together. Some parents are there constantly, but still don't have a good relationship with their kids.'

'True,' replied Oldroyd. 'I think—' The conversation was suddenly interrupted.

'It's ready!' called Deborah.

They sat at the large oak dining table, where the centrepiece was a delicious vegetarian lasagne, and tucked in heartily, drinking wine. Oldroyd was the only meat-eater present, but he was quite happy to eat veggie food when it was as good as this. He had never been much of a cook himself, but Deborah enjoyed it, and he was very grateful for the fare she served.

'Going back to landlords,' said Louise. 'I know there are some excellent ones around, but many of the women who come to us at the refuge have been so badly treated and forced to live in terrible places: damp, cold, dangerous. They often just get evicted for no reason. Well, except that it maybe benefits the landlord financially.'

Oldroyd took a sip from his glass of red wine. 'Well, I think this character would definitely fall into the rogue landlord category. He seems like a regular Scrooge.' He laughed. 'But if he got visitations from the spirits like Scrooge gets in the story, they didn't seem to change him.'

'By the way,' said Louise, 'I know someone in York who works for a housing organisation – I think it's called Roof. Her name's Saskia Middleton. She's brilliant, really dynamic. She was on the MA course with me in London. She might well crop up in your investigation if she had any dealings with your murder victim or his tenants. I expect she would have done – Roof is really involved in advocacy for people and families who are struggling with poor landlords.'

'Thanks, love, I'll bear that in mind,' said Oldroyd, thinking that this may very well be a useful lead into finding out more about Marlow's activities. Also – and he didn't say this to Louise – someone at Roof might have felt sufficiently outraged by Marlow's activities that they were prepared to do him harm.

~

The ghost tour during which the body had been discovered was operated by a small company called Ebor Ghosts, based in a tiny office behind a shop in the old centre of the city. They offered a number of tours concentrated on different aspects of the city's history: Roman York, Viking York, etc. All these tours were well patronised as tourism in York continued to expand, but the ghost tour operated by Gary Owen was particularly popular. It was based around the core medieval streets, which always seemed rather spooky at night, even in the summer months.

Gary walked to the office in the cold early evening. He passed a number of homeless people, one of whom looked at him closely, but he was scarcely aware of them as he was still feeling rather shaken after the events of the previous night. He was hoping that his boss might tell him to take the evening off, but knew that was very unlikely.

Craig Jordan, Gary's boss, was a tough character in his fifties who had made a living over the years in various jobs from fairgrounds to – sometimes illegal – betting shops. He had gained a reputation as being something of an enforcer, and had even served time for assault. After this, he'd decided to go for something less rough and opted to run ghost tours, since it related to his background in entertainment. He had started leading the tours himself – he made an intimidating figure in a black Victorian frock coat, top hat and a silver-topped walking cane that he used to point out the various ghostly landmarks – and it wasn't long before the business expanded sufficiently to be able to employ other people to lead the tours. He drove a shiny red Jaguar and lived in a large Georgian house near the racecourse, so it seemed his new business dealings were financially very successful. Some people were puzzled and suspicious about this, wondering if ghost tours could really be so lucrative.

Craig was a smoker – so much so that whenever he was working, the office always stank of tobacco. He was sitting at a small table with a cigarette in his mouth when Gary came in and started coughing due to the smoke. Craig looked at him with contempt. He was powerfully built, with a bald head and the smashed-up face of a boxer, though the whites of his eyes had a yellowish tinge.

'What's the matter wi' you? Pull yourself together. T'public don't want folk coughing all over 'em.'

'Do you think there'll be many turning up tonight? It's freezing out there and after the murder it doesn't—'

'On the contrary,' Craig cut him off. 'They'll be out in force. There's nothing t'public like more than summat ghoulish they can gape at.'

'But we can't go down that snickelway again – the police have closed it.'

'Obviously, you dumbo. But you can take 'em near it and tell 'em what happened in juicy detail. Make sure you elaborate a bit, use your imagination. I've put a message on social media saying that a witness to last night's murder is leading t'tour tonight. They'll be rolling in.' He laughed as he stubbed out his cigarette.

59

Gary's heart sank, but there was no way out of it if he wanted to keep his job. And he needed the money. He took his coat off and started to put on his costume: black coat, cloak and hat, which had been hanging against the wall on a peg. Then he suddenly remembered something.

'You know who the victim was, don't you?' he said.

'I do, it wa' that miserly old sod Marlow. Whoever did it gave th'ole o' York a great Christmas present, if you ask me.'

'Well, wasn't he the one you've had trouble with? He tried to stop us taking the tour down that snickelway, didn't he?'

'Aye, he did. He owned that run-down little place where he was found dead. I imagine he was trying to flog it off or rent it out to somebody. What a dump! Whoever it was probably got fed up of the old bastard wasting their time and finished him off.' Craig roared with laughter. 'He said us going down there with tourists was too noisy and it "lowered the tone of the neighbourhood". I told him to get lost and so did t'council when he complained to them. T'council will never stop us – we help bring in too much tourist money.'

Gary thought for a moment. 'So now he's helping us, in a way. Because he can become one of the ghosts on the tour.'

Craig looked at him and laughed. 'Well, I suppose you could say that.' He glanced at the clock. 'Anyway, you'd better get off. T'crowds'll be waiting.' He laughed again and lit another cigarette.

Without another word, Gary left the office and began the walk to his tour's starting point. He hunched up against the damp cold of another December evening and became lost in some interesting thoughts. Marlow had been murdered, and you could say that Craig had a motive – his landlord was threatening his livelihood. He didn't buy what Craig had said about having the council's support; people like Marlow were powerful and could pull strings. What if Craig had tricked Marlow into meeting him in that snickelway and then bumped him off? No more trouble and a new addition to the attractions of the ghost tour. What's more, he was physically capable of it. Was this just Gary's imagination running away with him? It was worth pursuing because if his boss was involved in some way, it would be a useful thing to use in order to extract more money from him. Gary had a room in a shared house and could scarcely afford the rent. He'd looked for work to supplement his earnings from the ghost tours, but hadn't found any. Blackmail was an ugly word, but Craig was an ugly character, and needs must.

He looked around and stopped, realising that he had walked past the street down to the riverside where the tour began. He quickly re-traced his steps and looked down the slope towards the black river. Craig was right. There was a big crowd of people waiting.

∿

Andy arrived home at the flat in Leeds which he shared with Steph, overlooking the River Aire. Inside, there were lamps on but no sign of Steph.

Then he heard a voice. 'Andy, I'm in here.' Steph sounded croaky. It came from the bedroom. He went in to find her in bed. She partially sat up with a struggle.

He sat on the edge of the mattress. 'Whoa, you don't look good at all,' he said when he saw her pale face and heavy eyes.

'I'm not. I wasn't so good this morning, then it got worse in the afternoon and Inspector Wood said I should go home. I only just made it back I was so knackered, and I could hardly get up the stairs.'

'That's bad.' He leaned over her but she pulled away.

'Don't come too near, I don't want you to get this when it's not long until Christmas. I want to get rid of it before then.'

'Well, you'll definitely have to take some time off. I'm sure Inspector Wood will manage without you.'

'He'll have to.' She sank into the bed again. The effort of sitting up was too much.

'I'm sorry, but I'm going to have to leave the shopping to you. I've done some lists for presents and food. Remember, your mum's coming up to stay over Christmas, and my mum and sister are coming over on Boxing Day.'

'Right. Don't worry, I'll manage. York is a good place to shop for presents.' Privately his heart sank at the prospect of the responsibility; he disliked shopping at the best of times, anyway.

'I'll go through the lists with you tomorrow,' she murmured from the bed. 'Get some treats but don't go mad. I think I'm going back to sleep now.'

'Do you want me to bring you anything?'

'No, thanks. Maybe later.' After a pause she said, 'How was your day?'

'OK. I think we're already making progress – quite a few suspects. The inspector is good. She reminds me of you. I think the boss thinks so too. I could imagine you doing her job.' There was no response. 'Steph?'

She was already asleep.

Andy got up from the bed and left the room, quietly cursing his luck. If only this had happened at a less crucial time. He was not looking forward to his role as chief Christmas shopper. Striking the right balance between a bit of luxury and spending too much would not be easy.

∼

Janice Marlow and Justin Hayward met at a smart Italian restaurant near Micklegate Bar. They were regulars and well known by the owners. The place was special to them – they had eaten there on their first date.

Janice looked around the restaurant. She still found it difficult sometimes to believe that she ate in places like this. Her upbringing in Leeds had been hard: her father had worked in an engineering plant, and never earned very much to support the four of them living in a little house in Armley.

But now, here she was, eating well and in the company of a very handsome man. Justin was tall, with an athletic build. He refilled her glass with wine as they ate their starter of tomato salad and burrata with focaccia bread.

'Well, it's been a strange day, hasn't it?' he said, shaking his head. 'Henry murdered. I can't believe it! Obviously I wasn't fond of him because of the way he treated you, but I wouldn't wish that fate on my worst enemy.'

'No,' replied Janice tersely as she fiddled with the stem of her wine glass. She was still struggling to deal with her feelings about what had happened. She wanted to talk to Justin about it but didn't know where to start.

'Have the police been round to interview you yet?' he asked.

'Yes, they came to the flat this afternoon – a police inspector and a detective constable: two women. I found that easier; men always think it was the grasping wife who's bumped her husband off.'

'And was it?' said Justin with a laugh.

Janice was strangely nonplussed by this for a moment or two, which surprised Justin. 'No, of course not. I told the police I was still fond of Henry, in a way. I would never have done him any harm.'

'But they're obviously treating you as a suspect?'

'I stand to gain more than anybody else, so from their point of view I have the clearest motive. They'll be paying you a visit soon. But . . .' She stopped speaking.

'What? Are you OK?'

Janice put down her knife and fork. 'Yes, but I feel really weird about it all, Justin. No, I didn't kill him, but it almost feels as if I did. I married him for money, didn't I? So was I wishing him away so I could get my hands on it?' She shrugged her shoulders.

Justin looked at her with concern. 'That's very deep.'

'Yes. Well, it's made me think about a lot of things – mostly about myself. What kind of a person am I?'

Justin extended his hand over the table and laid it on hers. 'I think you're a lovely person, or I wouldn't be here.'

Janice smiled weakly. 'Oh, Justin, that's so nice. I . . .' Again she faltered. Justin saw that there were tears in her eyes. 'I'm not worthy of you.'

'That's not true. You've had a big shock today and the police have been round and everything. You need to take it easy.'

Janice looked at him. 'It's different with you, Justin. I'm not interested in your money – you know that, don't you?'

'Of course I do.'

'It's just that I'm beginning to realise how badly I've behaved, treating marriage as a way to get financial security. Then I wonder why they all failed.'

'Look, that was in the past. We've got the future ahead of us now and things will be different. So, here's to us.' He raised his glass and Janice joined him, still feeling very shaken by what had happened and how it had made her confront her own behaviour and attitudes.

～

Next morning, Ailsa Braithwaite took Sam to school. The school was one of the few bright points in their daily lives. The staff worked hard in difficult circumstances in a deprived part of the city to make a difference to the lives of their pupils. It was close to the end of term and the building was bright with decorations and even had a tree in the entrance hall. Sam loved school and, as usual, he ran across the playground to a group of his friends. Ailsa was pleased but also sad as she watched him go; school was a warmer, brighter and more comfortable place than his home – no wonder he was keen to go every day.

As the bell went and the children lined up to walk in, she waved to Sam before talking to one or two of the other parents for a while. She valued this time as one of the few points of social contact that she had with other people, when she could feel normal and forget her troubles. Often they were the only people she saw all day if Terry was out working.

'Hi, Ailsa,' said Jody, one of the other mothers. She always seemed bright and cheerful, and was very good for morale. 'And how's Rosie today?' She knelt down by the pushchair and made a face at the little girl, who smiled.

'She's not bad today, thanks, Jody, but she's been a bit up and down. I think it's the cold weather and the bloody damp in our flat.'

Jody shook her head. 'That's awful, especially at this time of year. Have you got anywhere with the council?'

'No, but didn't you hear? Marlow, our landlord, has been murdered.'

Jody put a hand to her mouth. 'Oh my God! I did hear about a murder but I didn't connect the name with you.'

'We don't know what's going to happen now,' said Ailsa, taking a deep breath. Talking about the murder made her feel anxious again, so she said she needed to get to a meeting. Pushing Rosie in the pushchair, she headed for the nearby office of Roof. She needed to talk to someone there, hopefully Saskia Middleton.

Saskia had not been in the office long before Ailsa arrived, and could see that something was wrong as soon as Ailsa came in, due to the tense expression on the other woman's face. Luckily Rosie was asleep in her pushchair, so Ailsa parked it in the corner of the office, sat down, and promptly burst into tears.

Saskia had known the Braithwaite family for some time, helping them with their housing problems and their struggle with Henry Marlow to get repairs done to their flat. She had recently drafted a letter to the council with them, complaining about Marlow's neglect. She sat down next to Ailsa, and gave her a tissue to wipe her eyes.

'What's the matter, Ailsa?' Saskia asked. 'Is Rosie still keeping you awake at night?'

Ailsa shook her head. 'No, she sleeps through most nights now, at least until about six, but she still coughs a lot. She was really bad last night. But it's not that, it's what's happened with Mr Marlow. What will it mean for us? Will we be kicked out of our flat? Where would we go?'

Saskia looked at the mother and her ill child. So many people in their position felt that they had no power over their own lives and it was frightening. She tried to reassure Ailsa.

'No, I'm sure you won't. You've got some rights as the tenant. I wouldn't worry about that. Things could be much better for you after this. Whoever takes over will surely be a better landlord than Marlow.'

Ailsa looked down and started to cry again. 'That's what I'm afraid of.'

'What do you mean?' asked Saskia.

Ailsa shook her head as she dried her eyes. She looked exhausted. 'I didn't know who to speak to. I came here because you've been so good to us . . . and—' She stopped and didn't seem to know what to say next.

'What is it?'

'I'm . . . I'm worried that Terry . . . he might have done something. He was out working last night when . . . when he was killed . . . I mean, Mr Marlow . . . and . . .' She collapsed into tears again. Saskia put her arm around Ailsa's shoulders.

'You're thinking Terry could have been involved in that?'

Ailsa nodded.

Saskia spoke gently but firmly. 'Listen to me, Ailsa.' She waited until Ailsa stopped crying and took hold of her hand with both of hers. 'I'm sure he wasn't. He wouldn't do anything that would damage you and the family. You're just really tired because of Rosie and all the worry about her health and the flat. You're getting things out of proportion. Terry's not stupid – he knows that attacking Marlow wouldn't solve your problems.'

Ailsa continued to look down, but she nodded.

Saskia continued. 'Look, I'm going to make you a cup of coffee and I want you to stay here for a while and rest. Rosie's still asleep; I expect she's tired if she had a poor night, so you sit where you are and relax. And don't worry about Terry. He's a sensible man and he loves you all.'

Ailsa didn't argue. She slumped in the chair and closed her eyes. She stayed for an hour while the other staff arrived for work and kept an eye on Rosie. She left, thanking Saskia and saying she felt much better. She was going home to put a wash on and when Terry got back in the late afternoon, she would do her shift at the supermarket.

'Remember, we're here to help you,' said Saskia, smiling. 'You can come back any time to talk to us about what's happening with your flat. Let's see how the council respond to that letter. They may be able to do more now that Marlow has gone. We won't give up.'

Ailsa gave her a weak smile and Saskia watched the young woman walk away, pushing the pushchair. She'd seen this scenario so many times and felt angry. Why were these cruel Dickensian landlords allowed to get away with how they treated people like this? The system didn't protect the vulnerable.

She didn't think that Terry Braithwaite had killed Marlow, and believed what she'd said to Ailsa. Nonetheless, Terry was the kind of person who was capable of doing something like this if he lost his temper. For the sake of that family, she desperately hoped that was not what had happened.

She also found herself, a bit guiltily, agreeing more and more with her colleague Linda that it was a good thing that somebody had disposed of Marlow. Maybe there was now a chance for something better for people like the Braithwaites.

DI Anne Hopkins held an early press conference at the York police station. She stood on the front steps so that she was above the reporters. From this vantage point, she could see Christmas lights attached to the lamp-posts in the street and hear the distant sound of a Christmas playlist coming from a nearby shop. It made her think how unpleasant it was to be dealing with such a dark and violent crime at a time when everyone wanted to enjoy themselves, but such was the fate of police detectives.

Anne had done many press conferences and was confident in handling people from the media. She began by outlining what had happened.

'Yesterday evening, at about nine p.m., the body of Henry Marlow – a local landlord and property developer – was found in one of his properties, an empty former dwelling and slaughterhouse in Butcher Lane off Stonegate.'

'Good name for a place to find a body, Inspector!' piped up a typically cheeky voice from one of the tabloid journalists.

'I suppose you could say that,' said Anne with a smile but she refused to be deflected from her plan. 'He had been stabbed through the back with a sharp implement and had been dead for about three hours.'

'That's the companion to the blunt instrument, isn't it, Inspector? It's usually one or the other: stab 'em or smash 'em over the head,' commented another reporter.

'I must say, you're very lively and sharp for a dull winter's morning. I take it you must be looking forward to Christmas.'

This provoked some laughter. If DCI Oldroyd had been watching, he would have approved: humour got them on your side and showed you were unflappable.

'So, we are asking for anyone who saw or heard anything unusual around Stonegate and Butcher Lane between approximately five and seven o'clock yesterday evening to come forward. Also, it appears that Mr Marlow received a call in the late afternoon from someone calling himself Donald Hutchinson, asking to meet in the property in which Mr Marlow was killed. If anyone has information about this man, they should also contact us.'

'Is it true that the body was found by people on a ghost tour, Inspector?' enquired a voice near the front.

They loved that kind of thing. Anne could visualise the dramatic and outlandish headlines: 'Ghoulish Ghost Tour Finds Man Stabbed to Death. Was Murder Victim Killed by a Ghost?'

'Yes, but as far as we know there's no connection. I don't think the ghost tour organisers are trying to create their own ghosts, and it certainly wasn't some kind of prop.'

This went down really well, and there was raucous laughter before the questioning continued.

'This Henry Marlow, he was a nasty piece of work, wasn't he?'
'Treated his poor tenants badly, didn't he?'
'Have you got a lot of suspects, Inspector?'

'I can't comment in detail on all that. We are at a very early stage in the investigation, but it is true to say that we are following a number of leads.'

'Is it anything to do with that Asquith case, Inspector?'

'I take it you mean the case of Emily Asquith, who died in a flat owned by Henry Marlow? The answer is that we don't know. I'm about to discuss that with my team.'

'Do you think the murderer will strike again?'

'The evidence suggests that Mr Marlow was probably targeted for a specific and personal reason, which would mean that the general public are not in danger. Nevertheless, a dangerous person is at large, so people should take extra care.' She looked around. There was nothing else to be said at this point, but Anne knew they would return for more soon. 'No more questions – I think we should draw things to a close.'

She went into the police station to discover that DCI Oldroyd and DS Carter had arrived.

'How was it?' asked Oldroyd as they entered the incident room along with the usual DCs.

'Fine, sir,' replied Anne, as she took her place before the information board.

'They'll be back, as you'll know. I'm sure you've done hundreds of media conferences,' Oldroyd said with a smile.

'I have, and I'll be ready for them, sir, don't worry.'

The room filled up and Anne began the briefing. 'Good morning, everyone. Welcome to day two. Work has already begun. I've got people out taking statements and checking alibis, and I've just finished speaking to the press. There's quite an interest in this case, judging by what's already been on the local media. Marlow was clearly quite a controversial figure in this city. I've got a team analysing the material we found yesterday and looking into Marlow's past in relation to his dealings with clients and tenants.

I've told them to work backwards and start with the more recent issues that crop up, purely on the basis that if anyone from the more distant past had a grudge against Marlow they were more likely to have done something about it before now.'

Oldroyd and Andy nodded.

'Having said that, there was a notorious case a few years back which someone at the press conference mentioned, concerning a person called Emily Asquith. She was a young woman with mental health problems who lived alone in one of Marlow's flats, and she died due to fumes being given off by a faulty gas fire. She had drink problems and Marlow blamed that – said she hadn't operated the fire properly. He was found guilty of not having the fire properly serviced, for which he received a fine, but not of being responsible for her death. It caused a minor scandal, but Marlow seems to have toughed it out and not really changed his ways.'

'So, it's possible that someone connected with that woman could be involved, ma'am?' asked Andy.

'Yes, but, as I said, why would they wait so long?' Anne shrugged her shoulders and then continued. 'Anyway, I think we have to continue with our main suspects, the people we know had a clear motive: Janice Marlow, her boyfriend Justin Hayward, and the Braithwaites – who were in a prolonged dispute with Marlow and worried about the health of their child. There's no evidence so far that "Donald Hutchinson" actually exists. We traced the call Marlow's PA took to a call box in York, which doesn't narrow things down. I think it's more likely that was a false name used by the murderer to lure Marlow to his death.'

She turned to Oldroyd. 'I thought I would go to see the Braithwaites, sir. If you and DS Carter can catch up with Justin Hayward?'

'Sounds like a good plan to me,' Oldroyd replied, getting to his feet, eager to proceed. He was enjoying taking part in the investigation while not having the responsibility of organising it. Maybe this is what people meant by stepping down and lessening your workload before retirement? It was a tempting thought.

~

It would have been another quiet day at the Roman Hall Museum, except that a school party was booked in for an end-of-term visit. Philip Storey was not good with children, and left the party in the capable hands of Brian Lacey – the retired teacher and volunteer. Lacey had exactly the right approach for a group of Year 7 pupils. From his small office, Philip could see him firing the kids' imaginations, using the model of Roman York.

'Imagine you were a guard standing on duty on the walls here, looking out for invaders on a winter's day like this. You'd probably have come from Rome in what is now Italy, where it would be a lot warmer. You'd be freezing cold and having to wear extra clothes. And to add to your misery, you'd probably have left your family behind. Eboracum was right on the edge of the Roman Empire.' He pointed to a wall map. 'And it was a long way from Rome. It's still a long journey now, even when we have planes, but imagine marching for days and days across mountains and plains, or travelling by boat all around the coast. That would have been dangerous in the stormy seas. When they eventually got here, it must have felt like coming to a different world.'

Philip smiled. Brian made the history sound so interesting, he felt compelled to listen himself, even though he knew everything that his volunteer was telling the children.

But there was work to do. He got up from his desk. The museum was closed to the public for the duration of the school visit, so it was a good time to make a quick trip to the basement and sort out one or two things.

At the back of the office was a door that led to a steep stone staircase, and then down to a dark cellar which had been used to store wine and food when the hall was first built. Cold air met him as he descended, and there was a musty smell which somehow had an ancient feel about it. Philip pressed the light switch and a number of bare, dusty light bulbs came on. He continued slowly down the narrow, twisting staircase into the large, vaulted underground area – the oldest part of the building.

As with most museums, it was not possible to exhibit all the museum's stock at any given time, and what was not on display was stored here in boxes and piles: fragments of Roman pottery, metal tools, coins and pieces of sculptures. It had all been painstakingly catalogued by Philip over the years and he had recently completed some minor excavations down here to create more storage room.

Philip got out a torch to supplement the weak, shadowy light from the old bulbs. He was considering a change to the exhibition in the new year and getting some of these things out of storage so they could be seen by the public. It would be a dusty job sorting through the boxes but he didn't mind. His torch illuminated all the darker parts of the gloomy cellar. A large stone eye, once part of the head on a large statue, came suddenly and rather sinisterly into view in one corner. Philip enjoyed all this stuff. There were great treasures down here and he was privileged to be able to see and be the curator of them.

As he looked around and assessed what he might bring upstairs to the exhibition, he heard Brian Lacey's voice, and some laughter from the children.

It was a sobering moment. He felt a great sense of duty in caring for all these artifacts from Roman Britain for future generations like the children above.

His face contorted into a kind of snarl when he considered how so many people were indifferent to history. The idea made him angry. People needed to know where they came from and they were too distracted by the banalities of modern so-called entertainments. He would fight to preserve everything in the museum, no matter what kind of uncertain future there was about where it would be housed.

~

'Terry! Terry! I'm frightened! The police are outside and they're coming to the door. What's going on? Why are they here? You haven't done anything wrong, have you? No, they might not be coming here, but I just think they— OK, well . . . Please be quick!'

Ailsa looked with alarm out of the window of their decaying flat on the second floor of Rowntree Mansions as she spoke to Terry on the phone. Anne and DC Warren had just arrived and were leaving the police car. Terry, who had tried to reassure her, was fortunately in the neighbourhood without a fare in his cab, and was coming straight home.

Ailsa pulled back from the window, praying that the officers were going elsewhere. Her stomach lurched at the buzzer – a loud, rasping sound. What if it *was* Terry they were after? They might arrest him! She was frozen in fear, and it was only the repeated sound of the buzzer that prompted her into action. She pressed the button to reply.

'Yes?' she asked in a quavering voice.

Anne's voice came over the crackly speaker. 'Good morning, is that Ailsa Braithwaite?'

'Yes.'

'I'm Inspector Anne Hopkins from York Police. We're here to talk to you about your landlord, Henry Marlow. It won't take long.'

Ailsa felt faint. So, they *were* here about the murder! But what could she do? She had to let them in. Without a word, she pressed the button to release the door and waited. Fortunately, Rosie woke up from her nap, coughed and started to cry, which was a welcome distraction as she had to go over to comfort the little girl.

The door opened and she was relieved to see Terry walking in with the detectives. At least she wouldn't have to face them by herself.

Anne and DC Kate Warren sat in two rather worn armchairs while the Braithwaites sat on a battered sofa. The room needed decorating and the dark stain of mould was visible on the walls. Ailsa held Rosie, and looked suspiciously at the detectives.

'I'm sure you're aware that your landlord Henry Marlow was found dead on Wednesday evening in the centre of York. He was murdered,' began Anne.

Terry scowled. 'Yes, we knew that, but I don't know what it's got to do with us.'

'We have to speak to everyone who knew Mr Marlow, and especially people who had conflicts with him. You had disputes with him, didn't you?'

Terry was immediately angry. 'I should think we bloody well did. So would you if you had to live in a poxy flat like this with a poorly daughter.' He glanced round at the room with contempt. 'That man should have been in jail for the way he treated his tenants. He point blank refused for the two years we've been here to do any repairs. Look at the mould and damp.' He pointed to the wall. 'And it's worse in the bedrooms. Our daughter's got asthma. She coughs and struggles with her breath so hard sometimes it frightens you.'

'I understand. Try to remain calm, Mr Braithwaite. I'm sure you had good cause to feel very hostile towards Mr Marlow, but what we are exploring is whether this hostility led you to harm him?'

'I can't say I didn't feel like doing something. It's hard when your child is unwell and that bastard . . .' He stopped himself. 'But no, I didn't kill him, if that's what you're getting at.' He turned to look at Ailsa and Rosie. 'Why would I do that? I'd never risk going to prison, leaving my family to fend for themselves. I wouldn't allow him to get to me to that extent.' He reached out and took Ailsa's hand. She felt very much relieved to hear him say it, confirming what Saskia had said to reassure her. She cuddled Rosie close.

Anne nodded. 'I understand, Mr Braithwaite, but I have to ask you where you were on Wednesday evening between five o'clock and seven.'

Terry shook his head. 'I was out working. I'm a taxi driver.'

'Can anyone support that?'

'I don't know. I work alone. But if my fares could be contacted, they could tell you where we were. I can't remember them all – I drive dozens of people a week. I think I took someone to the train station, but that might have been Tuesday. I don't know. Can't you track them down with the company? They have all the records.'

'We will, Mr Braithwaite.' She turned to Ailsa. 'I assume you were here all evening with your daughter?'

'Yes – and our son, who's at school right now.'

'Wait a minute,' said Terry, feeling angry again. 'You're surely not accusing my wife of having anything to do with Marlow's murder? How would she even get chance to do it looking after the children?'

Anne remained unruffled. 'We have to consider every possibility, Mr Braithwaite, but she's obviously not a key suspect.'

'Unlike me.'

'I didn't say that. You have a motive and maybe an opportunity, but if we can establish that your alibi is sound then that will take suspicion away from you.'

Terry nodded. He seemed to finally accept that Anne was only doing her job.

'As far as you know, have any of the people in the other flats had arguments with Mr Marlow?'

Terry shrugged his shoulders. 'Naw, some of them are too old and haven't got the energy, and some are too scared that they'll get evicted if they complain.'

'I see. I suppose it's understandable.'

Terry looked at her. 'Do you have any idea what's going to happen to us now?' he asked.

'I'm afraid not. It will all depend on who takes over the ownership of these flats.'

He nodded. 'That's typical. Rich people argue over things, pass them about and exchange money. But meanwhile we've got to live here in this damp hole and the winter's only just started.'

Anne felt sympathetic but there was only so much she could say. 'Are you getting support from anyone?'

Ailsa spoke for the first time. 'Saskia at Roof helps us. It's just down the road.'

'Good. Well, I'd stay with that. I've heard good things about them.' She got up, followed by DC Warren. 'Thank you very much. We'll be in touch again, and here's my number if you need to call me about anything.' Anne looked over at Ailsa and Rosie and smiled. 'I hope she gets rid of that nasty cough soon.'

'Thanks,' said Ailsa. 'Rosie would be a lot better if we weren't living here.'

'Can your doctor do anything?'

'He gave us a letter about Rosie to send to the landlord but it didn't help. Saskia helped us write a letter to the council and she put his letter with it. But we haven't heard anything yet.'

And it will probably be some time before you do, thought Anne, given that local councils were utterly strapped for cash. At times like this she felt helpless. She was a detective, not a social worker, but she found it very hard to see people in these circumstances, and wished she could do more to help.

She felt sorry for Ailsa, who clearly also had a volatile husband to deal with. But she could understand why Terry was so angry. He would be frustrated at not being able to improve things for his family, and angry at being at the mercy of a rogue like Marlow.

'OK, I have just one more question. Have either of you heard of a man called Donald Hutchinson?'

Ailsa and Terry shook their heads.

'Well, best of luck,' she said. 'We'll see ourselves out.'

The next day Justin Hayward arrived early for work at the showroom. He thought it set a good example to his employees, as did the way he dressed. He always wore a smart suit, and his hair was cut short at the sides and combed back at the front to create a sleek professional appearance.

His business sold high-quality kitchens imported from Germany, and was sited in a retail park on the outskirts of the city. The showroom was large and modern, modelled around a central office enclosed in glass panels.

It was dark when Justin arrived, so he switched on all the lights. There were still forty-five minutes before they opened to the public, but none of his employees had yet arrived. He had timed this deliberately.

The showroom, with its varied and extensive range of kitchens was now fully illuminated. He had a quick look round and then went into his office. It was likely to be a quiet day; people were not planning their new kitchens in the last days before Christmas – they had other shopping priorities on their minds.

Justin was proud of the business he had worked so hard to build. He came from a poor background, but unlike some people – in particular, he thought of both Marlow and Janice – who wanted to forget their origins, he remembered what it was like to struggle with lack of money and he always paid his staff well and valued their contribution.

He sat at his desk and yawned. It had been quite a late night with Janice. They'd talked things over for a long time. He paused before turning on his computer. The quiet at this time of the morning gave him the opportunity to try to digest a little more about what had happened to Janice's husband, and the implications of the fact that he was her new man. He was obviously a prime suspect, standing to gain significantly – if indirectly – from Janice's inheritance of her husband's assets. He needed to get his thoughts in order before he expected the police to arrive.

He made coffee in the gleaming new Nespresso machine he'd bought to serve staff and customers, and sat down in his comfortable desk chair. He gazed into space and frowned. It had been unpleasant to see how upset Janice had been about Marlow's death. It appeared to have triggered a disturbing bout of soul-searching but maybe that was good if she came out of it happier and with greater self-knowledge.

When he had learned about Marlow's murder, he had suffered a pang of anxiety. He loved Janice for her vivacity and sense of fun. He'd been divorced for a number of years before they met, and his life had been very dull before she showed up. But he had always been aware that she was what some people called 'high maintenance' in terms of lifestyle.

She had no job, and constantly complained to him that her husband's allowance was not sufficient. Henry was her second husband – or third? She had always been a little vague about that. She had a son and a daughter from a previous relationship, and they were also constantly in need of cash, and asking her for financial help. Money seemed to dominate her to an unhealthy extent and the thought had crossed his mind that her financial problems were solved with Henry's death.

When he'd joked in the restaurant about her being the grasping wife who'd killed her husband, she looked very uncomfortable and then told him about how she'd been feeling bad about herself. That wasn't guilt, was it? He shook his head. No, he didn't believe that Janice could ever kill anyone.

Other members of staff arrived and then he got the message that the police had arrived and wanted to speak to him. Hayward went out to greet Andy and Oldroyd, and ushered them quickly into his private office, noticing the curious and embarrassing looks from his staff as the detectives crossed the floor. They introduced themselves, accepted coffee made by his Nespresso machine, and sat in chairs in front of Justin's desk as he sat behind it. Justin tried to appear complacent, but from the expression on Oldroyd's face, he was not endearing himself.

'What can I do for you gentlemen?' he said with a smile, relaxing back.

'I'm sure you know why we're here,' began Oldroyd, with an assessing look.

'I think so,' replied Justin.

'You are in a relationship with Janice Marlow, the wife of Henry Marlow, who was found murdered on Wednesday evening . . .'

'And as such I have a motive to kill him,' said Justin succinctly. 'I can see the logic of it, Chief Inspector, but I assure you that I had nothing to do with it.'

Oldroyd smiled. 'But it's true that Mrs Marlow will inherit her husband's money and properties, isn't it?'

'I expect so.'

Oldroyd looked around. 'This is your business? Selling kitchens.'

'Yes.'

'And how is it doing at the moment?'

'This is not a busy time of year, but generally we're doing OK.'

'Do you have any cash flow problems? Problems that might be solved with an immediate injection of money?'

Justin smiled. 'I can see what you're getting at, Chief Inspector, but the business is fine. We certainly don't need to murder someone to get their money.'

'This is a personal question, but I have to ask you: what was Mrs Marlow's relationship with her estranged husband?'

'I don't think it was acrimonious. Janice never expressed any animosity towards him. She just felt that their relationship was over. I think Henry was very sad that she'd left.'

'So, it's unlikely that he would have changed his will if he was still fond of his wife. I'm assuming he left everything to her?'

'Well, I don't know . . .'

'Presumably now Marlow is out of the way, she'll be a very rich woman?'

Belatedly, Justin saw where this was leading. 'That may be true, but—'

'Was she restless? Keen to get her hands on all that cash? Did she persuade you to get rid of her husband? You wouldn't be the first lover to dispatch a husband who was in the way.' Oldroyd's manner had become more hawkish, his voice harsher and more insistent.

For the first time Justin felt tense and defensive, partly because what Oldroyd was saying echoed some of his own fears about Janice. However, he wasn't going to reveal any of that to the detectives.

'Really, Chief Inspector, you're portraying Janice as an evil money-grabber who wanted her own husband killed so she could get her hands on his estate. That's outrageous.'

'Is it? It must have been very tempting. I understand Mrs Marlow is accustomed to a certain standard of living. Perhaps you were there to do the dirty work.'

Justin raised his hands. 'No, I did not kill Mr Marlow.'

Oldroyd looked at him. 'Have you ever heard of anyone called Donald Hutchinson?'

'No, I haven't.'

'Where were you on Wednesday evening between five and seven o'clock?'

'I was here until half five, then I went home and spent the rest of the evening there. I'm afraid no one saw me as I live alone and have done since my marriage broke down.'

Oldroyd finished his coffee and got up. Andy followed. 'OK,' Oldroyd said. 'An officer will come round to take a statement from you, so I will need your home address. Thank you for your time.' Oldroyd smiled before he left.

When they were gone, Justin sighed with relief and brushed his hand over his forehead. That had been more difficult than he expected. The hand was damp; he'd been sweating. That chief inspector was a shrewd character who would certainly penetrate to the truth of what had happened to Marlow. Justin would have to confront Janice with his concerns. But that would be difficult; she would not react well and it was likely to be a difficult scene. He felt restless and went to the office door to watch the detectives leave by the main entrance. Through the windows he could see them walking towards their car. Then he noticed several members of his staff looking at him and hastily turned and walked back into the office, closing the door behind him.

∽

'What did you think of him, sir?' asked Andy as they drove back to the station along streets busy with shoppers. There were not many of the infamous 'shopping days before Christmas' left – the slogan beloved by the commercial world. December progressed fast. Pressure increased on shoppers, especially those with children and limited resources.

Oldroyd frowned. 'I think I shook him a bit with my approach. He's obviously got one of the strongest motives, and if he didn't kill Marlow directly for his own benefit, from what we know of Janice Marlow, I think she could be very manipulative and persuasive. It's also possible that either of them or both, if they were acting together, could have hired someone to take Marlow out.'

'That's always dangerous, isn't it, sir? It leaves you vulnerable to blackmail.'

'True, but I'm finding it difficult to imagine either of them luring Marlow to a dark snickelway and stabbing him. In Hayward's case, he would be risking a lot to get involved in murder – especially when he has a flourishing business and a comfortable lifestyle. Despite what I said to him, I don't see Hayward as someone who would be blinded by strong romantic feelings and persuaded into murdering his partner's husband. I was fairly fierce in my questioning.'

'You were, sir.'

'Often when you do that and present the suspect with truths, they react and flinch in a way that tells you that they are concealing things. But Hayward didn't, even when I used the name Donald Hutchinson.'

'No, I agree. Anyway, sir, I have a question. What exactly is a snickelway?'

Oldroyd laughed. 'It was a term coined by a writer called Mark Jones, who wrote a wonderful guidebook for walking around the narrow passageways of York. It was a combination of the word 'alleyway" with two northern dialect words – snicket, meaning a narrow lane between walls or fences, and ginnel, which is a narrow passageway between buildings. Anyway, the word caught on, and it's used a lot round here.'

Andy smiled. His boss loved to talk about his beloved county and give little lectures about its history.

'It sounds pleasantly twee, sir. Not a place for a murder.'

Oldroyd nodded. 'Maybe, but some very dark and nasty things have happened over the centuries in the old parts of this city. I was learning about some on that ghost tour when we discovered the body. It was very interesting.'

'Don't you think those ghost tour people ham it up a bit, sir? You know, "After dark, the headless horseman appears riding down the street and then goes into the Hangman's Arms for a pint, except he has no head and can't drink it." Anyway, you don't believe in ghosts, do you, sir?'

'No, but we thought we'd seen one in that church in Knaresborough, didn't we?' replied Oldroyd, referring to a previous case in which he and Andy had been confronted by what appeared to be the ghost of a monk. 'I've never seen you looking so white.' He laughed.

'Yes, sir, it was the closest I've come to believing in spirits. I was telling DC Warren about it because Marlow's house was a spooky place, like that church.'

'And we had to spend the night there because of the snow!'

Both men grinned. It was one of many memories they had of working together ever since Andy had come to Yorkshire from London several years before.

'How is Steph, by the way? I'm sure she would like to be here. She likes the challenge of a mysterious case like this.'

'Yes, sir. But she's not well at the moment – down with a very bad cold. I left her in bed this morning.'

'Oh, I'm sorry to hear that. Give her my regards for a quick recovery before Christmas.'

'I will, sir. Talking of Christmas, I'm in charge of shopping now that Steph's poorly. Is it OK if I take a bit of a lunch break now and go and do a bit?'

Oldroyd chuckled. 'Do I detect a bit of reluctance?'

'You do, sir. I hate shopping at the best of times, but this is much worse. It's such a responsibility, somehow. We've got parents coming to stay, and stuff like that.'

'Well, a modern bloke like you should be sharing the "mental load", as my daughter calls it. You know – not leaving all the domestic planning and preparations to the women. I'm guilty of it myself, but I'm trying to change my ways. I think you would be advised to do the same. Anyway, of course you can go shopping for an hour. We have to take breaks in this job, like any other.'

They were just driving around the periphery of the centre near to Clifford's Tower. Oldroyd pulled into a lay-by. Andy got out and, looking harassed, headed towards the shops in Coney Street.

Anthea Marston was also taking a lunch break. The situation in the office had become weirdly frantic and also lonely. She was there by herself and the phone didn't seem to stop ringing – with people who rented homes or commercial properties, wanting to know what their situation was. Not surprisingly, some were anxious while others were angrily demanding answers. Unfortunately, she had no information – she had not yet been contacted by the solicitors, or Janice Marlow, or anyone who could tell her what was happening.

Anthea had decided to take a break from it all by shopping, but at the supermarket for food rather than for expensive Christmas presents. Money was probably about to become very tight if she lost her job. Her husband was crippled with arthritis and couldn't work. His benefits were not enough for them to live on. It was not a pleasant prospect to face in the run up to Christmas.

As she shuffled round the store, adding things to her trolley, her phone rang. It was Janice Marlow.

'Anthea, how are you? Oh, it's all dreadful, isn't it?'

'I'm fine, Mrs Marlow. And how are you?'

'Oh, please call me Janice. I know we've never met, but Henry said a lot about you – very complimentary things. I know he valued you and your efficiency very much. And thank you for asking. Henry and I were not together any more, but it's still a terrible blow.'

'Yes.'

'I just wanted to say how grateful I am that you are holding the fort. I'm sure it's difficult. I expect people are calling in wanting to know what's going to happen.'

'Yes, they are.'

'Well, about that. I don't really know much myself yet. I need to talk to the solicitors, of course, and see exactly what Henry put in his will, but I'm confident I will be his inheritor. But I'm no businesswoman. I'll have to talk to my partner, who knows a lot more about such things than me, and then we'll think about how to proceed. But I want you to know that I'll do my very best for you, whatever we decide to do about the business. Anyway, I won't keep you. Bye for now and I'll let you know more when I know myself.'

Charming, thought Anthea, when the call ended. So I have to carry on 'holding the fort', with no guarantee of a job when things are sorted out. Janice had been very careful not to make any commitments, although she had been very complimentary and sounded concerned. Was this genuine?

Anthea sighed. She was not really any clearer as to where she stood. But at least she'd finished her shopping and reached the checkout. She'd been careful about what she'd put into the trolley – only supermarket own brands and Christmas treats on special offer. She'd managed to find two duck breasts with a big reduction because the use by date was the next day. She'd freeze them to cook on Christmas Day with an orange sauce. She consoled herself by thinking that there were many people far worse off than her. This was brought home to her as she walked past a number of homeless people outside the supermarket.

～

Back in New Bridge, the weak winter sun had forced itself through the mist. Louise and Patrick, having risen late and enjoyed a leisurely breakfast, had just set out on their walk, leaving Deborah to see a client in the small downstairs room she'd converted into a welcoming space.

A mile or so away, Louise breathed in the air as she and Patrick walked across the wet winter fields.

'Get a lungful of that,' she said to Patrick. 'It's cool and refreshing – what we call "bracing" in Yorkshire.'

'Bracing!' replied Patrick with a laugh and took in a deep breath. 'It certainly is.' He looked around. They were walking on a ridge above the wide spread of Lower Wharfedale, heading towards the prominent landmark of Almscliffe Crag. Otley Chevin and Ilkley Moor stood out in the distance.

'Look at that,' said Louise, pointing across the dale. 'That's why they call Yorkshire the county of the broad acres – because there are all these big, sweeping landscapes and fabulous views.'

'Yes, it's beautiful.' Patrick turned to Louise with a smile. He had heard Oldroyd wax lyrical about Yorkshire. 'I can see it's very much "like father, like daughter" with you and your dad as far as Yorkshire is concerned.'

Louise laughed. 'Well, we were brought up to revere our county, but it's not just empty feelings – Yorkshire is a great place in many ways.' She took in another deep breath. 'It's so good to be here and away from the big city, though I have to confess I feel a bit guilty.'

'Guilty? What for?'

'For leaving the centre and the women with their children who need it. Christmas is a difficult time for them. Many of them don't have families and a lot of services are shut.'

'The refuge will be staffed by people who've volunteered to cover Christmas, so you shouldn't worry. Don't you think you deserve some time with your own family? To have a break? It's very stressful work, isn't it?'

Louise smiled at him. 'Yes, you're right.' She knew that she had to recharge her batteries if she was going to be effective in the refuge and in her academic work.

They walked on, and after a while reached a farm. They passed a field where sheep were gathered around a mound of hay put out by the farmer.

'This way – we're going over this stile and down the hill, across a stream and into the next little valley.'

'You seem to know this route well.'

'Yes, we used to do this walk a lot – it was one of Dad's favourite Harrogate walks and now it's on his doorstep.' They stepped over the stile and into the next field. 'Anyway, yes, we all need a break, but it's a responsibility, you know. I find it hard just to put those women out of my mind when I know they're struggling.'

Patrick turned her face to his and kissed her. 'You're such a caring person. It's one of the reasons I love you.'

'That and many other reasons, I should think!' she replied with a laugh as they walked down a hillside towards a bridge. 'You remember Dad mentioned Saskia Middleton? I think I might give her a ring. It would be nice to catch up and also see how she deals with these dilemmas.'

'Good idea. She's in York, isn't she? We could go over to see her.'

'Oh, that would be good, as long as we keep out of Dad's way.'

'We will. I don't want to get involved in a murder inquiry just before Christmas.'

'Me neither!'

They held hands as they crossed the stream and walked up into the next field. When they reached a road, they sat on a wooden bench for a short rest. Louise took out her phone and scrolled through her contact numbers.

'Yes, here it is. I knew I had Saskia's number,' she said, dialling it.

'Hello,' said a voice she recognised.

'Hi, Sas, it's Louise – Louise Oldroyd.'

'Oh, wow! Louise, great to hear from you. It's been a while. How are you?'

'OK, thanks. The thing is, I'm up in Yorkshire for Christmas at my dad's near Harrogate and I wondered if we could meet? You know, catch up a bit.'

'That would be great.'

'I'd really like to come over and see Roof. I've heard a lot about it and I bet you're doing a great job.'

'Well, we do our best,' Saskia laughed. 'I'm off this weekend but Monday would be good if you're free. We could meet here in the morning and have a good talk. First thing on Monday is usually quiet.'

'Fantastic. I'll bring Patrick along, if that's OK.'

'Ooh, who's Patrick, then?'

'Well, you'll find out on Monday!'

Saskia laughed again. 'OK, see you! Can't wait!'

When the call ended, Saskia went back to the computer screen feeling upbeat. She was looking forward to seeing Louise again. It was a while since they'd been in London together and she remembered the fun times they had when they were students. Unfortunately, her good mood did not last long.

Linda Black came into the office looking downcast.

'Cheer up, it's nearly Christmas,' said Saskia and smiled.

Linda sat down. 'Some bad news, I'm afraid. Our anonymous donor rang. She says that there won't be any more donations.'

'Bloody hell! Did she say why?'

'No. Just that she was sorry but can't give us any more money.'

Saskia grimaced. Donations from this person had been regular and substantial. But the donor would not reveal their identity, which made things difficult: if an organisation like Roof accepted donations, they were supposed to make careful checks that there was no suspicious activity involved. The problem was that, like many relatively small groups helping people on the margins of society, Roof was perpetually surviving on the edge financially, so donations like this were very difficult to refuse. And how was it possible to check a donor like this, anyway, when by definition you knew nothing about the person?

Saskia had decided that they would accept the money, which had been very useful. Unfortunately, Roof had become too reliant on this source of revenue and now they would be in difficulties.

'Great news just before Christmas,' she said to Linda, wondering if this loss of money would mean that she would have to let her assistant go. There was no way she was even going to consider that until the new year. Then she would have to begin the hard slog of trying to find alternative sources of funding. It was not a pleasant prospect, but she tried to put it out of her mind. She was not going to let anything spoil the festive season.

~

As Andy wandered in and out of shops, his sense of frustration mounted. He noticed that other shoppers seemed purposeful and confident, while he consulted his list and found it difficult to make any decisions. It would have been helpful if Steph could have been more specific. 'A nice scarf for your mum, a pale shade of green' didn't really help. He needed more detail. He couldn't really complain, though, because his failure to take the initiative with birthday and Christmas presents was one of the few things that caused tension between them.

Eventually he came to Marks and Spencer's, his mum's favourite store. He was certain they would sell scarves and they did – too many, in fact. Six different pale green ones. He almost picked one at random but then wondered about the material. Some were thin and silky, and the others were woolly and thick. Steph would like the woolly ones, he was certain of this, but he really couldn't remember what kind of scarves his mum wore. The problem was that there was far too much choice of everything and it was just bewildering.

There was a woman who looked about the same age as his mum and he plucked up courage to ask her for advice.

'Oh, a silky one, definitely. I'm sure she'll love it,' she said with a smile.

So, the pale green paisley patterned scarf went into his basket. Second on the list: Steph's mum. A definite challenge here as she was very particular and '8 x 10 inch photograph frame' was very vague. He decided to go for a silver frame to fit in with her formal lounge.

Two presents down and two to go, and Andy was already tired and ready to go back to work. He couldn't get everything today but would he manage to complete the list before Christmas, and would the things he got be right? It was much more stressful than being a detective!

'I can tell you, after I spoke to the Braithwaites, I was almost glad that Marlow had been murdered.' Anne Hopkins shook her head. 'There they live, in a damp flat, and their little daughter is ill. What parent wouldn't feel like killing someone to protect their child's life?'

The team had reconvened in the incident room at York station, where they shared a sandwich lunch and drank coffee.

'They have a motive, alright,' Anne went on. 'The husband is a taxi driver, so he could have easily got to the scene of the murder between picking people up. He also has a record of violence, so on the face of it he's an ideal suspect. We'll have to corroborate his alibi by checking the records of his fares, but in fact I'd be surprised if it was him. I think he's too devoted to his family to make things worse for them by risking arrest, and I can't see that his wife would be capable of such a violent act no matter how angry she was. They had that hapless, downtrodden feel about them – like they've lost hope that their lives could be any better.' She looked at her notes. 'Another point is that they mentioned an organisation called Roof, who have been helping them. I think we need to visit them and see what else they can tell us about Marlow. I bet they have other clients who had difficulties with him.'

Oldroyd was impressed by Anne's speech, which combined compassion and anger about social injustice with clear thinking about the case. It was interesting that Roof had come up in her enquiries.

'By coincidence,' he said, 'my daughter, who's up visiting us from London, knows the person who runs Roof. I can't remember her name now. They were on a course together in London. I agree it will be interesting to talk to them. But, to be honest, I'm hoping we get a breakthrough with our existing suspects or this could go on a long time.' He took a bite from his cheese and pickle sandwich and a sip of coffee before continuing. 'Andy and I spoke to Justin

Hayward. He had a cool exterior but I could tell he was jumpy. I don't know what's going on there, but he and Janice Marlow clearly have the strongest motive. We'll have to see how their alibis stand up.'

'The team is on that as we speak,' said Anne. 'And I'm expecting more information about that Asquith case soon.' She looked up at the whiteboard, which now contained more details about each suspect, with lines and arrows showing connections between them. Again, Oldroyd was impressed. He'd never been one for visuals, but he had to admit that Anne's diagram presented the key information very clearly.

'We've been looking at the details of his commercial properties. That stuff you brought from Bishopthorpe Manor was useful,' continued Anne, looking at Andy. 'They're mostly offices and shops, and no sign of any conflicts, but there is one that is more unusual. Marlow owned an old building in the centre of York called Roman Hall, which houses a museum about Roman York. Marlow kept files on all his properties and sometimes put in handwritten comments on things like the state of the building, what he thought about the tenant and so on. Against Roman Hall, he's written, "Storey is a damned nuisance. Must get rid of that place."' She passed around photocopies of the page.

'Who's Storey, ma'am?' asked Andy.

'Philip Storey. He's the curator of the museum, so it seems we've got something to investigate – there was clearly something antagonistic between him and our victim.'

'Sounds like a good one for me,' said Oldroyd. 'There's nothing I like better than a museum, and I know Andy here feels the same.'

Andy grinned and when the meeting was over he went over to his boss. 'Thanks, sir – you've volunteered us to go to some dusty museum about Romans in York two thousand years ago. I can't wait.'

'You've no sense of history, that's your problem,' replied Oldroyd with a laugh. 'Anyway, how did the shopping go?'

'Oh, don't talk about it, sir. I've made a bit of progress but I was exhausted at the end of it. I hate shopping at the best of times, but the pressure now to get everything done before Christmas is intense. I just hope Steph recovers in time to finish it off, before it finishes me off.'

'I know how you feel,' said Oldroyd. 'I'm grateful that Deborah seems to enjoy shopping for presents and doesn't want my help. Although I've not thought of what to buy her yet.'

'Well,' said Andy, 'I've had a brainwave regarding Steph's present. I'm buying her an "experience".'

'I'm intrigued. Go on.'

'A voucher for a paddleboarding lesson on Yeadon Tarn.'

'I've heard of paddle tennis but what on earth is paddleboarding?'

Andy explained and suggested that Deborah and Steph could enjoy such an experience together. Oldroyd, whilst grateful for the idea, was not so sure. Deborah had bought some amazing presents for him in the past, so he didn't want to take a risk with hers.

'However, you have given me an idea. Maybe an experience involving Pilates or yoga in a country house – with a delicious lunch thrown in?'

'Sounds good, sir.'

∾

Down along the River Ouse, the leafless branches of the weeping willow trees brushed the surface of the water – still high and swirling along downstream from York. A cold mist clung to the fields nearby, making the cows and sheep in the fields appear like ghosts.

Melanie Jackson arrived at Bishopthorpe Manor in the early afternoon. There was nothing much to do in terms of cleaning, but she had come for a different reason. She had not told the police about the true nature of her relationship with Henry Marlow.

The truth was that she'd had an affair with him after he split with his wife. She was divorced, with two teenage children, and it had all begun with her feeling sorry for her employer who had seemed so lonely after his wife departed. Things had slowly developed from there until they'd become lovers. It seemed a very unlikely relationship: the wealthy late-middle-aged property owner and his much younger cleaner. But she felt that she saw a different side to him from the public view of a miserly, cold-hearted man. She saw a more vulnerable and gentler aspect to his personality. And he, so it seemed, valued her ordinariness. He told her how he came from a poor family in York and had worked his way up to be a wealthy man who owned a large number of properties. He didn't like a lot of the people he dealt with who came from well-off backgrounds and had been to private schools. But she couldn't get him to say a word against his wife. He still seemed to be devoted to her.

Nevertheless, although she was fond of him, she had another, less romantic, motive for starting the relationship – his loneliness had also been her opportunity. Supporting two teenagers was difficult and her ex-husband refused to pay maintenance, despite being taken through the courts. Marlow had helped her financially, which had been very welcome, but now she hoped for a great deal more. He had promised that he would leave her money in his will, but that would be a long time coming. In the meantime, there were quite a number of valuable things in the house that she could help herself to. Who was in a better position than her to know about the cutlery, vases and ornaments and what they were worth? Not only did she clean them every week, but she had slowly found out from Marlow which items were valuable and which were not. She had brought a couple of sturdy bags. The trick was not to be too greedy, so that people were less likely to notice.

She went slowly around the house, selecting items. When she reached the bedroom, she felt some nostalgia for the times she had spent there. The relationship with Henry had improved her life but that was the past; there was no point in being sentimental. Now he was going to improve it still further, she thought, as she picked up a couple of expensive porcelain candlesticks and stuffed them into one of the bags. She knew a place where she could sell them, no questions asked. In fact, this would not be the first time she had done things like this. Cleaning for wealthy people had its perks.

She smiled. It was a shame that Henry was dead. She had enjoyed their time together. But every cloud had a silver lining – quite literally in the case of a lot of this stuff.

∼

Anne Hopkins was tired when she got home that Friday evening at half past six. The responsibility of leading a case like this was big, and though she welcomed the presence of DCI Oldroyd, she was anxious not to make a mess of things in front of the revered detective, whose reputation was kind of a legend among police forces across Yorkshire.

Anne lived in a modern detached house in a suburb on the edge of York. Her husband was a GP, and they had a son and a daughter who were both in secondary school. She was determined that work would not interfere with her family life and had set the team of detective constables to work on various matters connected with the case so she could take time with her family. Tomorrow was Saturday, and they were all going into York to see the Christmas market.

The lights were on and the house looked cosy. After interviewing the Braithwaites, she was acutely aware of how fortunate she was. She was also lucky with her teenage kids – they caused few problems in terms of staying out late and being argumentative and awkward. Her sixteen-year-old son, Paul, was interested in food and cooking, and he would have started to prepare the family meal. He was already thinking about being a chef. By contrast, his fourteen-year-old sister Amy was not interested in food; her passion was music, and she was learning to play the guitar.

Anne opened the door and went inside. She could smell food being prepared and heard Amy practising upstairs. 'Hi, everyone!' she called.

'Hi, Mum!' came the sound of Paul's voice.

She went into the living room and found her husband Peter watching the television news. She sat down next to him and sighed. He gave her a kiss.

'Busy day?' he asked.

'Very. This case is full on.'

'Yes, well, look at the local news.' He pointed to the television. 'It's been mentioned. You just missed the report. It was all about "prominent local property owner Henry Marlow" with photographs of him and an account of where his body was found. No mention of the police investigation.'

'They'll be waiting to see if it's all sorted out quickly. If it isn't and it gets complicated, the press will be asking us awkward questions. There's nothing the media like better than the police struggling or being outwitted.' She sat back and yawned. 'Anyway, fancy a drink? It's Friday night, after all.'

'Good idea.'

'OK. I'll open a bottle of red and I'll see what Paul's cooking. He might need a hand.'

'I don't think so. He can follow a recipe quite easily. He'll have a restaurant with Michelin stars when he's older.'

Anne laughed and went into the kitchen, where she found her son hard at work.

'Hi, Mum – I'm making a pasta sauce, but I think everything's a bit watery.'

She looked at the pans, one of ragu and one of white sauce. 'Just reduce the ragu with a gentle boil and keep stirring the sauce. It looks good and smells great.'

'Thanks.' A smile widened under hair as blond as his father's. 'Are you in charge of that murder thing where that man was found stabbed in an old building?'

Anne hesitated. What exactly she could tell her family about her work was always difficult. She couldn't keep it a complete secret because the crimes were reported, but she had to be careful what she said.

'Yes, but you know I can't tell you anything about it.'

'No, but we talked about it a bit in History today.'

'History?'

'Yeah, you know – we're doing social and economic history for GCSE and the teacher was telling us about the Rowntree family. They ran one of those places that made chocolate, didn't they?'

'Yes, and the other was Terry's. Both mostly gone now. I remember, when I was little, you could smell the chocolate up Haxby Road where the Rowntrees factory was.'

'But they also looked after their workers and they built a village of good-quality houses at New Earswick, because a lot of workers were living in slums. Joseph Rowntree's son did a study of it.'

'Yes, he did – Seebohm.'

'Yeah, that's a funny name. Well, our teacher Mr Hardwick said that there is a lot of bad housing in York again now and some bad landlords. He said that Mr Marlow had been in the papers a few years ago when someone died in one of his houses.'

'That's true, but be careful what you say to people. I don't think Mr Hardwick will want you going round saying Mr Marlow was a bad landlord.'

'But he was, though, wasn't he, Mum?'

'I'm saying nothing. But I'm pleased you're becoming aware that not everyone is as lucky as we are to live in a house like this. Poor people are often hidden away on run-down estates where they're forgotten about or dismissed as being lazy or at fault for their situation. As it happens, I'll probably be visiting the Deepwood estate next week. That's a run-down area, but there's a charity group called Roof who campaign on housing issues and try to make things better.'

'Roof? That's a cool name,' said Paul. 'So, did that Mr Marlow have some bad houses there too?'

'I'm not answering that, Paul. Don't burn your sauce!'

'Oh no!'

Paul dashed to the stove as his mother opened the wine and poured two glasses. Then she went back into the living room.

'Is he trying to pump you for information about your work again?' asked Peter.

'A bit. Henry Marlow cropped up in a History lesson, apparently. They've been studying the Rowntrees and the social problems in York at that time. I was a bit surprised the teacher mentioned Marlow being a bad landlord.'

'It's that Mr Hardwick, isn't it? I think he's well on the left politically, and he'll have to watch it if any parent complains.'

'I suppose so, but on the other hand why shouldn't he point these things out? It's certainly made Paul think, so he's doing a good job.'

'Absolutely! Good wine, by the way.'

Anne took a sip and remembered the Asquith case that Paul had mentioned. Her team had not reported on that yet. She must follow that up first thing on Monday. Then she shook her head – no more of that. It was the weekend and family time. She sat back and relaxed.

Three

In the sixteenth century there was resistance in the north to the English Protestant Reformation, the split from Rome and the Dissolution of the Monasteries. A rebellion began in York led by Robert Aske, a local barrister. It raised an army of over 30,000 and forced concessions from Henry VIII. When the rebels dispersed, Henry arrested the leaders and they were executed. Robert Aske was hung in chains from Clifford's Tower in York. Later in the century, in 1570, Guy Fawkes, a famous member of the 1605 Gunpowder Plot conspiracy to blow up the houses of parliament, was born in York.

The centre of York is colourful, vibrant and full of historical sights that pull in the tourists. But, like most British towns and cities, it also has a population of homeless people who live on the streets, in shop doorways, old tents and cardboard boxes.

It was late on Sunday night, and in another snickelway not far from Butcher Lane, called White Horse Passage, an unfortunate man – an alcoholic who had lost his job and home – was lying against the wall. He had a small dog crouched next to him, and a stained blanket over his dirty clothes, but despite this he was starting to shiver. He regretted not trying to get into a hostel for the night, but it was too late, and some of them did not admit animals.

The homeless man had a paper cup for donations and he held this up as people went past. But the number of people going through the snickelway had gradually reduced, until now it was very quiet and dark. His head slowly slumped forward as weariness overcame him, but then he became conscious of a person looming over him. He looked up and there was a dark shape, a figure wearing some kind of cape. It was impossible to see the face.

'Can you help me?' he asked, holding up the paper cup.

There was no reply. Instead, the figure produced a knife which they plunged downwards into the homeless man's body, as their other hand pressed the victim against the wall. Then, retrieving the weapon, they walked briskly away down the snickelway. It was all over in seconds.

The dog snuffled up to its owner but got no response. Then it smelled the blood trickling across the alleyway. It started to whimper, and then to howl.

~

It was early Monday morning before the body was discovered with the exhausted dog lying beside its dead owner and licking his face. It was taken away by the police to be cared for at local kennels.

The snickelway was cordoned off and pathologist Eve Redgrave was fast at work, dressed in gloves and protective clothing. Anne Hopkins had been contacted by local police officers as soon as they reached the scene. It was clearly another murder. She watched grim faced for a while before Dr Redgrave came over.

'Well, it's another stabbing. Similar type of knife to our other murder, only this time the wound was in the front rather than the back. The knife severed major arteries in the abdomen. He would have bled to death very quickly. There are copious amounts of blood on the ground and his clothes are soaked in it.'

Anne took a deep breath in and then out. 'Right. Does it look like the work of the same killer as the one in Butcher Lane?'

'Difficult to be sure at this stage. The knife wound is about the same size, but there are no other marks left on the body – nothing like a serial killer identifying their work. When I get the body to the lab, I'll see if there are any microscopic similarities – you know, fibres or patterns on the knife.'

'Thanks,' said Anne and frowned. This was an unexpected twist in the case they were investigating. The two stabbings could be completely unconnected. On the other hand, if it was the work of the same person, then maybe there was some kind of serial knife killer at large. Marlow was lured to his death, but the second victim appeared to have been killed where he was on the street.

Or maybe Marlow hadn't been lured to his death. Maybe he really had met a Mr Hutchinson, and was stabbed after that encounter? In that case, they would need to track down this Hutchinson, who might have vital information. If so, why hadn't he come forward? Scared he might be accused of the murder? Or maybe 'Hutchinson' was a total fabrication. They only had Marlow's secretary's word that someone of that name had rung.

The possibilities were suddenly bewildering, and Anne considered that they might have to reassess their whole approach to the case. The murderer might not, in fact, have had any kind of grudge against Marlow; if this homeless man was a random kill, perhaps Marlow was too, and that had implications for the safety of the public. She would have to prepare for a more searching and difficult press conference after this development.

～

Louise and Patrick hitched a lift with Oldroyd into York. They left early, as Oldroyd had received a message from Anne Hopkins about the latest murder. It was a drier and brighter day as they drove round the Knaresborough bypass and across the flat countryside of the Vale of York, past Green Hammerton. Some of the fields were flooded after the recent rains.

'So, there's been another murder, Dad,' said Louise. She was in the back of the car, holding hands with Patrick, which made Oldroyd smile – what it was to be young and in love!

'Yes. DI Hopkins sounded very downbeat. This could complicate things a lot if we decide the crimes are linked. Have you been to York before, Patrick?'

'Only briefly, to a training course in a hotel.'

Oldroyd winced slightly as he remembered his recent experience with DCS Walker. 'Oh, well. Louise, you'll have to show him round. Why don't you walk along the walls? And don't forget the Christmas market in Parliament Street – and, of course, the minster.'

Louise laughed. 'We can't do everything in one go, Dad. The main aim today is to see Saskia. By the way, turn right here.'

Louise was following the directions on Google Maps on her phone. Needless to say, Oldroyd's ancient Saab had no electronic devices. The car turned off the attractive, tree-lined road leading into the city centre, and on to less opulent streets as they made their way to the Roof office.

'Right, this is it, Dad. I'll call you later, and see if it's possible for you to pick us up from wherever we get to. Otherwise, we'll get the train.'

'OK, have a good day!' Oldroyd waved as he drove off. It was so good to have her around and, as he saw her wave back, he thought how much she reminded him of her mother. These reflections brought both pleasure and pain to Oldroyd. He had fond memories of his son and daughter when they were growing up, but he blamed himself for neglecting his family.

As he headed for the police station, he shook his head. There was no point dwelling on the mistakes of the past. The truth was that things had turned out well for everyone. Louise and her brother, Robert, were in settled jobs and relationships, and he and Julia both had new partners who were good for them. There was a lot to be thankful for.

~

Steph was feeling a lot better by Monday and, despite Andy trying to persuade her otherwise, she was determined to go back to work as she was getting bored being stuck at home. He drove her to Harrogate police station before he continued on to York, and insisted on picking her up in the evening.

On the way to the station, she gave him another list.

'I've been very impressed so far with your shopping,' she said in her familiar teasing way. 'So, I'm sure you'll manage a few extras. You need to get something for Ralph and Ian.' These were Andy's sister's sons in London. 'That should be easier for you. Aren't they Tottenham supporters? You could get them something football related.'

'Fine.'

'And I want you to get this perfume for Mum. I've written it down; you've just got to go in and ask for it. That won't tax your poor brain too much, will it?'

'Don't be so patronising. I'm capable of more than you think if I put my mind to it.'

'Well, make sure you do then.'

They reached the police station car park. 'Anyway, I hope it goes well today. Don't worry about me overworking and getting too excited. Things go at a slow pace with Inspector Wood, and nothing dramatic ever happens. I'm more likely to get bored and want to go home again, especially if he mentions his train set. Do you know what his nickname is?'

'No.'

'Timber.'

'What? I don't get it.'

'John Spence made it up. Apparently people shout out "Timber!" at the dramatic moment when a tree is being felled. But nothing exciting ever happens with Inspector Wood, so it's like a cheeky play on his surname.'

'That's a bit obscure, isn't it?'

'I suppose so, but it's still funny. Right, I'll see you tonight.' She got out of the car.

'Oh, I forgot to tell you, the boss rang when you were getting ready. Another body's been found.'

'Bloody hell! Well, it's all drama over there, isn't it? I'm so jealous. I spend my time going through boring documents looking for clues.'

'And learning about old steam engines. Never mind, I hope you get a "timber" moment today.'

She stuck her tongue out at him as she shut the car door.

'Look – Penny, darling, I don't know when everything will come through. We haven't even buried your stepfather yet. I had to go and identify his body the other day. Don't you think it's a bit premature to be asking these questions? . . . I know, I know, but you should have thought of that before you committed yourself . . . I don't see why you didn't realise it, that's what prices are in London, surely . . . Well, of course I want to help, but you'll just have to be patient and you're not the only one . . . Yes, of course I mean Alex . . . Alex and Maisie may be better off than you and Simon, but that doesn't mean Alex isn't entitled to help as well if he needs it . . . Well, I think it is fair . . . Look, I don't want to talk about this at the moment, I've got too much on my mind and it's giving me a headache . . . OK, if that's how you feel about it, I'm going.'

Janice Marlow abruptly ended the call to her daughter Penny before sighing with exasperation. Penny worked for a literary agent, and was paid a meagre salary by London standards. She had a useless boyfriend who called himself an artist, earned virtually nothing, and seemed content to drift through life relying on Penny. They lived in a tiny hovel of a flat in Shoreditch, but Penny was keen to move to a better place. She had found somewhere, although it was a lot more expensive than where they currently lived, and at astronomical London prices their Shoreditch place was already above their means. She assumed her mother was going to be rich with the inheritance from her third husband, and expected help with the rent.

Janice sat back on the sofa in her living room, kicked her shoes off and put her feet up on the coffee table. Once again she was wearing clothes from charity shops – admittedly ones with fancy labels, like today's pure wool jumper from Hobbs and Sweaty Betty leggings (very satisfying finds in Oxfam, York). But really she was sick of not being able to get much newer stuff. Her daughter's cheek had made her angry, particularly when Penny would not hear a word against Simon, her lazy boyfriend. Janice didn't feel like supporting a layabout. But it also made her sad and thoughtful – she felt that her main use to her daughter was as a source of money, which somehow Penny felt she had a right to. Was it her fault that Penny behaved like this? The painful truth was probably, yes.

Despite her air of being the rich woman accustomed to high living, things were actually very different. She thought about her childhood in Leeds, where her father left the family before she went to school. Her mother worked as a seamstress and struggled to support Janice and her siblings. Shortage of money was a constant problem, and Janice remembered all the times she had wanted things but was told they couldn't afford them. She didn't blame her mother, but she was determined that, whatever it took, she would not be short of money when she grew up. She was beginning to realise more and more just how strong that determination had been over the years and how it had affected her relationships.

As an adult, she had realised that men were a good source of cash. She cultivated rich ones with a view to marrying into money, which she had done three times. However, her first two husbands had been wily enough to prevent her taking too much money from them. But Henry had been different. She didn't like his miserly approach; he was unwilling to enjoy the money he had accumulated and she disliked his attitude towards poorer tenants. But there was a kind of bond between them, because he had also come from an unprivileged background, which had formed his attitudes to money.

She made herself a gin and tonic. It was a bad habit to start drinking in the morning. She would have to watch herself, but the conversation had turned her mood sour.

She saw herself in Penny. Her daughter seemed cold hearted and indifferent to Henry's death. It wasn't a pleasant feeling. She had valued money over people and relationships, and now that attitude was coming back to haunt her in the way her daughter was behaving. Could she blame her? These were bitter truths to face up to.

And what of Justin? What did she really feel for him? Was she going to enter another relationship and maybe a marriage with the same mercenary attitude? No, as she'd told Justin when they went out the other night, her feelings for him were deeper than for any of her former partners, and it wasn't just all about money.

These deep reflections were interrupted by her phone ringing. It was her son, Alex. No doubt he was after money too.

~

Once again the team were assembled in the incident room at the York station, where Anne Hopkins outlined the ways in which the discovery of the homeless man's body in White Horse Passage had the potential to change the course of the investigation.

'So, ma'am,' said Andy, 'you think this could be the work of some kind of serial killer, like Jack the Ripper, murdering people with a knife in dark alleyways?'

'We can't rule it out. The idea of imitating famous killers does enter the minds of certain criminals, although mercifully they haven't mutilated the bodies like the Ripper did. I've also had the report from Eve Redgrave on the knife wounds. Apparently they were similar enough in both cases to suggest that the same knife could have been used.'

'What's your instinct about whether or not the crimes are linked?' asked Oldroyd, who believed that, although evidence was paramount, sometimes your gut told you something important about a case, especially when you had years of experience.

'Well, sir, despite the knife evidence, which is suggestive but not conclusive, it's odd that we have one victim who appears to have been lured to his death, and another killed where he was already. Unless, of course we find that Jeffrey Smith – that was the name of the homeless victim, according to ID on him – had enemies who wanted to kill him and went looking for him. So, I'd say the pattern isn't clear yet.'

'I agree,' continued Oldroyd. 'But I think you will have to alert the public to the threat. We might have a serial killer at work.'

Anne frowned. 'I will, sir. I've already called another press conference for later this morning. It'll be trickier than the last one.'

'Not to worry,' said Oldroyd. 'You'll cope fine.'

This expression of confidence improved Anne's mood. 'OK,' she said with renewed energy. 'We've got the team working on Smith's background and continuing to check the alibis we've been given for Marlow's death. So far, the accounts of Anthea Marston and Janice Marlow seem sound. Janice's friend, Daphne Allison, has been found and she confirmed that they watched TV on the night of Henry Marlow's murder. Marston was at home with her disabled husband, confirmed by him. We've tracked the fares that Terry Braithwaite had on Wednesday evening and they suggest he was driving his cab during much of the timeframe that Marlow was killed, but that doesn't rule him out because there were some gaps of time.'

'Good work,' said Oldroyd. 'So, it's him and Justin Hayward who have the weakest alibis?'

'Yes. We might have to revisit some of them to check their whereabouts last night. Anyway, I'm going to see Anthea Marston briefly today to check on the story of Mr Hutchinson, and then I'm going to Roof to see if they have any useful information. Can you go to the museum, sir?'

'Yes, I'm looking forward to it.' He glanced at Andy, who groaned a little. 'And it will be better if you go to the charity.' He explained that Louise was visiting her friend Saskia, so he didn't want to get involved at Roof. Anne agreed.

Oldroyd stood up. 'Right, never mind the setbacks – let's all go and get on with it,' he said.

It was a moment in which Anne was glad that he was involved in the investigation.

∽

Gary Owen had gone into the ghost tour office early. Craig Jordan wouldn't be there, as the business operated mostly in the evenings. He had a key to let himself in and, once inside, made his way to Craig's stinking little office and sat at the desk. His eyes flickered round the shabby room. What was he looking for? He wasn't exactly sure, but it was something that would show that Craig had a motive to get rid of Marlow. There was a computer, but he didn't know the password. His hope was that he could find some printed correspondence that might incriminate his boss.

There was a pile of box files on a table, and he rummaged through them whilst keeping a wary eye on the outside door. After a long and fruitless search, he finally found a square cut folder with the single word 'Marlow' written on the front. Inside were letters from Marlow and the council regarding Butcher Lane.

Marlow had objected to the ghost tour going through the snickelway and past his property. Apparently, there were too many people jammed into a small space and it was changing the atmosphere of the quiet and secluded courtyard. Craig had presumably written back and told Marlow where to go. Several letters more, and Gary found what he was looking for. In a recent letter, Marlow threatened that if the ghost tour wasn't limited to ten people, he would ask the council to revoke Craig's licence on the grounds of causing a nuisance. He hinted subtly that he had influence with the council. Gary considered this – a limit of ten people per group would effectively make the tour uneconomical. Craig had scribbled in the margin: 'Interfering bastard! Like to turn him into a bloody ghost.'

Gary put down the letter and smiled. So, he was right, it wasn't like Craig had told him. There wasn't necessarily support from the council, and there had been a real chance that he would lose his licence or see the ghost tour ruined. He hadn't said anything about it due to pride. He didn't want people to know that Marlow had beaten him. And his comment was threatening. If the police found out about this, he would become a suspect in the murder.

Anyway, he thought, this letter could be very useful to him. Gary had been in the army for a number of years and had struggled to find work since leaving. He was now developing a plan that might enable him to acquire money more easily. Craig was an awful boss, and now he could get one over on him. He would take this letter, copy it, and return it without Craig knowing. Then things would get interesting. He stuffed it into his pocket, closed the file and cautiously left the office. In the street, a homeless man came up to him with a begging cup, but he strode past.

～

'Sas, it's absolutely great to see you!'

In Saskia's office at Roof, Louise flung her arms round her old friend and then introduced her to Patrick.

'Oh, it's great to see you too, Louise – but you've been keeping quiet about him!' Sas said jokingly and pointed at Patrick, who laughed.

'Well, it's only been six months and he's still on probation!' said Louise, joining the laughter.

'Do I get a report at the end of that period, whenever it is?' asked Patrick. 'And can I have some time to correct my weak points?'

'We'll see!' Louise continued, gazing around Saskia's office with interest. 'Anyway, look at you running an organisation like this! It's fantastic! How are you finding things?'

Saskia smiled. 'I think we do OK. We're helping a lot of people, even if what we can do is sometimes limited. We can be an advocate for people in their struggles with rogue landlords and with the council, and it does make a difference. Without us and our knowledge of the law and people's rights, they would find it very difficult. Of course, there's a lot more we could do if we had the resources. It's harder to get funding here than in London.'

'I'm sure it is, especially in York. People think it's a wealthy place that doesn't have any housing problems.'

'Yes, but it has the same structure as most British urban areas, including the beautiful cathedral and market towns. And there's a big irony there. Remember that unit we did on the master's course about the sociology of housing? Seebohm Rowntree, son of Joseph the chocolate maker, did some of the first sociological studies of poverty and bad housing here in York, and they showed that poverty was structural. People were poor due to low wages and bad housing, not because they were intrinsically lazy.'

'Hear, hear,' said Patrick and he clapped at the end of Saskia's little speech.

'Hey, sarky!' Louise gave him a playful cuff on the shoulder and Saskia laughed.

'Yes, of course I remember that,' said Louise, steering the conversation back to what Saskia had been saying. 'It made me feel proud that it was done in Yorkshire. I remember the lecturer saying that it showed that abject poverty was not confined to London, as many people thought at the time.' She shook her head. 'Anyway, tell me more about how you run things here, and the profile of this area. How do the housing problems intersect with other issues?' She turned to Patrick. 'Sorry, are you OK while Sas and I talk about this stuff?'

'Sure, go ahead. If I get bored or out of my depth, I'll read my book,' he said teasingly and produced a novel from his coat pocket. 'But, seriously, I find it all really interesting, so don't worry.'

There was an intense discussion for an hour or so over coffee and biscuits. Then Louise and Patrick got up to leave and catch the bus into the city centre.

'Oh, by the way,' said Louise as they opened the door, 'I mentioned to my dad that I knew you, and that you worked here at Roof. He said someone would probably come round here to interview you today. It's to do with that murder case he's involved with.'

'Henry Marlow?'

'Yes, I think so.'

'He was one of the worst landlords in the city and we had lots of clients who had problems with him. I can't say I'm sorry to see him gone.'

'That's what it will be about, then, but I don't think he'll come himself because of your connection with me.'

'That's fine . . . It's been great to see you, Louise. I hope we can meet again before you go back down to London. I've got some time off over Christmas.'

'That would be great.'

'So, what do you fancy doing now?' Louise asked her boyfriend as they waited for the bus into the city centre.

'Walking round the walls sounds good.'

'It is – you get to see a lot of the city from there. Let's go for that. I think the best place to start is Monk Bar. You'll love it – it still has a portcullis, and from there, the path goes behind the minster.'

∼

'Come in, gentlemen. I've been expecting you.' Philip Storey greeted Oldroyd and Andy at the door to the museum with only the ghost of a smile to brighten his rather austere demeanour.

As Philip led them into his office, Oldroyd looked around. He loved the unusual nature of the building in which different parts had been constructed in different styles over the centuries.

'You're lucky to have your museum in this historic building,' said Oldroyd as he sat down in Philip's office. 'It seems appropriate somehow.'

'Yes,' replied Storey. 'It's a fascinating building.'

'How old?'

'Oh, it goes back to the medieval period – the fourteenth century or earlier. It was a private house for rich merchants and businessmen for centuries. Then, in Victorian times, it housed some council department. As you can see, it's been rebuilt and added to many times. That's why it doesn't feature in lists of buildings of the most architectural quality in the city – it's not an intact version of any particular style, which is what a lot of architectural historians prefer.'

'Neither is York Minster.'

'That's very true, but that is a building of much greater importance and visual impact than Roman Hall. I suppose you could say that its sum is greater than its parts, and, anyway, most people don't notice that it's a mixture of styles.'

Oldroyd nodded. Philip struck him as a learned and serious person, lacking in humour and lightness. He decided to bring their discussion back to the matter at hand. 'As you say you were expecting us, I assume you meant in relation to the murder of Henry Marlow. He was your landlord, wasn't he?'

'Yes.'

'How would you describe your relationship with him?'

Philip shrugged. 'Not particularly good.' He was suddenly very laconic.

'In what way?'

Philip thought for a moment before answering. 'Marlow acquired Roman Hall a while ago. I think his plan was to refurbish it and then sell at a big profit to a hotel company or something like that. We were sitting tenants.'

'So you're saying he wanted you out of here?'

'Oh yes, he made no attempt to conceal that. He had complete contempt for the museum – called it a pile of old stones and broken pots with no relevance to the modern world. All he was interested in was money.'

'That attitude must have made you angry.'

'Of course, but Marlow is not the only person around these days who expresses such philistine views. We seem to have lost much of the great antiquarian tradition of the Victorian period in the pursuit of money. Do you remember Oscar Wilde – "the price of everything and the value of nothing"?'

'But in that period, wasn't there a lot of pinching stuff from other countries and putting them in our museums?' said Andy. 'I remember going to see the Elgin Marbles in the British Museum. They were lifted from Athens, weren't they?'

'Yes, from the Parthenon, Sergeant. And I agree that kind of behaviour is controversial, but at least they saw the value of those things back then.'

'We've seen evidence in Marlow's paperwork that you and he did not get along. In fact, he called you' – Oldroyd glanced at his notebook – '"a damned nuisance". Did you have rows with him? Did they get acrimonious?'

Philip looked at Oldroyd, but his gaze gave little away. 'I stood up to him, Chief Inspector, and he didn't like it. He tried to get us to leave here voluntarily, but I was having none of it.'

'I assume if Marlow had succeeded in evicting you, it would have caused major problems. Where would the museum have gone?'

'Oh, we would have found somewhere. I would never have allowed that man to close us down.'

For a brief moment, Oldroyd saw a glint of anger in Philip's eyes. 'When you say "would have", it sounds as if you're confident you will be able to stay here now that Marlow's gone.'

Philip shrugged. 'Maybe. I'm hoping that whoever takes over has a more positive attitude to culture and history, but there's no guarantee. I was talking to my volunteer Brian Lacey about this. I'm confident that the council would step in and save the museum if the situation got desperate. We're an asset to the city.'

Oldroyd paused before asking, 'Do you know anyone called Hutchinson?' He watched Storey carefully.

'No.'

'And where were you on Wednesday evening between five and seven p.m.?'

'In other words, do I have an alibi, Chief Inspector? It's not an easy one for me. I live by myself and I'm a bit of a loner.' He thought for a moment. 'Actually, on Wednesday I called in for a drink at my local pub on the way home. It's the Queen's Arms in Albion Street. I spoke to Kevin, the landlord. He might remember. I was in there from about half past five, and stayed for over an hour.'

'OK.' Oldroyd stopped his questioning and looked out of the office window. There were a few people wandering around the exhibits. He turned to Philip. 'You know . . . I wouldn't mind a quick look around the museum. It looks interesting.' Oldroyd caught Andy raising his eyes to the heavens and shook his head. Andy likely had secret sympathy with Marlow's attitude to the museum: he wasn't the sort of person to raise any curiosity about a lot of ancient coins and bits of stone. But then Oldroyd reckoned Andy also knew his boss couldn't resist learning something about a new area of local history, especially when it was connected to Yorkshire, and would cope with a little tour.

Philip was clearly delighted, and showed the detectives round with enthusiasm, explaining the history and significance of various objects. He pointed out some large pieces of blue glass with some white figures.

'Now this is part of a cameo vase which, when it was complete, would have been similar to the famous Portland Vase in the British Museum. The fascinating thing, I think, is how this would have been made. They probably had a bubble of the blue glass and dipped that into white glass and then blew them together. The design was produced by removing parts of the outer white glass.'

'Fascinating,' said Oldroyd. 'It's amazing what they could do in those times, isn't it?'

'Oh, indeed, Chief Inspector. They were very advanced technologically. And over here we've got some pieces of what we call tablets – thin pieces of wood on which people wrote things. These contain facts about life in Eboracum.'

'Well, that is interesting,' said Oldroyd, who found Philip compelling and well informed. Andy was slouching behind with a very tired expression on his face, clearly finding the man a bore and wondering when this would end.

'Of course, we have a lot more things in storage,' he said.

Oldroyd stifled a smirk at Andy's panicked expression. 'I can imagine,' he replied. 'Where do you keep them?'

'There is a large space underneath here – everything's boxed up or piled in corners. I try to rotate the display as much as I can, but space is limited.'

'I see.'

The guided tour continued for a while longer, much to Andy's dismay. His relief was evident when his boss finally said they must be on their way.

'Bloody hell, sir, that went on a bit,' Andy said when they left Roman Hall. 'And, God, that bloke was tedious! What he could tell you about bits of stone, glass and wood. I can't get interested in that kind of stuff.'

Oldroyd laughed. 'Well, I found the whole thing very fascinating,' he said. 'Both the exhibition and Storey himself.' It was bright but cold outside and he clapped his hands together. 'Come on, let's get back to the station.'

～

Anne Hopkins was about to leave for Anthea Marston's house, to speak to her again about the telephone call from the mysterious Hutchinson, when DC Kate Warren came over to her.

'Ma'am, before we go, I think you need to see this. The team have discovered some information about that Asquith case. They've sent it to you.'

She led Anne over to her computer. On the screen was a picture of a group of people and underneath was the headline, 'Troubled Woman Dies in Flat'. The photograph looked as if it had been taken at a family occasion some years before Emily died.

'Those older people are her parents, but look there, ma'am.' DC Warren pointed to another woman to the side of Emily. 'And look what the caption says.'

Anne nodded her head.

The caption read, 'Emily Asquith with her parents Fred and Elsie, and her sister, Anthea.'

The woman in the picture was clearly Anthea Marston.

～

'Yes, Emily was my sister.' Anthea Marston was as controlled as ever as she sat in the office of Marlow Holdings, despite the fact

119

that Anne's visit had been unexpected – and the revelation that the police knew about her connection to Emily Asquith even more so.

Anne and DC Warren sat opposite her. 'Tell us all about it, and how you ended up working here for Henry Marlow,' said Anne.

Anthea took a deep breath and frowned. It was a moment of reckoning but she remained composed. 'You won't be surprised to learn that I blamed that awful man for Emily's death. And then he got away with it.' She was fiddling with a pen and her grip suddenly tightened.

'You obviously felt very angry about what happened.'

'Furious. Emily was a few years younger than me and very vulnerable. She suffered from depression and started to drink heavily as a teenager. She always fought hard to control it. At first we were pleased that she managed to get this small flat and live independently after years of languishing with my parents. She got herself a part-time job in a supermarket. But it soon became apparent that the landlord, Marlow, was a classic rogue.

'There were lots of things wrong in the flat: damp, taps not working, old window frames that were rotten and draughty. It was badly in need of decoration. But Marlow wouldn't do anything.'

'And then she died in an accident,' said Anne.

Anthea looked up sharply. 'To me, it was not an accident. He had not had that gas fire serviced and he was found guilty of that. So whose fault was it?'

Anne noted she was finally showing her feelings: the anger in her face was clear. 'But he was not found responsible for her death.'

Anthea made a gesture of contempt. 'Huh. He had all these fancy lawyers that he must have paid a lot of money for. I'll bet that hurt the miserable skinflint. They dredged up all the wretched details about Emily's alcoholism and said she was incapable of living safely by herself, that it couldn't be proved she hadn't operated the fire properly due to being drunk. There was some alcohol in her blood, but not enough that she'd be unable to function.' She stopped talking for a moment, and tears formed in her eyes. 'It was very painful to hear Emily so maligned and heartlessly blamed for her own death. It was enough to create doubts in people's minds, so Marlow was found not guilty. He was fined and warned. He should have been banned from being a landlord.' She stopped and wiped her eyes with a tissue. 'He was just too powerful. That's how the law works in this country, isn't it? The rich get away with things.'

Anne looked at her. It clearly took a lot to get Anthea upset. 'So, what were your motives in getting a job with Marlow?'

'I wanted to get him to pay back something for what he did. I couldn't think of how I could get to him until one day I saw an advert for a job in his office. I had the right skills and I knew he wouldn't recognise me; we'd never had any contact. I got the job because I said all the right things about being efficient and not wasting money and resources – things I knew would please him.'

'And what did you do?'

Anthea looked at her. 'Since you've found out about this, I may as well tell you everything. You'll find out soon enough for yourselves. I devised a very cunning way of siphoning money from the company. He prided himself on being in control of all his affairs. It was very satisfying to outwit him. I did it with many small amounts, which he never noticed.'

'Did you keep the money?'

'No, I donated it anonymously, to a housing charity called Roof.' She smiled grimly. 'I loved the idea that Marlow was helping poor people, even some of his own tenants, and he knew nothing about it.' She frowned. 'Unfortunately, I don't know what's going to happen now as I can't really continue stealing money from a new owner. I rang Roof to tell them that there wouldn't be any more donations.'

Anne was secretly impressed by Anthea's plan, but of course it was against the law. And had it been enough for her? 'You took one kind of revenge on Marlow, but I'm wondering if you thought that it was sufficient retribution. Did you still want to get rid of him?'

Anthea looked at her. 'No, Inspector. I didn't kill him. I humiliated him without him knowing and his money helped struggling people in the name of Emily. He was more use to me alive than dead.'

'OK . . . I want to ask you about this call from Donald Hutchinson.'

'What about it?'

'Well, we've only got your word that anyone of that name rang. We've traced the call, but it was to a call box. It could have been you, or an accomplice, in a plan to get rid of Marlow. Your alibi for that evening might be sound but that doesn't mean you weren't involved.'

Anthea smiled and shook her head. 'That seems a bit far-fetched,' she said. 'Who is this accomplice I'm supposed to have?'

'Maybe you could tell me.'

Anthea was calm again. 'No, Inspector, you're wasting your time on this. I got my satisfaction by deceiving Marlow into helping the kind of people he damaged. I'm not a murderer. That call was real. I don't know who Hutchinson was – and even if that was the caller's real name – but I had nothing to do with it, apart from taking the call.'

'I see. Well, I think you need to come down to the station for an interview about your embezzlement of the money, and then we'll have to investigate it.'

Without another word, Anthea reached for her bag, put on her coat, and locked the office as they left. She was as composed as ever. She hoped she would be treated leniently, but she didn't regret what she'd done.

$$\sim$$

Terry Braithwaite cruised around the city, waiting for assignments from the HQ of his taxi firm. It wasn't a hard life compared to some of his friends who were roofers and builders – out in all weathers, sometimes doing dangerous things. But the hours were long and anti-social. He did shifts during the night and when he was working days it usually meant leaving the house very early. He was often absent for meals and the kids' bedtime. He hated this because he missed seeing them, and it left Ailsa to cope on her own.

He received a pick-up, and drove to a Georgian terraced house just out of the centre. A well-dressed family came out, closing the imposing dark blue wooden door with its gleaming brass knocker behind them. A beautiful wreath, of the kind he knew Ailsa would like to buy, hung on the door. Two primary-school-aged children and their parents got into the taxi as he loaded their bags into the boot. The fare was to the station, and during the journey they ignored him as they chatted on about the Christmas show they were going to see in the West End: *The Snowman*. He couldn't imagine what they'd paid for all four of them to see this. The chat quickly switched to Christmas presents – Grandad was getting a new gardening spade and Grandma a National Trust membership for a whole year, and so it went on. He thought how he would love to take Ailsa and the kids to Fountains Abbey, but it was just too expensive.

It was difficult not to feel envious. They seemed nice people, but what a relief it must be to live in such a beautiful house and not to have to worry all the time about money and the safety of your children. He knew he was lucky to have Ailsa and the kids, but he couldn't get the idea out of his mind that somehow he had let them down. No matter how many hours he worked, it never seemed to be quite enough to meet their needs. Ailsa's job at the supermarket didn't bring in much and childcare costs were high. In any case, she didn't want to leave Rosie for long as she was often unwell. It was a constant struggle to pay the bills and buy everything the kids needed. What kind of Christmas were they going to have? They could barely afford a few food treats, let alone theatre trips and expensive presents. It was a difficult time of year, and he felt like crying with frustration and anger. Part of him wanted to stop the cab, tell the family to get out, but instead he drove over Lendal Bridge, turned right through a gap in the city walls, then right again into the drop-off point at the city's magnificent Victorian railway station. After he'd unloaded the bags, the father gave him a generous tip. He watched the family laughing and talking as they went on to the station concourse, then he got back into his cab.

His face was tense and he gripped the steering wheel tightly as he drove away from the station to pick up another fare. Now he felt angry with Marlow again. That bastard had made things so much more difficult for them and endangered his daughter's health. A grim smile came to his face. Thank God the man was dead.

The second press conference outside York police station was much better attended than the first. The media people now had the prospect of a long-running and tense investigation and were keen to draw out the dramatic possibilities of the situation. Anne faced the cameras feeling less confident than before, but trying not to show it.

'Two murders now, Inspector.' A reporter barely let her get to the microphone before the questions started. 'Are you looking for a serial killer? Might they strike again?'

Straight for the jugular, thought Anne. 'It's too early to say for sure that the two murders are connected. There are significant differences between them, but given that two people have been stabbed to death in similar locations, it's possible that the murders were committed by the same person.'

There was a cacophony of voices trying to ask her questions but she waited a moment and then continued. 'So, it is important that everyone stays alert and avoids going alone into the darker areas of the city, and that anyone who saw anything suspicious near White Horse Passage comes forward.'

'That's not far from the scene of the first murder, is it, Inspector?' asked another journalist. 'Have we got a Jack the Ripper-style killer in York? You know, all these bodies in dark alleyways and close to each other?'

'We had Peter Sutcliffe, the Yorkshire Ripper, back in the seventies . . . Have we got the York Ripper now?' called another voice, and there were a few guffaws, which made Anne angry at the bad taste of joking about such things. Goodness knows what kind of headlines they might write. No doubt DCI Oldroyd would produce a witty and barbed put-down at this point, but Anne was content to move things on. She had her own way of doing things.

'I think speculation of that nature is not helpful. We are also appealing for any information about the victim of this murder who was an apparently homeless man called Jeffrey Smith. Did anyone know him? Has anyone seen him recently? Was anyone aware that he had any enemies?'

'The victims were very different, weren't they, Inspector? A homeless man and a rich property owner?' asked a reporter with a more serious demeanour.

This was a more sensible contribution. 'You're right. This difference in victim type is one of the things making us pause in assuming that the attacks are the work of the same person. On the other hand, the method of killing is similar in both cases and, as you say, both victims were murdered in the same area. That's about as far as we can draw them together at the moment.'

After a few more questions, Anne brought the conference to an end, and went back into the building and into the incident room, where the team were waiting.

'How did it go?' asked Oldroyd, who had thought about attending the conference with her, but decided not to interfere or give the impression that Anne couldn't cope by herself.

'OK. They're licking their lips at the possibility of there being a serial killer on the loose, but some of the more sensible ones have their doubts. I think we may have some lurid headlines tomorrow. "Is There a York Ripper on the Prowl in the City?" Stuff like that. I just hope they don't. It will be dreadful if they stoke up fear just before Christmas.'

Oldroyd shook his head. 'Yes . . . Once this kind of thing starts, people get more frightened and start barricading themselves in their houses. I've seen it many times. Then the press start saying we're being too alarmist. It's very difficult to win. Anyway, what's the latest?'

Anne gave an account of the interview with Anthea Marston – how her sister had been a victim of Marlow and how they had arrested her for stealing money from Marlow's business.

'It's one of those cases where you sympathise more with the criminal,' she added. 'She obviously got great satisfaction from handing Marlow's money over to Roof, but we had to bring her in. Despite confessing about that, she vehemently denied being involved in his murder.'

'I think we have to keep her on the list of suspects, though. Even if her own alibi is sound, she could have worked with an accomplice. They could have been Donald Hutchinson. Maybe, in the end, stealing the money wasn't sufficient revenge for what happened to her sister,' suggested Oldroyd. 'It can't have been easy for her to work with him every day and watch him treat his tenants in the same way he treated her sister.'

'You're right, sir. How did you get on at the museum?'

Oldroyd looked at Andy and put his head on one side. 'Sergeant Carter was not impressed – too many old artifacts and pieces of stone. Unfortunately, he lacks an interest in history.'

Andy grinned. 'I like more recent history, sir – you know, the second world war and stuff like that. But Roman times are too far back for me – all those fragments of pottery and bits of coloured tiles in dusty display cabinets. It doesn't give me an idea of what it was really like in those days.'

Oldroyd thought for a moment before he replied. 'Yes . . . anyway, the curator of that museum, Philip Storey, was quite open about the fact that he was in a dispute with Marlow, who wanted them to leave so the building could be developed. He called Marlow a philistine who was only interested in money. He came across as someone deeply committed to the museum and its collection and I could imagine him getting very angry with Marlow. But I'm not sure that I could see him killing his landlord. He insisted that if Marlow evicted them they would find another venue, although that might have been bravado. What do you think, Andy?'

'I agree, sir. He was a boring bloke, but didn't seem the violent type. Even if he did get rid of Marlow, it wouldn't guarantee that the museum would be able to stay in that building, so why go to all that bother?'

'Where do we go from here?' asked Oldroyd, looking at Anne.

'Well, sir,' Anne said, 'in the absence of a chief suspect, we just have to keep trying to find more information about people, like the link we discovered between Anthea Marston and Emily Asquith. In the end, we'll be able to narrow the investigation down. I'm going to Roof, to see if they have anything useful. They will know as much as anyone about Marlow's poorer tenants and their problems. They might be able to provide us with more suspects.'

Oldroyd nodded and when the meeting ended he went to have a word with Anne.

'By the way,' he began, 'talking of finding things out, I'd like your team to look into this.'

When he told Anne what he wanted, she looked puzzled. 'OK, sir, but I'm not sure why that would be important.'

'I'll explain another time,' he said, but wouldn't elaborate further on his request. It was one of Oldroyd's characteristics that he sometimes kept his theories to himself until he was sure that he was right. This was just one of his hunches, but he had a feeling he could be on to something.

Justin Hayward's demanding job meant that he often only snatched a quick sandwich for lunch and ate it at his desk. Today, however, he felt the need to get away from the office and have a proper break so, at one o'clock, he got up from his desk, put on his coat and walked out.

There was a cosy pub off the main street which usually wasn't too busy at lunchtime. Outside, he passed a homeless man sat on the ground, leaning against the wall. Justin dropped some money in the man's plastic cup. Inside, he sat by himself in the corner after ordering a tuna mayonnaise wrap to eat with his pint of beer.

He was worried about Janice and had been unable to concentrate all morning for thinking about her. He was still slightly concerned about her possible involvement in her husband's death, especially because of her response to the news, which had plunged her into a crisis of self-identity. Her disturbing reaction seemed related to her upbringing, which was something they both had in common.

Justin had grown up in Bradford in a large family. His father had been a garage mechanic and earned just enough to enable the family to scrape by without many luxuries. They lived in a terraced house and their landlord refused to do basic repairs. Justin's father had ended up doing them himself.

Justin was so deeply immersed in his thoughts that he hardly noticed the arrival of his tuna wrap, leaving it uneaten for some time. He noticed an old man in a flat cap sitting opposite and drinking half a pint of beer. Flat caps were becoming rare now amongst ordinary people, and the man reminded Justin of his father.

Although Justin was a successful businessman selling expensive products to rich people, he'd never forgotten his upbringing and it made him sympathetic to people who were having a hard time paying bills and raising children. He loved Janice's fun-loving attitude to life; she had re-energised him after the failure of his marriage.

Half-heartedly, he took a bite of the wrap and a sip of his beer. The lessons that Janice had taken from her childhood seemed to be different from the ones he'd absorbed. Although he sensed her attitudes were changing, he and Janice were going to have to have a serious conversation about this.

∼

Back in Harrogate, Steph was struggling. She hadn't realised how much her energy had been depleted by the illness – though at least she was sure now that was what was wrong. She felt very tired but she was only halfway through the day. It wasn't helped by the tedium of working with Inspector Wood. It was a hard slog reading through dull material looking for discrepancies between accounts. In the afternoon she felt her energy levels sag even more and felt drowsy. She put her mouse to one side, leaned forward on to her desk and shut her eyes for a power nap.

After what seemed like only a few seconds, she heard a voice break through the darkness. 'Hi, sarge, are you OK?' Steph sprang awake to see Sharon Warner standing over her and looking concerned.

'Oh, Sharon. Hello. I was just having a rest.' Steph yawned.

'You must have been asleep for a while. We heard you snoring and somebody joked that you must have had a big night out last night.'

Steph looked across the room to see other officers watching them with curiosity. 'What? Oh no! How embarrassing! I was feeling really tired. No big night out, though.'

Sharon smiled. 'It's nice to see you back, sarge, but maybe you've returned to work too early. Have you got the energy for it?'

Steph shook her head, trying to clear it and yawned again. 'I think you may be right, but I can't bear it at home after a day or so. It's too boring and quiet. I'm not a great telly watcher.'

'Are you sure you're OK?'

'Yes, I'll be fine, don't worry. Thanks for coming over.'

Steph tried to get back to work but still found it hard to concentrate. After a while, she got up from her chair to get a glass of water. As she was walking across the room, she suddenly felt very dizzy, and moments later she passed out and fell on to the floor.

◦⁓

Anne Hopkins and DC Warren finally made it to the offices of Roof, where Saskia had been expecting them after Louise had told her to expect a visit. They sat in the office and the first thing that Anne did was to inform Saskia about who her anonymous donor had been and why the donations had to stop.

Saskia grimaced. 'Oh no . . . Does that mean we have to pay it all back? We had no idea that the money had been stolen.'

'I believe you. It's why a lot of charities won't accept anonymous donations. But you're in the clear as long as you were unaware that the money was stolen. As far as returning it goes, whoever inherits Marlow's estate has the right to demand the return of the money, should they wish to do so. That will probably be his wife. But we can't be sure until the will is sorted out.'

'What's his wife like?'

'I have met her but, obviously, I can't comment on someone's character.'

'No, I understand.' Saskia sat back in her office chair and sighed. 'We learned on Friday that the donations were going to stop. It will cause us difficulties; we came to rely on that money. Maybe I should have found out more about the donor but when resources are coming in to help our desperate clients, I tend not to ask too many questions.'

'I understand. But there's more, I'm afraid. I haven't told you why Anthea Marston was giving you the money.'

Anne explained that Anthea was Emily Asquith's sister. Saskia put her hand to her mouth. 'Oh my God! I had no idea. So siphoning money off to us was a kind of revenge for how Marlow treated her sister.'

'It appears so, yes. So . . . you're sure that you had no idea that Anthea Marston was the donor? And no knowledge of where she was getting the money from, or her connection to Emily Asquith?'

'No, absolutely none, it was all done anonymously right up to the final phone call. I will try to be more diligent in future, but, as I say, it's hard to turn money down when there are people out there who are badly in need of help.'

'I know. Do you have trustees here? What do they think about accepting anonymous donations?'

Saskia looked a little sheepish. 'To be honest, they trust me to make the right decisions.' She frowned. 'Maybe they shouldn't. I will have to talk to them and see if we should put further rules in place. I feel as if I've let them down.'

'Don't be too hard on yourself. Everything you do is for the good of Roof and the people it serves. It's not that you are making any personal gain out of it or that Roof is getting some commercial advantage.'

Saskia smiled. 'Thanks.'

'Moving on,' said Anne. 'I also need to ask you if you've had dealings with Marlow here at Roof through your clients. The only people we know about are the Braithwaites, who were in a dispute with Marlow when he was murdered. We understand that the health of their child was being affected by the damp in the flat.' She looked at Saskia and gave her a rueful little smile. 'I'm afraid this makes them suspects, or at least Terry Braithwaite, as his wife was occupied with the children when Marlow was murdered.'

'I understand,' said Saskia, 'but I can't believe that Terry would do anything like that.'

'Did you ever witness him threatening Marlow, or getting angry in a way that would suggest he might become violent?'

'I never saw them together. Of course he said some unrepeatable things about Marlow to me, but I don't blame him. Not when his little girl was being made ill by Marlow's inaction.'

'OK. I want to know if any of your other clients were tenants of Marlow, and if they were in conflict with him. We are in the process of searching Marlow's records to find out who his tenants were, but not all of them may have been in a nasty situation like the Braithwaites. It would help if you are able to identify anyone known to you as having difficulties with Marlow.'

Saskia looked uneasy. 'I find that very difficult, Inspector. I would be breaking client confidentiality if I start telling you about people's circumstances and what they said to me about other people.'

'I understand, but I have to remind you that this is a murder investigation – indeed, a double murder investigation, if we establish that the two recent killings are linked.' Anne thought for a moment. 'I would be happy if you just supplied me with a list of your clients who were tenants of Marlow without going into detail, as long as you indicate any person who expressed violent intentions towards Marlow and who you think could have committed the crime. That information is vital. It could save lives.'

Saskia nodded. 'OK, I can do that. There are a number of Marlow's tenants among our clients, and they've all had similar problems of neglect, refusal to do repairs and stuff like that, but I can honestly say that, as far as I know, none of them have expressed any threats towards him. I'll put a list together and send it to you, and I'll also speak to the staff in case anyone has witnessed something that I didn't.'

'Thanks for your co-operation,' said Anne. 'There's just one more thing that I have to ask. I understand that there must have been some hostility towards Marlow amongst the staff here at Roof. Has anyone ever expressed any violent intentions towards Marlow?'

Saskia was shocked at this question and paused before answering. 'No, certainly not in my hearing, but you are right – he was not the most popular person here.'

The detectives got up to leave, and Saskia showed them out. Once they were gone, she came back into the office to sit down and think about these unexpected developments. It was sobering to think the people who worked for Roof – including her, presumably – were possible suspects. But of course the inspector was just being thorough. Saskia didn't imagine that they were very serious suspects. She managed to smile. It was a good job the inspector hadn't heard Linda sounding off against Marlow when she brought in the news that he was dead.

She also reflected on what the inspector had said about the sisters – Emily and Anthea – and how the ramifications of the bad actions of someone like Marlow could continue for years and affect so many people.

It made her all the more determined to fight for the victims. Marlow's death, in her mind, wasn't any kind of real justice for them.

There was an explanation as to where Craig Jordan acquired the money which allowed him to live a rather luxurious lifestyle, and it had nothing to do with running ghost tours. That was his respectable and legal business. But he was also what the criminal world called a fence – in other words, a receiver of stolen goods. Burglars, thieves and robbers brought what they had stolen to him, and he then sold it on to other people: dealers, dodgy market traders and members of the public who were often unaware that what they had bought was stolen.

He ran this most lucrative of his many money-making ventures from a group of old warehouses, lock-up garages and run-down offices in an industrial park some distance away from the city centre. He had a large portacabin with a small office and a big storage area. The premises were presented as a pawnshop complete with the three-ball sign hung above the door. Craig kept this place a secret, known only to his regular customers. He was usually there during the day before he transferred to the ghost tour office in the late afternoon.

One of his regular customers was Melanie Jackson. She turned up in the late morning and proceeded to bring in several bags of miscellaneous stuff from her car. Jordan smiled at her as the bags piled up.

'Where on earth have you got all this bloody stuff from, Mel?!'

'Never you mind,' she said and tapped her nose. 'Keep it out. It's not part of our deal that I tell you where things come from.'

Despite her warning not to ask, Craig said, with a knowing smile on his face, 'I'll bet it's all from Bishopthorpe Manor. I know you used to do cleaning for that old miser, Marlow. You've taken the opportunity to lift some stuff while there's no one living there. You don't hang around, do you? He's only been dead a few days.'

'Ha ha – very clever! So what if I did? He and I were close, and he'd have wanted me to have a few things. He wasn't as mean as people think. Not to me, anyway.'

Craig looked at the bags and laughed. 'A few things?! It looks as if you've emptied the bloody place!'

'Nowhere near. There's plenty more where these came from. But . . . don't be greedy is my philosophy. Then it's less likely that they'll notice things are missing until it's too late. Anyway, I don't think anybody knew exactly what Henry had in that house so they won't know what's been taken.'

Craig chuckled. 'I have to hand it to you, Mel, you're a good operator. Let's have a look, then.' He began to take things out of the bags: cutlery, ornaments, jewellery. 'Good Lord, look at all this! Are you saying none of it will be missed?'

'Trust me. His wife hasn't been around for a while and he had no kids to visit him, poor sod. Janice wasn't interested in antiques and stuff. I'm the only person apart from Henry who knew about all the expensive stuff in that house. I've left the most obvious things and the most valuable.'

'Why?'

'Because they won't think a thief has been at work if the diamond rings and gold watches are still there. If anyone misses anything, they will assume Marlow sold it.'

Craig laughed and shook his head. 'You're a wily piece of work, Mel.'

'You have to be sharp when you've got a family to support like me. You've got to look after yourself and them. The way I look at it is that the government should be grateful for people like me. I look after myself and my kids, and I don't have to rely on benefits. Not that they would be enough – even with my wages – for us to have a decent life. I don't feel bad about taking stuff from rich people like Henry; it's a hard world, and you have to survive. But I'd never nick anything from somebody who was struggling.'

'Hmm, I suppose you're right,' said Craig, although he didn't really care where his money came from. *Put yourself first in this tough world*, was his motto. 'Let's talk about what it's all worth, then.'

It took over two hours before he'd considered everything she'd brought, and they finally agreed a price after a great deal of bartering.

'This should set you up for Christmas,' said Craig, as he counted out the money and handed it over. Then he looked at her. 'Hey, you didn't bump him off so you could get your hands on this stuff, did you?'

Melanie turned on him as she checked the cash. 'No, I didn't, you cheeky bugger. I told you, I was quite fond of him, really.'

Craig looked at her suspiciously. 'You were shagging him, weren't you?'

'Mind your own business, you creepy sod. Are you some kind of perv who gets off on knowing about other people's sex lives?'

Craig ignored this. 'I know your game – you were hoping that he'd leave you stuff in his will, but inconveniently he got bumped off before he'd changed it in your favour.'

'Well, make your mind up. One minute you think I've killed him, and the next you think my plan's failed so I'm pinching stuff. Which is it?'

'You tell me.'

'Get lost. Anyway, I'm off. I might be back with more soon, so not a word to anyone.'

'As if I would.'

Craig smiled and shook his head as Melanie drove away. You had to hand it to her, she was a tough character and a shrewd operator. And one of his best suppliers.

'Just lean forward, Steph. Put your head between your knees. Everybody move back, please, and give her some air.'

Steph had regained consciousness, and was sitting on a chair in the office. Cynthia Carey – another detective sergeant older and more experienced than Steph, and also first-aid trained – was attending her. 'Drink some of this,' she said, offering Steph a glass of water. 'How are you now?'

Steph blinked. 'Better. A bit woozy.'

'OK, sit there for while with your head forward. If you still feel weak, you can lie down in the break room. Let's have a look at your head.'

Steph had caught her head on the edge of a table as she fell. 'Ouch!' she exclaimed as Cynthia examined the spot.

'No bleeding. You'll just have a bit of a bump there.' She stood back and looked at Steph. 'Sharon was right. She said she'd told you that you'd come back to work too early. You do look very pale.' She looked at the work desks. 'And too much leaning over the keyboard. It doesn't do any of us any good.'

Steph nodded and drank some more water.

'I'm going to contact that partner of yours,' Cynthia said, 'and get him to pick you up. There's no way that you're driving to Leeds. You'll just have to leave your car here until you're fit to drive.'

Steph nodded. 'It's OK, I don't have the car. Andy gave me a lift in and he's picking me up later.'

'Good, well, I'm still going to contact him and see if he can come earlier. You need to be at home.'

Steph closed her eyes and felt too tired to talk, but not that she might faint again. After a moment or two she said, 'I think I will lie down for a while.'

Cynthia helped her to the break room and Steph lay on the sofa.

'Don't even consider coming into work tomorrow. If you don't feel better in a couple of days, you should see a doctor. OK? It's obviously a nasty virus you've got. It's going round at the moment.'

Steph nodded again, then closed her eyes. She soon fell asleep.

At the York station, Oldroyd was engaged in some research, assisted by a member of Anne Hopkins' team, when he received a call from Tom Walker.

'How's it going, Jim? As I predicted, you didn't miss anything at that bloody conference. The last session was some twerp trying to get us to meditate on our vision of the path ahead and imagining all our problems melting away as we walked through a wood with birds singing. Then we went on an "energising fantasy journey" as he called it, and imagined we were surfing on the waves and into our places of work. Have you ever heard such a load of twaddle? And the tax-payer funded it all. The next thing will be Watkins proposing cuts to staffing because we can't afford them. Is there any bloody wonder we can't afford them when we're wasting money like that? Anyway, I'll shut up and let you answer the question.'

This was a big relief to Oldroyd, who had been steeling himself for one of Walker's long rants.

'Progress is slow, Tom. The case keeps getting more complex. Most of the obvious suspects appear to have good alibis for the night of the first murder, but now we've had a second killing, which has forced us to re-think everything.'

'Yes, so you think the crimes are connected?'

'Maybe, Tom. There's no clear evidence either way, but it's such a big coincidence, and the crimes are sufficiently similar, that we can't ignore the possibility.'

Walker grunted. 'Hmm . . . well, it sounds as if you've got a way to go yet. The problem is, I can't spare you and Carter for too much longer. We're a bit under pressure here. Stephanie Johnson's not been well, as I'm sure you know from Carter, and the caseloads are piling up. So, unless there's some kind of positive development in the next few days, you'll have to come back. I've spoken to DCS Hainsworth and he understands. I know you'll be doing a great job and I don't like to pull you away, but needs must, I'm afraid.'

Oldroyd had been half expecting this, but it was still a blow. He hated to leave an investigation that was incomplete. 'OK, Tom. We'll do our best to get to the bottom of it as quickly as we can.'

'Good man. I'll let you get on with it then while I sit here and meditate about a country lane with twittering birds.' Walker laughed uproariously. Nothing amused him more than one of his own jokes. 'What an idiot that man is! Bye for now.'

Mercifully, Walker ended the call without launching into another diatribe, leaving Oldroyd thoughtful. This time constraint added to the pressure. They would have to redouble their efforts and push for a breakthrough.

'Sir.'

He turned round and saw Andy looking very serious.

'What's happened?' he asked.

'Cynthia Carey just called, sir. It's Steph. She's fainted at work – collapsed on to the floor of the office.'

'No! Is she OK?'

'I think so. Apparently she's resting in the break room. I'll have to pick her up on the way home.'

'I see. Well, look, we're not doing any interviews this afternoon. You've been helping Inspector Hopkins' team to go through statements, haven't you?'

'Yes, sir.'

'Well, they can manage without you. Get off and take her home. And tell her from me not to come back to work until she's properly better.'

'Are you sure, sir? I think she'll be OK there resting for a while.'

'Yes, but you won't be much good while you're worried about her, so off you go. I'll explain everything to Inspector Hopkins.' He didn't say anything about them being called back to Harrogate. He knew Andy would feel the same as he did, and he had enough to worry about.

Andy looked relieved and got his coat on.

'Give her my regards,' said Oldroyd.

'I will, sir,' replied Andy and walked quickly out of the building.

Oldroyd had not missed how worried Andy looked. Fainting sounded serious.

~

It was dark by the time Oldroyd picked up Louise and Patrick by Bootham Bar – one of the medieval gates in the walls, which still had its portcullis. They'd obviously had a good time, as they got into the car laughing and in high spirits.

'Thanks, Dad. We've had a great day. We walked right round the walls. I absolutely love the section from here to Monk Bar, where you get a great view of the minster, the old library and the deanery. We started there so it was still very light.'

'It's great. How did you find York, Patrick?'

'Wonderful! I've never walked around original city walls like that. It's amazing that they're still intact.'

'We had some street food for lunch at the market,' continued Louise with great enthusiasm. 'What a choice there is! We had some mulled wine – it's really got me in the mood for Christmas.'

Oldroyd turned right to drive over Lendal Bridge. The street lamps were reflected in the dark waters of the Ouse. The river was still high and threatening, though mercifully a dry few days had led to a slight drop in the water level. As long as there was no more heavy rain, the city would escape serious flooding over the Christmas period.

'We also visited the Viking Centre and did the "trip to the past" thing.'

'What did you think of that?'

'It's very unusual,' said Patrick. 'And we enjoyed it. It's clever how they show you the archaeological dig and the sort of strata levels there are in the city, one on top of the other, going back to Roman times.'

'Yes,' said Oldroyd. 'That is interesting.' He paused for a moment, finding it hard to take his mind off the investigation. 'Good,' he continued. 'And how was Saskia?'

'Oh, it was lovely to see her again. She hasn't changed; just as committed as ever. I told her that you were on the case of Henry Marlow's murder. She confirmed that he was a problem landlord.'

'I think Inspector Hopkins will have been out to interview her this afternoon. I don't know whether your friend had any useful information or not.'

'I'm sure she would be helpful if she could.' Louise sat back. They had been on their feet all day. 'I already feel so rested getting away from London and work. I'm sorry you're having to deal with a serious case like this just before Christmas, Dad.'

'It's what the job is like, I'm afraid. It's happened before at Christmas and lots of other inconvenient times. It's very unpredictable and it's the kind of thing that your mother found hard to deal with, especially when you were little, and I don't blame her. By the way, I presume you'll be going to see her while you're up here?'

'Yes, of course. I need to ring her to arrange a time.'

'What is she doing for Christmas?'

'I don't know. She hasn't said anything. We'll go on Boxing Day if she's in Leeds. She might be going to Auntie Caroline's.'

'Right.' Caroline was Julia's sister who lived in St Alban's.

'Do you know if . . . she's . . . you know, OK with her new partner?' Oldroyd found it a difficult question to ask but he was curious. He held himself responsible for the breakdown of the marriage and felt no bitterness towards Julia. He wanted her to be happy.

'She hasn't said anything about that either. You know what she's like; doesn't say much about her private life, even to me. But it seems to be going well.'

'Good.' Oldroyd reflected and was overcome with nostalgia for a moment, remembering the family Christmases at their house in Harrogate when Louise and Robert were little. He would get a bit of that when he and Deborah went down to stay with Robert and his wife for New Year.

Oldroyd took in the scene around the car. They were now out in the flat countryside, back towards Green Hammerton and Knaresborough. The sky was clear and the moon was reflected on the still-flooded fields. Oldroyd smiled to himself. He remembered the Christmases of his childhood and the overwhelming excitement he felt as a small boy. There was something about the Christmas period that made you look back and evaluate your life. Was it because of the getting together and talking about the good times and the sad times? But when he did look back, he had to admit that, overall, he'd had a pretty good deal.

Four

During the Civil War, the parliamentarians besieged York in July 1644. Prince Rupert arrived with a Royalist army and the parliamentarians retreated six miles from the city. Unwisely, Rupert pursued them and his army was soundly defeated at the Battle of Marston Moor – one of the key battles in the English Civil War. After their defeat, the Royalists abandoned the north of England, which proved a handicap in the years ahead. York surrendered to the parliamentarian Sir Robert Fairfax on 15 July.

It was a clear and cold night in York. Down the dark snickelways, homeless people were hunkering down in sheltered spots and staying together in groups for safety. News of the murder of Jeffrey Smith had filtered through, and there was a sense of fear amongst the men and women on the streets who were detached from society, but vulnerable to attack.

One member of the homeless community was Samantha. She was twenty years old, thin, with long, straggly hair, dressed in frayed jeans and a dirty long coat. She had been thrown out of her home by an abusive stepfather, and had turned to alcohol to cope. She was unable to hold down a job at the moment, and was alone except for her little dog called Lucy, who was always with her. She was constantly looking out for people on the streets who were worse off than her, older, or in bad health.

Samantha was walking around the streets and snickelways near the river. There was one person in particular she was worried about. Lucy trotted after her as they passed people queuing to enter a nightclub. Samantha rattled her polystyrene begging cup.

'Bugger off and get a job!' one of them said.

'If you're hungry, why don't you eat that dog?' called another, and several people beside them laughed.

Samantha was used to the abuse and walked on. A young, heavily made-up girl dressed in a tight short skirt, spangly tights and high heels followed her. 'I'm sorry,' she said. 'Don't take any notice of them, they're just pigs. Here take this.' She gave Samantha a five-pound note.

'Thanks,' said Samantha, and then turned down a narrow snickelway which led towards the river. She went slowly, checking the grimy doorways and keeping Lucy on a short lead. Eventually she found what looked like a pile of rags in a doorway near to another nightclub entrance.

'Fraser? Fraser? Are you there?' she whispered. She didn't want to attract any unwanted attention.

The pile moved and the face of a man appeared. He was grubby, with long hair and a thickly matted beard.

'Aye, I'm here,' he said in a Glaswegian accent and began to cough in a harsh manner. His hands appeared out of a dirty blanket, trembling and holding the scrap of a rolled cigarette. 'Have you got a light?'

'No. I haven't got anything yet. A woman gave me a fiver and I'm going to get some food. Do you want some?'

'Naw, I'm not hungry. But I could do with a drink.'

'No chance, you need to lay off that. Me too.'

'Aye, I know. Where are you going tonight?'

'Railway arches. They won't allow pets in the hostel and I'm not leaving her. Are you staying here?'

'Aye.' The barking cough came back. 'I'm never sober so they won't let me in either. Here, Lucy!' He put his hand out and the dog came to be stroked. 'Good girl! You're lucky to have her. Hey, I was gonna tell you. I saw someone I knew today . . . but he didn't remember me or at least pretended he didn't, the arsehole. We used to be mates until he . . . aw, shit.' He was scrabbling around for a match in his chaotic pile of belongings.

Samantha didn't take much notice of what Fraser said – he often rambled on about things that couldn't have happened to him. Sometimes, she thought he was in his own fantasy world. She was concerned about his safety as he was a loner and that was dangerous in the present circumstances.

'Look, Fraser, you shouldn't be here by yourself. There's some maniac on the loose and there's no one else down this alley.'

'Aye, I heard, but I prefer it that way. I get some peace.'

'OK, well, I'll see yer. Look after yerself.'

'Aye, you too. Don't worry about me, I've got this.' He rummaged in his belongings and produced an iron bar.

'Right, well, be careful.'

Samantha and Lucy walked back up the road towards the brighter lights. Halfway up, the dog stopped and started to growl and yap. She seemed to be looking down a narrow yard to the side door of an old run-down building.

Samantha got ahead and then called back. 'Lucy! Come on, girl!'

The dog cowered down and growled again. 'Lucy!' Samantha shouted louder. This time the dog got up and ran to catch up with her mistress. Fraser was now alert and sat up watching people go past. And suddenly there was that person again. The one he'd recognised. He called out. 'Hey, look who it is. Yer remember me, don't ya?'

~

Oldroyd's expression was very sombre as he stood by the entrance to the snickelway where a body had been found that night, and looked into the face of Anne Hopkins. The inspector had lost all her vivacity, and appeared very stressed and tired. After this third murder, the situation was extremely serious, and they were looking at the possibility of a case review and new officers being brought in if there was no breakthrough soon. Also, Walker would recall himself and Andy to the Harrogate station. He felt that he had let Anne down.

'It's bad, sir,' was all she said.

'Yes,' agreed Oldroyd.

As with the murder of Jeffrey Smith, the snickelway was cordoned off with blue and white incident tape. Oldroyd and Anne stood watching and waiting for Dr Redgrave to report back to them. It felt like a defeat. Whoever was doing this, if it was one person, was well ahead of them. It seemed that they could strike at will.

Dr Redgrave ducked under the tape, and walked over to them. She, too, seemed dispirited by this latest murder. 'Similar story I'm afraid – stabbed. Probably with the same knife that was used before. It penetrated the heart. He's been dead for several hours, so the attack was at a similar time in the evening to the others.' She looked at Anne and Oldroyd with pity in her expression. She was glad she didn't have the responsibility of having to catch the perpetrator. 'There are some differences. In this case, the victim has been roughed up, as if there was a struggle, and there's an iron bar near the body, which the victim might have been holding to try to defend himself. He's got some quite serious head wounds, which might have rendered him unconscious before he was stabbed.'

'OK,' replied Oldroyd, wondering if that information really changed anything. It would be natural for the victim to put up a fight. Jeffrey Smith must have been surprised by his attacker.

'Thanks,' said Anne, and the pathologist went to collect her things.

'I don't know where this leaves us, sir. I'm baffled. I suppose it must be a serial killer, someone preying on people who are alone in these snickelways.' She covered her face in her hands in a gesture of deep frustration.

'That may be what we're intended to think.'

'What do you mean, sir?' Anne murmured.

'Remember that the first murder was different. We haven't found this Hutchinson person, and I think if he was making a bona fide enquiry about that property and he met Marlow there and left him alive, he would have come forward by now. So, it does seem as if Marlow was lured to his death, whereas the two subsequent victims weren't.'

Anne took her hands away from her face. 'You mean, someone is trying to make us think a serial killer is at work? To throw us off track?'

'I think it's very possible,' Oldroyd said. 'All three men seem to have been killed by the same person. But I think the motive revolves around the murder of Marlow. The killer is hoping we will start looking in the wrong places: at people around here with a history of violence or a mental health problem that has caused them to threaten people or even attack them. But this killer is not like that; they are clever and calculating, and they have a plan. They are also ruthless, because if I'm right, they have killed two people for no reason other than to mislead us.'

'And maybe more if we don't get to them soon.'

'Yes. But we just have to hope that the killer thinks they have done enough to put us off the scent and won't attack anyone else.' Oldroyd looked around at the scene. He'd been called again in the early morning and informed of this third murder. He hadn't contacted Andy as he was probably still caring for Steph. There was no point in him arriving earlier than necessary.

'What's going on here?' A voice sounded distressed. Oldroyd turned to see a young woman dressed in dirty jeans and a scruffy, worn coat. She had a small dog on a lead.

'Someone's been killed. You can't go through there,' said Anne.

'Killed? You mean, murdered?' asked the woman.

'Yes.'

'Oh my God. Not again. Who? It wasn't Fraser, was it? I told him not to stay by himself.'

'You know some of the homeless people around here, do you?' asked Oldroyd.

'Yeah, I'm homeless myself, aren't I?' She stuck out her hand. 'Samantha.'

Anne shook it, introducing herself and Oldroyd. 'OK, Samantha,' continued Anne. 'There was nothing on the body or among his possessions to identify who the victim was. Can you come with me now and see if it was the person you mentioned?'

'You mean look at the body? What about Lucy?'

'Don't worry, I'll look after her,' said Oldroyd.

Samantha shrank back. 'I don't know. I've never seen a dead body.'

'It's OK,' reassured Anne. 'He's got some head-wounds but he's not badly disfigured. He just looks as if he's asleep. It would help the investigation a lot if you could identify him and, if it is him, tell us a bit about him.'

Samantha still looked unsure, but finally she nodded and handed Lucy's lead to Oldroyd. Anne led her through the cordon, making a note of her details on the scene log. The body was still in the position in which it had been found, but the paramedics were about to move it. Anne had a word with one of them and he pulled back the sheet covering the face.

Samantha looked briefly, then pulled away. 'Yes, it's him. Oh my God, what's going on? Is someone trying to kill us all?' She sat down on the ground, put her face in her hands and shed a few tears.

'What's his name?' asked Anne gently.

'Fraser. I think his surname was McLean or something. I've known him for a few months. He came down here from Glasgow. I don't know why. He drank a lot and said the hostels wouldn't let him in. He was a gentle bloke, he wouldn't have hurt anybody. He didn't deserve this.' She started to cry again. Anne left her for a moment and motioned to the paramedics to cover the body. Then she helped her to get up and led her back to where Oldroyd was waiting with Lucy. Samantha took the lead.

'Thank you for your help. Are you OK?' said Anne.

Samantha nodded but didn't reply, then she walked off with Lucy.

'Fraser McLean, although we have to confirm the surname,' said Anne. 'Another unfortunate homeless person, it seems – very much like Jeffrey Smith. I think it confirms that the murderer's choice is random.'

'That's what we expected, isn't it?'

'Yes, sir. I must say that woman turning up has really highlighted how homeless people in this city must now be feeling. Imagine being out on these streets at night when you know a murderer is on the prowl.'

'Yes – you'll have to give the order to increase night patrols in the city centre. What's the city's policy on providing accommodation for homeless people?'

'They have a strategy and are trying their best, but money is tight, as it is for all services.'

'I'm sure. Anyway, you'll want to finish up here. I'll see you back at the station.'

Oldroyd walked back slowly and thoughtfully to his car. They were in a tough position and he did what he always did when things were difficult. He put on a CD of a string quartet. It was Brahms' String Quartet No. 1 on this occasion and it contained one of his favourite slow movements, which always soothed and stilled his mind.

∿

Unaware of the latest developments in York, Andy was reluctantly preparing to leave for work. He didn't really want to leave Steph, who was still in bed.

'How are you now?' he asked, sitting beside her in the bedroom.

Steph yawned. 'I'm OK. I'm going to get up soon. My cold is a lot better. Thanks for the tea.'

'Are you sure? I mean, you fainted yesterday. You've never fainted before – at least, not since I've known you.'

'No, but I've been really run-down with this cold. I shouldn't have gone back to work. It was my own fault.'

'Maybe you should stay in bed and rest?'

'I don't think so. But I can always go back to bed if I feel bad again, can't I?'

'OK, well, make that appointment to see the doctor. You promised.'

'Yes, I will, so stop fussing and get off to work. I really feel OK.'

'Good.' He gave her a kiss. 'Don't forget to text me how you're getting on and make sure your phone is on for when I ring you.'

'Yes, yes – now off you go!'

He left the flat and Steph smiled. It was nice to have someone who really cared about you.

~

Andy arrived at the York station and was shocked to find that another murder had been committed. Oldroyd briefed him before they attended the latest case meeting.

'OK, good morning, everyone. Although there's not much that's good about it,' said a downbeat Anne Hopkins. 'Just to confirm what I know you will have heard: another homeless man has been murdered – this time in Water Alley, near the river. It was another stabbing – probably the work of the same person.' She stopped and looked up at her small audience. 'This obviously increases the pressure on us. I've already had DCS Hainsworth on to me asking what leads we have, do we think we're making progress, and so on. The force is under pressure when there's a risk to public safety with a dangerous killer on the loose and the brutal truth is that we'll be replaced on this case if we don't get some answers quickly. I don't have to tell you how humiliating that would be.'

People shuffled, looking uncomfortable, including Oldroyd. He hadn't yet told Anne that he and Andy would have to return to Harrogate soon if no progress was made. That would make it even more difficult for her.

Anne continued. 'So, progress on following things up: we got straight on to Philip Storey's alibi. The landlord at the Queen's Arms remembered chatting to Storey on the evening of the murder, but he can't be sure about the time. Looking at the map, it's not far from that pub to Butcher Lane where Henry Marlow was killed, so I don't think his alibi is watertight. Saskia Middleton at Roof has given us a list of people they worked with who had difficulties with Marlow, so we're pursuing those. Of the current suspects, the frontrunner must be Justin Hayward, who had the motive and no verifiable alibi for the night of Marlow's murder. The problem is that he's an intelligent man, so if he planned – with or without help – to kill Marlow, wouldn't he have been likely to construct some kind of plausible alibi?'

A number of people nodded.

'As far as the other murders go, we have no leads at all. DCI Oldroyd and I have discussed his theory that the murders of the homeless men could be an attempt to misdirect us into thinking all three killings have been committed by a deranged serial killer. I agree that it is a definite possibility, and so we are going to have to go back to all our suspects and see if they have alibis for the times when Jeffrey Smith and Fraser McLean were killed. It's just a hard slog, I'm afraid, but there's no way round it.'

No one said anything. It was a sombre message. Everyone was hoping for a breakthrough so that they could wrap the case up by Christmas.

When the meeting ended, Oldroyd went to speak to Anne. 'There'll be a clamour from the press for you to hold another conference,' he said. 'I would advise you to say something to them, but to keep it short – just the usual asking for people to come forward with any information and obviously best to not say anything about our theory that the killer might be trying to mislead us. In fact, stress the opposite: state that we are looking for someone who has been behaving strangely, who may have a grudge against people living rough. We want the killer to think that we've swallowed the bait – of course, that's assuming I'm right.'

Anne nodded. 'Yes, sir, I agree.'

'Try to do it without feeding their fantasies about serial killers too much, though we're definitely going to get some lurid headlines after this. "Serial Killer Stalks Alleyways in York" kind of thing. But if we can trick the killer, they may become complacent and start to make mistakes. I've seen it happen many times.'

'Well, I hope so, sir.'

'Sorry,' said Oldroyd. 'I seem to be taking over and telling you what to do. I'm so used to being in charge.'

Anne laughed. 'Don't worry, sir. I value your advice very much.'

'OK. But let me tell you . . . you're doing a brilliant job on a very tricky case.'

'Thanks.'

After this, Oldroyd went to speak to Andy. 'Sorry, I was in such a rush earlier to bring you up to speed that I forgot to ask about Steph. How is she?'

'Not too bad, sir. I left her still resting and insisted that she make a doctor's appointment, so we'll see what they say. I don't think it'll be anything serious. She's just got very run-down with this bad cold she's had, and she went back to work too quickly. I warned her, but there we are. She's not one for sitting at home doing nothing – she likes to be working.'

'I'm pleased to hear that. I'm very fond of her, as you know. She's worked with me ever since she joined us straight from school.'

'Yes, sir.'

'Louise is up for Christmas. I'll never forget that she wouldn't be here if it wasn't for Steph – all that business in Whitby.'

'I remember it well, sir.'

Oldroyd was getting quite nostalgic and a bit emotional – even if he didn't admit it out loud. He was worried for Steph, as he would be for his own daughter – so he reverted to talking about work. 'Anyway, another matter I have to tell you about is that, unfortunately, we only have a limited time left here in York. DCS Walker needs us to return to Harrogate soon. I haven't told Inspector Hopkins yet because I don't want to put more pressure on her, so don't say anything.'

'I won't, sir. I hope we can make a breakthrough before then. It'll be very disappointing to leave with the case still open and the killer not caught.'

'I agree. I can't stand leaving things unresolved. I suppose it's pride. It's our job to solve the puzzle of these crimes and if we don't, it's a failure. Also, we're not fulfilling our duty to protect the public.'

'I know, sir.'

'I think all detectives feel the same. I've heard of people who've retired but had a case that remained unsolved, maybe from years before. They were haunted by it for the rest of their lives and were still trying to work it out right up until they died.'

'It doesn't surprise me, sir. It sort of gets under your skin, doesn't it? And it feels personal.'

'Yes . . . Deborah is always warning me not to see a case as a personal struggle between me and the perpetrator; that can distort your view of things, but it's not easy, especially when other people's safety is at risk.'

They went silent as they reflected for a moment, and then realised that everyone else had left the incident room. They followed them out, ready to re-engage with their demanding but vital work.

Samantha wandered around the centre of York without a destination in mind. She was devastated by Fraser's death and knew that it would have a terrible effect on the homeless community. However shapeless and shifting that was, people knew other people in the same position as themselves and cared what happened to them.

After a while she slumped on to the ground in a doorway and someone bought her a coffee. Lucy lay still beside her. She knew her mistress was not feeling good. Samantha cried a little and then, revived by the hot drink, thought about what she could do.

There was no point just sitting around and moping; she had to do something practical. Why not try to organise a march in the city in support of homeless people? They needed a voice, and it could draw attention to their plight. The authorities needed to do more to protect people on the streets now that they were being threatened by this killer. It was bad enough being without a home without having to fear for your safety. The thing about sleeping rough was that there was no security, so you were very vulnerable. You couldn't lock yourself in anywhere and you were always exposed to danger.

She got up. She would go to the homeless shelters and talk to them. Also, Lucy was hungry and they stocked a bit of dog food even though you weren't allowed to take pets in when you stayed there. After that she would find other groups who were sympathetic.

There was a shelter nearby, based in an empty church. She'd stayed there before she acquired Lucy, and remembered the people running it as being very kind. When she arrived, there were two people on duty that she recognised: a youngish man with a black beard and a middle-aged woman with glasses and short hair. Some bedraggled people were leaving the sanctuary for the day.

Samantha explained her idea and asked them if they could help.

'I think it's a good idea,' said the woman, and the man nodded in agreement. 'It's an emergency. People living rough are not safe. Saturday would be the best day. It will allow you to publicise what's happening and people can take part who are working during the week.' Then she paused, reluctant to say what was coming next. 'But the thing is, you're supposed to get permission from the council for something like that.'

'There isn't time. It's got to be done soon. We can't wait weeks to get a letter from the council. This killer might strike again. We want better protection. We need it now.'

'I know,' the woman said, 'but Dave and I couldn't take part in anything illegal. We have to be very careful about campaigning for anything politically sensitive because we're a charity. It could affect the shelter here and the work that we're able to do.'

Samantha frowned. 'That's crap. The people who might come to you for help are at risk.'

The woman shook her head. 'I know, I'm sorry, but that's the way it is. We could lose our funding over something like that. I'll tell you where to go. Have you heard of Roof? They're an organisation dealing mostly with families who are having housing issues and problems with landlords. I'm sure they would be supportive – you could try them. The woman in charge, Saskia Middleton, is very committed to highlighting all housing issues and the problems people face. I can tell you how to get there.'

∾

Philip Storey was guiding a group of American visitors around the museum. They were elderly scholarly types who showed great interest in the exhibits. Philip loved groups like this. He had to have an audience that was attentive, not kids – he left those school parties to Brian. Philip relished an opportunity to show off his knowledge about Roman York and to tell stories about life and events in those times. They were looking at a series of statues and busts of Roman leaders. Each one had an information board explaining who they were and their relevance to York.

'Now,' announced Philip portentously. 'Do we have any ministers of the church here today?'

One man raised his hand and identified himself as Reverend Harris, a retired minister from the American Episcopal Church.

'Well, sir,' Philip said, 'something truly momentous in relation to the Christian church happened in Roman times here in York.' He pointed to one of the statues. 'This is Constantine the Great, who was proclaimed emperor by his father's soldiers here in York in 306 when his father died in this city. We know that Constantine became a Christian and halted the persecution of Christians. In fact, it was largely due to him that the Christianisation of the Roman Empire took place, and that Christianity was established as the religion of western Europe and in the eastern part of the Roman Empire in Constantinople – what is now Turkey. From these places, Christianity was eventually taken around the world, including to America.' He paused and turned to Reverend Harris. 'So, sir, it's not too far-fetched to say that if it wasn't for what happened here in York, early in the fourth century, you may never have been ordained into a Christian church. Western Christianity started here in York, with Constantine the Great.'

Philip's little audience loved this, and there was an excited hubbub of conversation. Of course they knew about Constantine, but hadn't known that he was proclaimed emperor in York, which they thought was amazing.

'This is a copy of the bronze statue in the street next to York Minster, which I recommend seeing. There is also a Roman column that was discovered in 1969, and if you go down into the crypt in the minster, you can see the remains of Roman pillars.'

'Oh wow!' said one of the group, clearly impressed.

When the tour was finished, the group thanked Philip profusely, with many of them even donating extra money to the museum.

Philip was beaming as he went back into the office. Brian was sitting there reading the paper. It was one of his volunteering days and there was another school party arriving soon. He looked up and smiled.

'You look as if you've been enjoying yourself. I heard you holding forth about Constantine.'

Philip laughed. 'You know me, Brian – there's nothing I like better than a receptive audience. When people are listening and you sense they are moved by what they are hearing and seeing, I think that is what we're all about.' He took a deep breath after this little speech. 'I know I'm a bit of a performer – it's why I like doing a bit of acting. Which reminds me – there's a panto rehearsal tonight.'

'What are you, then?'

'Widow Twanky! I've done it before. It's great fun. I like kids when they're laughing and enjoying themselves, not when I have to talk to them about this stuff and they look bored.' He gestured to the exhibition area.

Brian laughed. 'You're too formal when you talk to them. You can't give them a lecture. You have to make it interesting. Try to look at it from their point of view. You can entertain and educate them at the same time, you know?'

'Yes, well, I'll leave it to you. I could never have been a school teacher.'

'OK. By the way, I assume you've heard that there's been another murder?'

'Yes – same scenario, wasn't it? I overheard people talking about it on the way in. Those homeless people must be terrified. I hope the police get it sorted out soon. It's terrible to have this going on just before Christmas, and in York.'

'"Too cruel anywhere", to quote the bard,' replied Brian with a smile. 'But I know what you mean. You need to be careful yourself. I know you walk home through some of those dark snickelways. A serial killer might not care who the victim is. They don't have to be homeless – the first person wasn't, were they? It could be anyone who presents an opportunity.'

'You're right, but don't worry. I'll take care.'

～

At last, Janice Marlow made a visit to the office of Marlow Holdings to check in with Anthea Marston, who was back at work after her interview at the police station. Anthea had been hoping for this visit and was ready to confront her ex-employer's wife with one or two matters.

Janice had never been to the office before. She looked curiously around the two rooms: one where Henry had his desk and one in which Anthea was still working. 'So, this is where Henry worked? Very basic, isn't it? Typical of him and his frugal attitude. How do you find it, Anthea?'

Anthea was still at her computer. 'Fine. We got everything done from here.' She didn't say anything of what she'd told the police and the story of who she really was, nor her stealing of the money. She was waiting for the right time to tell Janice the truth.

'I take it you'll be busy answering enquiries?' said Janice as she sat down in a chair opposite Anthea.

'Yes, they're coming in all the time. Henry's tenants naturally want to know what's going to happen.'

'Of course. Well, things will be clearer when we go to the solicitors to hear the will. I have to say that I'm not a businesswoman. I shall be leaving the running of the business to my partner, who runs his own concern in retailing.'

'I see. So, you have no information about what he might do with the various properties in the portfolio?'

'Oh no! I'm afraid not. Justin, my partner, will be looking into it all when it's confirmed that I've inherited the estate. It will be a while before we decide what to do.'

Anthea looked at her directly. 'And what about my own situation? Can I ask if that has been discussed?'

Janice looked a little flustered. 'Well, not exactly, but, as I said to you before, we need you to keep things running at the moment – you're doing a great job. That doesn't mean that when things have settled down we intend to dispense with you, so please don't worry. I know you've worked here for a number of years and I value that service.'

Anthea smiled. Little did Janice know that, during those years of service, significant sums of money had been taken out of the company and given to organisations like Roof. She thought for a moment and decided that this was the time to speak her mind and make it clear where she stood. 'Thank you for that. I would obviously like to stay here. But not at any cost.'

'What do you mean?'

'I was often made to feel very uncomfortable by the way your husband dealt with his tenants, particularly the poorer ones. As you say, you didn't involve yourself with the details of his business, so you are probably unaware that some of the residential properties your husband owned are in a very poor condition: damp, run-down, and infested with mould and pests. He stubbornly refused to spend money on their upkeep. I've witnessed some very unpleasant scenes where desperate people came here to plead with him to do repairs but were turned away. Some of them have small children who are having to live in those conditions. There is a family with a little girl who has asthma, and her family are living in a damp flat because your husband had failed to assist with the upkeep of the property.'

'I see,' replied Janice. She was clearly surprised that Anthea was so outspoken, but looked like she actually admired her for doing it. Anthea reckoned that Janice must have been aware of what a mean person Henry could be, and suspect that he had made enemies. But it was unlikely she knew any specific details of his dealings with tenants, probably because she hadn't been interested. Might she feel ashamed of her ignorance? These were people and families, after all.

'I know my husband was no angel, although he was always kind to me. I'm sorry about the tenants he treated badly. The problem with Henry was that he thought of himself as a self-made man who'd worked himself up from a poor background. And he thought everyone should do the same. He didn't have much sympathy for those who didn't or couldn't.'

'It's one thing to believe that if people are poor it's their own fault, and quite another to abuse and exploit them, especially children,' observed Anthea.

Once again, Janice was taken aback by the other woman's forthrightness, but she nodded. 'You're right, and as far as going forward is concerned, I promise there will be changes. I'll speak about it with my partner.'

Anthea nodded. 'I suppose I've talked myself out of my job now. I've always been a straight speaker.'

'No, absolutely not. I'm pleased you spoke up. We'll find a place for you, I promise.'

'Thank you,' said Anthea. 'I do have something else to tell you. I wanted to find out what your attitude to Henry's treatment of his tenants was before I spoke about this. After what you've just said, I want to get everything out into the open.'

She told Janice about her sister's death and how she'd taken the money in revenge. Janice was shocked and, when Anthea had finished, shook her head and didn't seem to know how to respond.

'Bloody hell!' she eventually said. 'What a bastard! I had no idea that he'd behaved like that to your sister. Of course it was his fault – the poor woman. To be honest, I've been completely lax in finding out about things like this. It matters, even if it was before I met him. All I was interested in was Henry's money.' She looked down and hung her head, feeling ashamed and angry with herself. Then she looked up and smiled at Anthea. 'Do you know what? I'd have done exactly the same in your position. I'll tell the police I will not be pressing charges, and I still want you to work for us. The least I can do after your family has suffered so much at the hands of my husband is to keep you in a job.' She reached over and shook Anthea's hand. 'I admire your spirit.'

Anthea was a very composed person who didn't often show much emotion, but she was very much affected by Janice's response, which was unexpectedly understanding and generous. For the first time, she felt there could be a better, more moral and honest future working for the company.

~

Saskia was reading a report on her computer when Linda Black came in to have a word.

'There's a young woman at the door, asking to talk to us. She has a dog with her and says she's homeless.'

Saskia looked up. 'What is it she wants to talk about? Is she looking to be housed?'

'No, she says it's about the murders of homeless people.'

'Oh. OK, bring her in.'

The lady came into the office with her dog on a lead. She had the unkempt and unhealthy look of a homeless person and seemed nervous. She clearly wasn't used to office spaces.

'Sit!' the lady said to the dog, who obediently lay down on the floor. 'Are you two in charge here?' she asked.

'Yes, I'm Saskia, and this is Linda.'

'Oh right,' Samantha said. 'Well, pleased to meet yer. I'm Samantha, and I'm organising a march for us homeless people. You know we don't feel safe after these murders. You've heard there was another one last night?'

'Yes, it was on the radio. I'm sorry.'

'I knew the bloke who was murdered. Fraser. It's horrible – there's some maniac on the loose and we don't know where they'll strike next.'

'I understand,' said Saskia. 'But what do you need us to do?'

'Come and support us. We want as many people as we can. It will show that people on the streets matter. I've been to that church shelter, but they won't do anything because they're a charity or something. They said you'd be interested. People are just not safe out on the streets. We need the coppers to protect us more.'

Saskia looked at Linda. Samantha had an impressive pluckiness about her – it was impossible to say no. Roof was also a charity but sometimes you had to take some risks to further your cause.

'Of course we'll help. It's a great cause. You must all be scared stiff, and I think we do need to bring what's happening to people's attention.'

'Yeah . . . Will you print some flyers or something and put it on social media? None of us have got phones or anything.'

'Yes, we can do that. It's probably too late to attract a large number of people, but I'm sure there'll be enough to make the point – and it is urgent.'

'That woman at the shelter said you're supposed to get permission from the council. I can't do owt like that.'

'Well, don't worry. In a situation like this, I think the police will be sympathetic, as long as it's peaceful and you don't block any streets. I don't suppose there'll be a massive turnout. I've got some contacts in the police and I think I can make it OK.'

'Oh, good. Thanks,' Samantha said, looking surprised that she had actually been offered any help. 'I'll come back tomorrow for the flyers. I'll just write down what I want you to put on them.'

'If you're thinking of a day, I reckon Friday would be the best, because the streets will be packed with Christmas shoppers on Saturday. If we don't have official permission, then it would be better on a quieter day so there's less chance we could block a street or something like that.'

Samantha shrugged. 'OK.'

When Samantha had written down the text for the flyers, she motioned to Lucy to get up on her feet, and together the young woman and her dog left the office.

'She's got some spirit, hasn't she?' said Linda. 'Fancy organising that when you're homeless.'

'Absolutely,' agreed Saskia. 'We have to support things like this. How can we not? We're an organisation campaigning on housing issues and helping people.'

'True. Well, I'll definitely join you – and I'll see who else I can persuade to come along.'

In the afternoon, Steph was feeling well enough to attend the doctor's appointment she'd made in the morning, though she was still feeling a little light-headed.

She always found Dr Stevens to be very approachable. They were about the same age, and got on very well. Not that Steph went to the doctor's often – she was usually in very good health.

Dr Stevens performed the usual tests on heart rate and blood pressure, which were normal. She listened to her chest, which was fine.

'Have you ever fainted before, Steph?' Dr Stevens asked, entering some notes on her computer.

'Not that I can remember.'

'So, it's not happened repeatedly through your life? Never when you've been under stress or anything?'

'No.'

'And have you been under any unexpected or unusual pressure recently for any reason? Work?'

'No, but I've had a really bad cold recently, and it left me feeling very tired.'

Dr Stevens looked at her. 'Well, there're a lot of viruses around at the moment. OK – we'll do a couple more tests, see if anything shows up.'

Gary Owen got to the ghost tour office in the late afternoon before Craig arrived from his other 'job'. Having photocopied the letter from Marlow, he replaced the original in the file and waited for his boss to appear. He was a bit nervous, but he steeled himself. He desperately needed money, and to get away from York now. It was too small for him. Craig deserved what he got; he was a nasty boss who paid rubbish wages despite rolling in money. Gary didn't know where Craig got his money from, but a man who drove around in an expensive car could afford to pay his employees more.

He had to wait a while until Craig's Jaguar parked down the side of the building. A few minutes later, his boss came in and looked surprised to see Gary sitting on a chair near to where the costumes were hung.

Craig looked at his watch. 'What the hell are you doing here at this time? Not on the cadge again, are yer? It'll be a loan. I don't give money away.'

Craig had once loaned Gary some money and charged him interest, which had really angered Gary at the time.

'No,' Gary said, 'I want to have a word with you about something.'

Craig screwed up his craggy face. 'What? I'm not giving you a pay rise, if that's what yer after.'

Gary smiled. He was determined to stay calm throughout this encounter. 'No, I didn't expect you would, but it's not about that.' He paused and took a breath. 'I know about Marlow threatening to go to the council and have your licence removed.'

Craig had clearly not expected this. His mouth dropped open. 'What? How did you—? You've been going through my stuff here, haven't you?! Blast it! I should have made sure I locked everything away.' He looked at Gary, and his lip curled. 'You bloody little snooper. I'll . . .' He moved towards Gary, who stood up, put his arms out defensively, and stepped away.

'Steady on,' Gary said. 'What would the police think if they knew about that letter?' As he spoke, he tried to maintain his composure.

Craig stopped and looked uncertain for a moment until he realised the implications.

'Oh, so that's yer nasty little game, is it? Blackmail! Give me money or I'll tell t'coppers.'

'I just want to be paid a decent wage.'

Craig scoffed. 'Yeah . . . to begin with. But blackmailers always want more, don't they?'

Gary frowned; this wasn't going as he hoped. Craig didn't seem at all cowed by his threat. 'You can easily afford it,' he said. 'And you don't want to become a suspect in Marlow's murder, do you?'

Craig laughed. 'Marlow's murder? Huh! I'm glad t'bugger's dead alright – me and a lot more folk. I'm sure t'police have plenty of suspects already. And what would they think if I told them you'd been going through my private stuff?'

'They'd be more interested in you having a motive to bump him off. So, let's come to an arrangement. It'll be much better for you.'

Craig snarled like a dog and jabbed his finger at Gary. 'You can get out of here now with your bloody arrangement, and don't come back. You bastard, I've a good mind to—' He lunged at Gary, who ducked, evading Craig's grasp, and then ran to the door. He opened it quickly and bolted out, narrowly avoiding Craig's boot connecting with his rear end. 'Do what the hell you like and see if I care! And don't come back here!' Craig shouted after him before slamming the door.

'Shit!' Gary swore to himself as he walked quickly down the street, putting some distance between himself and the office, worried that Craig might decide to come after him. Gary was stronger than he looked. He wasn't frightened of his boss – more that he might lose his temper with Craig and cause him injury.

He kicked a tin can hard down the street in frustration. His scheme had been a disaster, and he'd lost his job. But, he thought, so what? It was a crap job and he was fed up of it anyway. He stopped to get his breath and glanced back towards the office with a sneer. He wasn't going to let Craig get the better of him. He would go to the police as he'd threatened. Craig wouldn't expect him to do that. Maybe there would be a reward for information.

~

The end of the autumn school term was very close to Christmas this year. Ailsa Braithwaite pushed the pram with Rosie along to the school gates to collect Sam. She wasn't looking forward to

Christmas; it was too expensive with all the food, presents and other treats. She'd managed to buy some things for the kids, but there would be no presents for herself and Terry, and the truth was there hadn't been for a number of years.

Rosie was asleep in the pushchair. The little girl slept a lot these days, and she always looked very pale. When she was awake, she often had bad coughing fits, and found it hard to catch her breath.

Ailsa tried not to think about what might happen if there was nothing done to the flat to stop the damp, or they were not offered somewhere better. The council had put them on to some kind of waiting list for a council flat, but there was never any news.

At the gates, some of the other mothers and fathers had gathered. She joined a group of people who were talking in low voices, looking serious and shaking their heads.

'What's wrong?' she asked. 'You don't look happy.'

'Hi, Ailsa,' said a blond-haired woman called Liz, who was rocking her twins in a double pushchair. 'We're just talking about all these murders; three of them now in a week. It's shocking, isn't it?'

'What? Has there been another?' Ailsa had not listened to any news bulletins. She found the news generally depressing.

'Yeah, haven't you heard? Another homeless man was stabbed in one of those dark snickelways.' Liz shuddered. 'Alan was saying why don't we go into the centre and see the Christmas market, but I don't want to go anywhere near the place while there's some maniac at large, certainly not at night. I feel sorry for those people with nowhere to go. They must be terrified at the moment.'

Another woman carrying a young child joined in. 'I think you'd be alright in the busy areas where it's well lit. I don't want to miss that market, it's great.'

'No,' said Ailsa absently as a fresh pang of anxiety went through her. She knew the stress of her life was making her anxious, but she'd never entirely got the idea out of her mind that Terry could somehow be involved with Marlow's death. Going out in his taxi at night gave him the opportunity to move around and . . .

She shook her head. She had to resist thoughts like this. But she was desperate for the police to find the killer and prove her husband really did have nothing to do with what had happened.

'Oh, they're coming out!' someone called, and suddenly there was a rush of children running down the path towards them. Ailsa's panicky train of thought was disrupted as Sam shot up to her, smiling and holding a Christmas card he'd made.

~

The reporters seemed positively exultant at the latest press conference. They had got what they wanted: an unpredictable and terrifying serial killer on the rampage in the cathedral city of York in the dark days of December leading up to Christmas. It was a dream story!

Anne felt some revulsion as she stood outside the station, sensing their excitement. What a job it was if it made you enthusiastic about frightening people, especially just before Christmas!

'Inspector! Inspector!' There was a huge scramble to ask questions.

'Are you going to catch this killer soon?'

'Will York be terrorised all over Christmas?'

'Is this mystery murderer a step ahead of you?'

Their questions were very provocative. They knew that she couldn't answer them in an affirmative way. She would have to do what Oldroyd suggested and keep to simple messages, even though it made her appear rather weak and evasive.

'My team and I are obviously working extremely hard to catch this killer, but they have struck a number of times over a very short period and we have not had the opportunity to follow up any leads.'

'We hear that you're getting help from DCI Oldroyd of West Riding police. He's got quite a reputation as a crack detective. Is he here because you're not capable of solving this case, Inspector?'

Anne took a deep breath. 'No. DCI Oldroyd has been involved from the beginning in a consultant role, and his help has been very useful, as has that of—' She was interrupted.

'Is it true that DCI Oldroyd discovered the body of Henry Marlow, the first victim?'

Anne frowned. They had kept this information back from the media as things like that were distractions that only fed their imaginations and speculations: 'Top Police Inspector Finds Body in York'. Clearly someone had been speaking to the press; somehow they always found these things out, no matter how hard you tried to keep them secret.

'Not by himself, no. Inspector Oldroyd was attending a conference in York and on the evening of the first murder he was part of the group of people who were on the ghost tour when the body was found in Butcher Lane. After that, DCI Oldroyd was interested in pursuing the case and police chiefs at Harrogate station have allowed him to be a part of my team.'

There was a buzz of conversation from the assembled reporters.

'If you're failing to solve it when someone like DCI Oldroyd is helping, then you're in big trouble, aren't you?' called out one.

'As I said, events in this case – and we are assuming that all three murders have been committed by the same suspect – have moved very fast. I don't think it's helpful to talk about "failing" and "trouble" at this relatively early stage of the investigation.' There was a cacophony of voices, all asking questions together. Anne had to raise her voice to be heard. 'If I can just continue, please.'

The hubbub quietened.

'It's very important that people stay alert and don't venture into any dark places such as yards and snickelways. The evidence suggests that we are looking for someone who is extremely dangerous, so I'm asking people to be alert to any signs that anyone they know has been behaving strangely. Have they been out at night when these crimes have taken place? Have there been any signs of blood on their clothing? Have they been handling knives? Does anyone know a person who has expressed negative views about homeless people or even threatened violence against them? If anyone has information that might connect to these murders, it is vital that they come forward. Cases like this are often solved by a member of the public being observant, but we understand that it can be difficult if a person suspects someone in their family, or a friend.'

'Do you think the killer will strike again, Inspector?' called someone at the front.

This was always the terrible but unanswerable question until the killer was in custody.

'Obviously I cannot be sure about that. Killers like this often continue until they are caught, but we can all make it much more difficult for whoever it is by keeping ourselves safe and by staying alert in the ways I spoke about earlier.'

'Are any special measures being taken by the police to protect people who are vulnerable?' asked a more sensible reporter.

Anne felt some relief – at last a practical and sensible question. 'Yes, we will be increasing the number of patrols by officers in the city centre, especially at night. We hope that the council and the charities who work with homeless people will increase their efforts to find safe places for them, but we know that these are difficult times financially.'

When the press conference ended, a tired Anne walked back into the station where she met Oldroyd in the incident room.

'How did it go?'

'Fine, sir, I think. I laid it on thick that we are looking for a dangerous killer who has committed three murders and people should report suspicious behaviour. I'm afraid it will result in a lot of bogus calls to us, which will waste our time, but it will be worth it if the killer believes they've got us on to the wrong trail.'

'Good,' said Oldroyd, who was sitting with a cup of coffee and looking at the diagram of the suspects on the white board. He got up and poured a mug for Anne before continuing. 'You know, I'm more than ever convinced that the murders after Marlow's have been intended as misdirection. I'm sticking my neck out, but I think there are unlikely to be more murders. Once the killer hears what you've said, and they'll be listening carefully, they'll believe that we've taken the bait and are off their track.'

'What makes you more confident, sir?' said Anne wearily. It had been an exhausting day so far and it was still only mid-afternoon.

Oldroyd leaned forward. He felt positive about his theory now. 'If you think about the pattern, we've not only got the differences between the first murder and the others, but the fact that the second and third murders have happened in very quick succession. I know people think about what happened in the famous Whitechapel Jack the Ripper murders, but even they were sometimes weeks apart. He did kill two women in one night but that was highly unusual. You would normally expect there to be much more of a gap between. A serial killer will tend to wait until the furore has died down and people are off their guard before taking their chance again. But this person is moving quickly in order to try to control things.'

Anne nodded. 'I see, sir. It makes sense, but it doesn't get us any nearer to catching the killer, does it?'

'Not yet, but it may do if we stay alert. Anyway, in the absence of any further leads, I'm going to help your team checking alibis for the nights of the last two murders. I have a feeling that they will probably all have them but some of them will turn out to be false.

No other strong leads have emerged, so it's very likely that the killer is one of the people we already know about.'

'Yes, sir. We've been working through the information about Marlow's clients we got from Saskia Middleton, Anthea Marston and Bishopthorpe Manor. Nothing suggests anyone who had a better motive than the suspects we already have.'

Oldroyd slapped his knees and got up. 'OK,' he said. 'I'm off to see Justin Hayward again. He's still a top suspect. I'll see what his alibi is for the recent murders and see if I can probe a bit deeper. Did we find out anything about his business?'

'Yes, sir, we looked into that. Bespoke Kitchens is solvent and making a modest profit, but I'm sure Hayward would welcome an injection of cash from Marlow's estate.'

'Yes.'

'Oh, before you go, sir, I got someone to do a bit of research on the thing you asked me about and I've printed off some information for you.' She went into her office and came back with a pocket file.

'Thanks,' said Oldroyd, and started glancing at the papers as he left the building.

Anne went back into the office, sat in her chair and closed her eyes for a moment. She was just distracting herself from the rigours of work by doing a bit of family meal planning in her head, when DC Jefferson knocked on the door.

'Come in!' she said.

Liam opened the door. 'A bloke's just come into the station, ma'am, and he's asking to see you.'

'Oh?'

'Yes. He says his name is Donald Hutchinson.'

～

174

After Gary Owen beat a hasty retreat from the ghost tour office, Craig Jordan turned back into the building, seething with anger. It was probable now that Gary had been sacked that he would go to the police and cause trouble. So what if he did? There was no way he would give Gary any blackmail money. He could tell the police what he wanted.

He picked up his phone and dialled Mel's number.

'Mel? It's Craig.'

'I know it's you, dumbo, your name and number come up on my phone.'

'Alright, you clever sod. Listen, I've just sacked Gary Owen and he's going to cause bother.'

'What did you sack him for?'

'He threatened to blackmail me. The bastard! Can you believe it?'

'Gary Owen? Is he that bloke I've seen around your office? One of your tour guides?'

'Yeah.'

'Bloody cheek! Blackmail about what?'

'He must have been going through me papers. It's my own fault for leaving stuff around. I'm no good wi' paperwork. Anyway, he found this letter from Marlow threatening to go to t'council and get them to remove me licence.'

'Why would they do that?'

'Aw, it's all crap. He said there are too many ghost tours going past that shambles of a building that he owned and its lowering t'tone of th'area. Can you believe it? It's that wreck of a place that's lowering t'tone. He was such a miserable bugger, he couldn't stand th'idea of anyone enjoying themselves. Anyway, listen. I think Gary will go to t'police to get his revenge and then there's a good chance they'll be back at that palace where Marlow lived looking for more evidence against me. So be careful. You don't want them to find you there pinching stuff.'

'Right, thanks for the heads up, but I already knew the police were nosying around. They were there the other day when I turned up to clean and a nice detective told me that Henry had been murdered. It was quite a shock. I've been back once to get the stuff I brought to you but I wasn't going to go again before Christmas. I'm trying to find out if anyone's going to live there. At the moment I can come and go as I please cos I don't think anybody knows I've still got a key. So I can select a bit more stuff at my leisure.' She chuckled. 'Don't worry, you can always tell if the police are there because their cars are parked outside.'

'OK, good. Glad to hear it. I look forward to you bringing some more things over. But don't get too greedy and get caught.'

'Oh, I won't – I know what I'm doing. Anyway, I'm too busy at the moment – I've got all my Christmas shopping to do, but least I've got more cash to do it with.'

∽

Anne Hopkins sat facing the elusive Mr Hutchinson. He turned out to be a tall man with a full beard, dressed in a large black overcoat.

'I've just heard about what's been going on here,' he said in a Scottish accent. 'And I found out you were looking for me in connection with the murder of Mr Marlow.'

'Yes,' replied Anne, still stunned that this man had turned up. This could demolish DCI Oldroyd's theory, and where the hell would they be then? 'Can you tell me exactly what happened on that day when you met him?'

Hutchinson took a deep breath. 'Yes . . . Well, I'm a property developer myself. I'm based in Scotland, but I'm on the look-out for stuff all over the British Isles, so I spend a lot of time travelling.

I was in the area looking at one or two properties when I saw this small place advertised for sale. I thought that, being in the centre of York, it might have, you know, some development potential. So I rang the office – Marlow Holdings, I think the company was called – and I spoke to a nice woman who said she would tell Mr Marlow I would be at the property at six o'clock. My phone was out of power, you see, so I was in a call box. I didn't want to miss the opportunity. I knew it would be dark but it would be OK for an initial viewing and I was shortly going back to Scotland.'

'Had you had any dealings with Mr Marlow before?'

'No . . . at least, I don't recall any. I have dealings with so many property owners and companies that it can be difficult to remember them all. Anyway, this place was in a very dark alley. Mr Marlow was there waiting with a torch and we went inside. There was no electric light. I had a brief look round, but I was disappointed. He said it was very old and had been a shop and a small house in its time. But, to be frank, it was little more than a shell. I wasn't even sure about the external structure. The asking price was low and the position was good, which is what had attracted me, but it seemed that just about everything needed doing. The investment would have to be big and then there was the question of conservation area status. That always makes things more difficult. I had a brief look round, thanked Mr Marlow and left. I think he knew I wasn't interested. But, I want to emphasise, he was very much alive when I left him. I don't think he would have stayed there much longer, so the killer must have struck quickly. It's a wonder I didn't see the person who did it.'

'Why has it taken you so long to come forward?'

'Aye, well, I heard someone had been murdered here in York, but I don't follow the media much. I find the news too depressing, so I didn't learn the details until yesterday when I was in a café and someone who was talking about the murder mentioned the name

Marlow. So I asked them about it and they told me the full story and about the other murders too. I was shocked, but I realised that I needed to come forward. I knew I was most probably the last person to see Mr Marlow alive, so I would obviously be a suspect. Then I found out that you were looking for me. But here I am. I've nothing to hide and I hope what I've said has been of help.'

'So, you didn't see anyone else in the vicinity of that property?'

'There were one or two people walking through the alley, but no one stopped. There was no one waiting around when I left. But, to be honest, it was so badly lit that there were shadows everywhere. It would have been very easy to hide.'

Anne looked at him. He seemed an ordinary guy, very believable.

'Do you have a company that develops your acquisitions?' she asked.

Hutchinson smiled. 'No, I'm a kind of middle man . . . freelance. I've always preferred to work alone. I select places, then I work with a number of building firms who trust my judgement. They buy the properties and when they sell them after refurbishment, I get a cut. It's not made me rich, but I enjoy the scouting.'

'OK,' Anne said. 'Thank you for coming in. I would like you to provide a statement and also leave your details in case we want to get back in touch with you.'

'Of course, I'll leave my phone number. I'm staying in a B&B here in York at the moment and I'll leave the address, but I'm heading up to Scotland shortly for Christmas and Hogmanay at my sister's in Edinburgh. I'm a bit of an . . . itinerant, I think the word is – never happy staying in the same place for very long. I'm hoping to be back in York in the New Year. There are some more properties I want to look at around here.'

'I see.'

Hutchinson left and Anne sat thinking with her head in her hands, and not about menus this time. Where did they go from here? Maybe they were looking for a serial killer after all. There was a knock on the door and in came DC Jefferson again.

'It's all happening this afternoon, ma'am.' Liam looked at his notes. 'We've just had an anonymous tip-off that there was a big row between Marlow and a man called Craig Jordan, who runs a ghost tour business in the city centre that goes down Butcher Lane. Marlow was threatening to get the council to revoke Jordan's permit, because the tours made too much noise near his property. Ironically, the property in question was the one in which Marlow's body was found. The caller alleges that Jordan threatened violence against Marlow, and he's got proof.'

Anne perked up a bit. Maybe this was the lead they'd been waiting for.

'Did the caller give their name?'

'No, ma'am.'

'OK, well, we need to check it out – and pretty quickly.'

Louise and Patrick were spending the day in Harrogate with Deborah. A clear sky and weak winter sun tried to illuminate the Valley Gardens as the three of them walked from the bottom gates alongside the stream where the gunnera plants were wrapped up for winter – their giant leaves roped down over the tender crowns to protect them. On the other side of the path were extensive flower beds, where the winter pansies were looking a little forlorn.

After a walk around the gardens, where they passed the remnants of the special dahlia display, they arrived at the beautiful, circular Edwardian-style Magnesia Well Tea Room. They didn't know that this café had been a regular place that Oldroyd visited in the lonely days when he had lived by himself in the flat overlooking the Harrogate Stray.

Patrick sat down in the café and looked at the menu. 'Well,' he grinned, 'I think I'll have a cappuccino – or anything except that stuff you had me drinking at that pump room last time.'

Louise laughed; like her father, she enjoyed the occasional practical joke. Patrick had been to Harrogate with Louise on a previous visit and she had tricked him into sampling the sulphurous water at the Royal Pump Room. In fact, Oldroyd had once persuaded Andy to drink the same water, resulting in Steph banning Andy from their bedroom that night due to the stink he was producing.

'She didn't get you to drink those spa waters?' said Deborah.

'She did. I've never tasted anything so vile in my life. It took me days to get it out of my system.' He shook his head. 'And people used to pay for that stuff?'

'They did,' said Louise. 'Drinking and bathing in the mineral waters and all sorts of weird stuff. I think they also did something called an intestinal lavage where they stuck a pipe up your bum.'

'No!' exclaimed Patrick, and Louise shrieked with laughter. 'They didn't squirt that water up, surely?'

'I don't know,' said Louise, who could hardly speak for laughing.

'They still do that, don't they?' said Deborah, who was also laughing. 'They call it colonic irrigation now, I think. I must say I've never fancied it.'

'I wouldn't want to see what came out!' exclaimed Louise and doubled up laughing again. 'And what a job doing it!'

They had all calmed down by the time they got their coffees and Louise became thoughtful.

'You know, Deborah . . . Dad's a lot happier since he got together with you. I just think you're so right for each other.'

Deborah smiled. 'Aww, it's really nice of you to say that.'

'Well, I mean it. You seem very tolerant about his weird working hours and the fact that he can get obsessed about what he does. Mum always found that really hard, especially when Robert and I were little.'

Deborah nodded. 'I'm not surprised. It must have been very difficult for her. I might feel differently if I was in her position, but I've only got your dad to handle, and not young children.'

'Well, he's enough!' said Louise, laughing again.

'Yes . . . but I can't say I didn't know what I was taking on, as he keeps reminding me. I think one of the things is that his work interests me, particularly from the psychological angle. I take it, from what he said, that your mum wasn't really interested in his job, and found it hard to relate to him on that level.'

'Yes, I think she did. She works in a sixth-form college. She enjoys History, and teaching it to young people. But I think she found police work grim.'

'Also, I don't mind if he comes home late and cancels things. I'm not that "couply", if you see what I mean. I like doing things by myself and with my friends. I don't think partners have to do everything together, which was expected more in the past. I do have to put my foot down occasionally, and he always comes into line.' She laughed. 'He doesn't want another relationship to be ruined by his work.'

Patrick nodded. 'I can understand that.'

Louise took a drink of her coffee. 'I do worry about him, though, as he's getting older. What he does is very demanding. So much is expected of him because he's solved so many difficult cases. Do you think he should retire?'

Deborah frowned. 'Well, we've talked about it. The problem is that he enjoys it so much, even though it's stressful. And I don't really know what he would do with himself. I've tried to encourage him to take up hobbies. He's got his music and he writes poems occasionally. We go to the theatre now and again and I've got him running. And of course he loves walking. I can't get him gardening, though – he always has an excuse for not doing it.' She laughed. 'I don't know if those things would be enough to get him out of bed in the morning. Maybe he could write his memoirs or something.'

'That would be good,' said Louise. 'He's been involved in so many famous cases, and there's so much interest in true crime – I think it would be a bestseller.'

'Yes. The problem is I think he'd rather still do it than write about it. He loves the challenge and the buzz of working with his team.' She shook her head. 'It's very hard to replicate that. Anyway, we'll see what happens. He might change his mind if he loses energy and it all becomes too much of a struggle.' She finished her coffee. 'Another thing I can't get him to do is shopping. I'm grateful to you two for coming to the supermarket with me.'

'You're welcome,' said Patrick. 'It's always a massive shop, the one before Christmas. I've helped my mum in the past.'

'Oh, isn't he marvellous?' said Deborah, laughing again. 'You're a lucky woman, Louise.'

∼

'Oh, hello, darling. What a nice surprise! I thought we weren't meeting until this evening. Come in.'

It was late afternoon and Justin was at the door of Janice's flat. They kissed in the hall, before he came in and sat down on the sofa, while she took the armchair opposite. She hadn't seen him since their meal on the night of the first murder, although they had spoken a few times on the phone.

'Two more murders,' said Justin. 'I can't believe it. Do the police think they're all connected?'

'I think so. I saw the police inspector on the telly holding a press conference. She looked very harassed.'

'I'm not surprised. I told you the police came to see me and I got the feeling that I was a chief suspect. Surely they don't think I would go around murdering homeless people?'

'No, but I think they're struggling.'

Justin paused before continuing. 'How are you, anyway? There are some things I want to talk to you about.'

'I'm OK. What things?'

'When we went for that meal, you were upset, and you seemed to be struggling with things you'd learned about yourself.'

Janice looked down. 'Yes, to do with relationships and my attitude to money, but I told you, Justin, it's different between you and me, I—'

'Yes, I know, but I thought maybe I could help you more. You see, we were both brought up in poor families where money was short, weren't we?'

'Yes. I've been blinded by the idea of having plenty of money and not having to worry about it. It's gone on for a long time.'

'Look, I understand. You had no money as a kid and you've never forgotten that – the disappointment and going without things. When you grew up, you were determined never to be poor again.'

She nodded.

'I was the same,' he continued. 'I worked so hard setting up this business that my marriage to Sheila broke down. And I wasn't really doing it for her or for Adrian and Kelly; it was for myself, so that I could feel secure with money in the bank. I realise now that it was more important to me than spending time with my family.' He shrugged. 'It's too late to change that now, but it's taught me to have a different attitude to money.'

Janice nodded. 'You're right. I've also had a sobering experience today. I went to see Anthea Marston in the office. She told me about Henry's behaviour towards her sister.' She shook her head. 'I won't go into details now, but it shocked me, and I realised that I've been awful. I never took any interest in how Henry made his money or how he treated people.

'Another thing that upset me was when I spoke to Penny and Alex on the phone yesterday about money. They didn't ask me how I was, or what I'd been doing – they just seemed to want me to hand over the cash. It was painful and disappointing, but then I realised that their attitude to money is only the same as mine has been: money comes first before anything else.' She looked at Justin and seemed to be on the verge of tears. 'They don't seem to want to see me, they just want my money.'

'I'm sure it's not as bad as all that.'

'Well, if it is, I've only got myself to blame. I went through three marriages and they all failed because I married for money each time. It's my fault.' She moved to sit on the sofa with him and held his hand. 'It's not going to happen to us. I admit I was attracted to you partly because you have a business and are comfortably off. But I'm telling you again that my feelings for you are deeper than that, and money is not going to spoil it this time.'

Justin was very moved. He embraced and kissed her. 'I think that's amazing. I'm so proud of you for saying those things. It's not easy to admit when we're wrong and that we want to change. I feel exactly the same about you, and this has brought us so much closer.'

'Oh, Justin, that's wonderful!'

'There's something you could do, however, that would really show that you want to put things right. Find out who the present tenants are that Henry was treating badly. Go round and tell them that things are going to be different now. That way you can draw a

184

line under the past and start to right the wrongs inflicted by Henry. It will be good for the tenants – and for you.'

'You're right,' she said. 'I will.'

~

Andy was feeling anxious as he drove home that night. He hadn't heard much from Steph apart from brief texts saying she was alright and her cold was a bit better. There had been no more fainting.

When he got to the flat, he made his way in gingerly, hoping that everything was OK.

'Hi, I'm back!'

'In here!' she called from the living room. He went in to find her sitting on the sofa reading a book, which she put down when she saw him. When he went over to give her a kiss, she smiled at him, and there was something in her expression that he couldn't quite place.

'How are you?'

'Oh, fine, the cold is definitely better.'

'How was the doctor's?'

'Good.'

What was it he could see in her expression? It was almost as if she was trying not to laugh.

'Was it Dr Stevens?'

'Yes.'

'What did she say?'

'Well, she did a few tests and the last one was quite revealing.'

Andy felt panicked. 'Oh? Why was that?'

Steph couldn't contain herself any longer. She burst into laughter. 'The poor man, he can't pick up any hints. The test showed that I'm pregnant, you twit, so you're going to be a daddy! Apparently pregnant women are prone to fainting – something to do with changes in the blood flow. I haven't felt any other symptoms, but often you don't. And my periods aren't very regular, so I didn't consider it.'

Andy was so surprised that his legs went weak and he had to sit down beside her. 'What? Me? Daddy?'

'Yes, you. At least, I think it was you but maybe it was one of the other men I've been having sex with recently.' She picked up her book and hit him lightly over the head, laughing. 'What a dolt you are! And look, I'm already reading all about it and getting prepared!'

She showed him the book, which was about pregnancy and childbirth, but he seemed speechless. 'Well, are you going to say anything else . . . Daddy?!'

Suddenly Andy's face broke into a massive smile. 'Oh – my – God! That's amazing!' he shouted. 'Come here.' He put his arms around her and gave her a huge kiss. Her blue eyes were sparkling with laughter, as they often did, and he loved her more than ever. 'When is it due?' he asked, feeling incredibly excited.

'Dr Stevens thinks I'm about a month gone, so that would make it sometime in August. She's signed me off work for a few days so I can completely recover from the cold. I have to have my blood pressure checked regularly.'

'Oh, next year,' said Andy still in a daze. He didn't seem to have heard what she said about having time off work. Steph looked at him and shook her head.

'No, a year in August, obviously. I'm going to be the first woman to be pregnant for over eighteen months.' She went for him playfully with her fists. 'You idiot! I don't know whether you're up to being a father – too dopey.'

'Well, we'll have to celebrate!' Andy got up. 'I'll get round to the shop and get some champagne, we'll—'

'Oh no, here he goes again. I can't drink, you fool. It's bad to have alcohol during pregnancy.'

Andy put his hand to his forehead. 'Oh, yes, I forgot. What shall we do? We must do something to celebrate. Oh, but we can't do . . . that . . . can we?'

'What?'

'Well, sex? Won't it harm the baby?'

Steph laughed again. 'Bloody hell, did they do any sex education at all at your school?'

'Yeah, but just the basics – you know, sperm and eggs and stuff like that.'

'Well, no, it doesn't harm the baby, but don't get excited, I'm still not very well. The cold is real and I'm not in the mood for that. What I'd really like to do is have a nice takeaway meal and sit here and talk about things like names and what we need to buy and who are we going to tell first and all that stuff.'

Andy rubbed his hands together. 'That sounds great!' He bowed. 'Your wish is my command.' He shook his head. 'But I still can't believe it!'

Five

In the eighteenth century, York declined as a trading hub due to competition from Leeds and Hull. It remained an important religious centre with the province of York and its archbishop being second only in importance to Canterbury. The city became a social and cultural centre, and a number of elegant townhouses and buildings were constructed: the Theatre Royal, Mansion House, Fairfax House, the Assembly Rooms and the racecourse. In 1839, George Hudson brought the railway to York, and by the 1850s the city was a busy railway centre on the East Coast Main Line halfway between London and Edinburgh. A magnificent new station was built in 1877 on a bend in the line. It has a soaring curved roof supported by wrought iron trusses and cast-iron columns. On completion, it was the largest station in the world, with thirteen platforms.

There was a case meeting early next morning, where Anne Hopkins described her encounter with Donald Hutchinson. Oldroyd raised his eyebrows and frowned as he digested what she had to say.

Andy, meanwhile, was only half listening, with a smile on his face. His mind was elsewhere after the previous night's news. He hadn't had the opportunity to tell his boss yet.

'It was obviously a great surprise that Hutchinson actually turned up to talk to us. I don't think that any of us were expecting it. We had all been working on the assumption that Hutchinson was a false name used by the murderer to lure Marlow to his death. The fact that he's a real person complicates things. If he is telling the truth, it leaves us with the possibility that Marlow was killed after Hutchinson left him – by probably the same opportunistic killer who murdered the two homeless men.'

'So, ma'am,' said DC Jefferson, 'that would mean that we're wasting our time looking at the motives and the alibis of the people who knew the victim and had a reason to kill him. Marlow was killed because he was in the wrong place at the wrong time.'

'I only said that was a possibility, Liam. We have to continue with all lines of enquiry where there is evidence.' She turned to Oldroyd. 'What do you think of this, sir?'

'Hmm . . .' Oldroyd screwed up his face in thought. 'Did Hutchinson say why it took him so long to come forward?'

'He's staying in a B&B here in York and said he wasn't following the news. He overheard someone talking in a café about a murder and heard Marlow's name mentioned, so he contacted us.' She shrugged. 'Sounds OK. In fact, he was generally very plausible, and he claimed that he left Marlow alive and didn't see anyone around that snickelway who seemed suspicious. He also claimed that he'd had no prior dealings with Marlow.'

'What was he like?'

'Tall, big beard, glasses, Scottish accent. He runs his business from Scotland, but spends a lot of time travelling round the country viewing properties. He acts as a kind of agent finding stuff for development companies to buy.'

'Has anyone seen him around in York before?' asked Oldroyd, but no one had.

'OK,' said Anne. 'We're going to have to find out more about him and whether he did have a motive to kill Marlow, despite his denials.' She paused and looked around at everyone. 'Now, I've looked at all your reports concerning alibis, Marlow's financial affairs and incidents concerning him and the suspects. Most of the suspects have some kind of alibi for all three murders.'

DC Jefferson raised his hand.

'Yes, Liam?'

'Ma'am, with respect, I don't think a lot of those alibis are worth much. People who are at home with someone, or in the pub and stuff like that. It's easily possible to slip away for a while, especially late at night when all these murders took place. You remember that case in Clifton where the bloke murdered his wife. He appeared to have a rock-solid alibi: with his mates in the pub, until we worked out that there was a period during the evening when no one had seen him and that's when he'd rushed home, killed her, and then gone back to the pub.'

'Yes, Liam, I do remember that case – and your point is valid. Alibis are only part of the picture. If lots of other evidence points to a certain person, an alibi has to be revisited. Anyway, we have a couple more leads to follow now. In addition to Hutchinson, we got a tip-off yesterday about the ghost tour organiser, Craig Jordan.' She looked at Oldroyd. 'He runs the tour you were on, sir, when the body was discovered.'

Oldroyd raised his eyebrows.

Anne continued, 'This anonymous caller alleges that Marlow was threatening to have Jordan's licence revoked and that Jordan had threatened violence.' Another hand was raised, and she turned her head towards the questioner. 'Yes, Kate?'

'Craig Jordan, ma'am? I've come across that name before. Isn't he the bloke suspected of a running a fence out near the ring road?'

Anne nodded. 'I think you're right. I wonder if Marlow knew about that as well? He could have used this information against Jordan. Anyway, we'll stick with what we've got. We haven't got the time or the resources to start looking into whether or not he's receiving stolen goods.'

'Did this informant offer any proof?' asked Andy, finally beginning to concentrate. 'He may be just a disgruntled employee trying to cause trouble.'

'We called back and said that we would take no action without some evidence, and that he would have to identify himself. So he came in this morning, looking sheepish, with a letter, said his name was Gary Owen.' She turned to Andy. 'You're right – he was employed by Jordan, who he had admitted sacked him, so we'll have to take that into account. Nevertheless, it needs to be investigated. The letter does contain comments threatening to do things to Jordan, but how serious it all is, I'm not sure.' This time she turned to Oldroyd. 'Could you and Andy root out this Craig Jordan, while the rest of us see what more we can find out about Hutchinson?'

Oldroyd gave the thumbs up but didn't say anything. He was still struggling with where these current developments left his theory about the murders.

Andy came over and sat by Oldroyd as the others in the room were talking among themselves. He had a beaming smile on his face.

'Well, something seems to have pleased you,' said Oldroyd. 'Have your lottery numbers come up?'

Andy spoke in a quiet voice. 'No, sir. Better than that, I've got some news for you – Steph's pregnant. I'm going to be a father!'

'What? Oh, that's fantastic!' replied Oldroyd, who grinned and shook Andy's hand.

Andy looked around the room and he gestured to his boss. 'Sir, if you don't mind, can we keep it quiet? Steph said I could tell you, but no one else yet.'

Oldroyd nodded. 'I see. Yes, of course, but congratulations! Wow, Steph a mother. That's great!' He shook his head. 'You know I still think of her as the young lass who joined the force straight from school. How old was she, seventeen? Eighteen? It's amazing how the time has passed so quickly.'

'Well, sir, I feel it too. When I first came up here, I'd no idea how much I'd love it – or that I'd meet Steph and love her even more. And now we're going to start a family. It's incredible.'

Oldroyd laughed. 'That is really good news, and we needed some at the moment. We'll have a drink to celebrate at the first opportunity.' He tapped his finger on his nose. 'But don't worry, I won't say anything to anyone.'

∼

At the house in New Bridge, Louise and Patrick were doing some housework while Deborah saw a client. Deborah had protested, but Louise had insisted that she and Patrick were not there to be waited on hand and foot. They wanted to help.

Louise was vacuuming the hall when her phone sounded. She switched the machine off and answered the call. It was Saskia on the other end of the line.

'Hi, Sas,' Louise said. 'How are you? It was so great to see you last week.'

'It was good to see you too,' replied Saskia. 'I'm just calling to ask a favour.'

'Oh?'

'Yes. This case that your dad's working on. It's got really nasty. Two homeless men have been killed in the centre of York.'

'Yes, I know. It's awful.'

'Well, we had a visit yesterday from a homeless woman called Samantha. She knew the second homeless victim, Fraser

McLean. She asked if we would help her to organise a march in York in support of the homeless people in the city. We don't usually deal with people on the streets directly – there are other charities doing that – but she is such an amazing character. So, the upshot is that there is going to be a march on Friday through the centre of York. Then we will gather at some point and hear a few speeches. I was wondering if you would come along and join in, say a few words at the end? It would be great to hear about your work at the hostel. Of course, bring Patrick along. You can imagine how homeless people in York are feeling – they're not only sleeping on the streets in December, but there's a threat of them being attacked. It's—'

'It's OK, Sas – stop there,' Louise said. 'You don't need to convince me. I think it's a great idea. I'll be there and I'm sure Patrick will want to come too.'

'Oh, Louise, that's great! I'll let you know the details once it's all been finalised but I think we'll be aiming for the middle of the day because it goes dark so quickly now. Probably about one. I'll let you know where we're meeting up. Thanks a lot. I'll see you on Friday.'

'Looking forward to it, Sas, and well done for getting involved. It will highlight the plight of vulnerable people on the streets of the cities in this country.'

'I know – and thanks.'

Patrick wandered into the hall holding a duster. 'Who was that?'

'Saskia. We're going on a march in York on Friday in support of homeless people.'

Patrick raised his eyebrows. 'Are we? Fine, sounds great. I'm always up for a bit of a protest.'

∽

When the police contacted Craig Jordan, he agreed to meet them at the ghost tour office. He didn't want them anywhere near his property on the outskirts of York, which was stashed with stolen goods. Even though most of them were carefully hidden away, it was still too dangerous.

Oldroyd and Andy entered the scruffy main room, which was barely big enough to contain the costumes, props, a few chairs and a table. Some signs advertising the ghost tours were propped against the wall.

Craig took them into his tiny office, which was a crush for the three of them.

'I don't know exactly what Gary Owen's been telling yer,' he said, a hostile scowl on his face. 'He came into this private office when I wasn't here and rummaged through my personal stuff. He stole a letter and then tried to blackmail me about it.'

Oldroyd produced a sheet of A4 paper. 'Is this the letter in question?'

Craig glanced at it quickly. 'Yes, the bastard made a copy.'

'So it's true that you were in conflict with Henry Marlow concerning your ghost tour? After all, the route did go down Butcher Lane and past one of his properties.'

Craig's scowl became even more angry. 'Yes, but that doesn't mean that I killed him, even if I scribbled something on that letter.'

Oldroyd read from the paper. '"Interfering bastard! Like to turn him into a bloody ghost." That sounds pretty threatening to me.'

Craig made a dismissive gesture with his hand. 'Ah, rubbish. T'bloke made me angry. Here we are trying to make an honest living by entertaining t'public and a mean, miserable sod who makes loads of money out of his poor tenants in those bloody awful flats tries to stop us. I just jotted those things down when I was in a bad temper.'

'But if he'd succeeded in having your licence removed,' Oldroyd looked at the letter again, 'and he implies that he's got friends in high places, then that would have had a big impact on your business, wouldn't it?'

'It would have caused problems, yeah. Butcher Lane's a good part of that tour. It's a spooky little snickelway – but we could have re-routed the tour somewhere else. What got me angry was him interfering for no good reason. I mean, have you seen that place he has in Butcher Lane? It's a right dump and nobody lives there.'

'Yes, we've seen it, alright,' replied Oldroyd. 'That's where Marlow's body was found. And I was there. I was on that ghost tour.'

'What? Bloody hell. Well, you've met Gary, then? He leads that tour. Or did. I've sacked him over this.'

'I see. Well, there are quite a few ironic coincidences here, aren't there? Did you decide to finish Marlow off in that building of his that caused all the problems? And then have his body discovered by people on your own ghost tour? That must have been very satisfying.'

'No.' Craig stabbed his finger at Oldroyd. 'I'm telling yer, I never touched him. Why would I risk going to jail over him?' He was lost for words.

'OK, where were you on the night of his murder?'

'I don't know. When was it? Last Wednesday? I was at home watching telly. My partner can vouch for me.'

'And what about when the two homeless men were killed?'

'What?! Are you accusing me of those murders too?'

'We believe one person was responsible for all those crimes. You need to give us your home address. An officer will come round to your house to take a statement and also speak to your partner.' Oldroyd fixed Craig with one of his hawkish stares. 'And by the way, don't consider taking any revenge against Mr Owen, however you feel about him speaking to us. It would be very unwise, and would confirm in our minds that you are a person capable of violence.'

'I never want to see that bastard again,' said Craig and returned Oldroyd's icy stare.

~

'Well, he's a bad-tempered bloke and – as you said, sir – capable of violence,' said Andy as he walked with Oldroyd through the streets back towards the station. Around them, people were still streaming in and out of the shops. Another shopping day – before the rapidly approaching Christmas – was coming to an end.

'Yes. But I worry about the motive. As he said, it wouldn't be the end of the world if they had to change the route of that ghost tour. Was it worth killing a man for?'

'He's the kind of bloke who hates being told what to do. He could have easily killed Marlow through sheer spite and anger.'

'Maybe. Despite what I said about the satisfaction of him killing Marlow in that property, it creates such a strong link between himself and the murder, I think it's more likely that he would have killed Marlow somewhere else.'

They were near the Christmas market, and street-food vendors were doing a brisk trade in curries, German sausages and Swedish meatballs.

'Look, I'll treat you to some lunch – fancy a bratwurst sandwich?' Oldroyd lowered his voice in a mock whisper. 'They can't see us here.'

'No, sir,' Andy laughed. Steph and Deborah both monitored the diets of their partners, who had a tendency to put on weight due to their weakness for junk food. Like a pair of naughty schoolboys, Oldroyd and Andy enjoyed an occasional escape from their surveillance.

As they ate their long sandwiches, Oldroyd looked around at the people carrying bulging bags. 'By the way, how's the shopping going? I ought to be doing some myself. At least you've got the consolation of knowing that you're better at it than me.'

Andy swallowed a mouthful of sausage and bread. 'I don't know about that, sir, and I'd completely forgotten about it after yesterday's news. I can't even remember what I've done with the list.' He went through his pockets and found it crumpled up in the breast pocket of his jacket. 'Phew! That's a relief. Steph's going to need even more help now, so I'd better pull my finger out.'

'Well, take a quick break. We've been at it all day and here we are in the shopping area. I'll see you back at the station.'

'Thanks, sir. I won't be long.' He finished his sandwich and licked his fingers. 'That was very tasty.'

Oldroyd smiled as he watched him go off much more enthusiastically than last time. The prospect of fatherhood was clearly putting a spring in his step.

~

Anne Hopkins and DC Kate Warren located the address that Donald Hutchinson had given them. It was a B&B just out of the centre of York in a gentrified area of large three-storied Victorian terraced houses. There was a bed-and-breakfast sign in the window with the word 'Vacancies'. Anne pressed on the buzzer, but there was no answer. She pressed again and a middle-aged woman appeared at the door.

Anne introduced herself and Kate and they showed their warrant cards. The woman looked alarmed.

'We're looking for a Mr Hutchinson. We understand he's staying with you.'

'Oh, yes, but I don't think he's in. He's out working.'

'I assume you live here as well?'

'Yes, my husband and I own the house. We've run a B&B for many years now, never short of visitors in York – so many tourists. Is Mr Hutchinson in trouble?'

'We're just making enquiries in connection to a murder investigation, and we need to have a look at his room.'

'I see . . . I'm Mrs Richardson, by the way. Come in. A murder, you say? Of course I've seen something about it on the telly. I can't imagine Mr Hutchinson getting involved in anything like that – such a polite, friendly man. It's this way. I'll just get the spare key.'

Anne smiled at the woman's naivety as she fiddled with the lock to open the door to the room. Inside, everything was neat and orderly, with a suitcase by the wardrobe and clothes hung inside. There was a toiletries bag and a copy of a novel – a spy story by John le Carré – on the bedside table. Other than that, there were no personal items laid out anywhere. Inside the suitcase were underwear, socks, a mobile phone charger and a glasses case, presumably containing a spare pair.

Anne looked round, noting everything. Hutchinson obviously travelled lightly, which was consistent with a man who moved around a lot and knew exactly what he would and wouldn't need on a trip.

'How long has he been staying here?' she asked.

'Three days now. He's booked for another two. He's paid cash in advance. He said he's going back to Edinburgh to his sister's for Christmas. I don't know the details about what he's been doing here in York.'

'Yes, he told us about his sister. Has he stayed here before?'

'No, this is the first time, but as you can see he's a good guest – he looks after the place and generally keeps himself to himself.'

'Has he said he might come back sometime?'

'Yes. When he's got more properties to look at.'

'Do you know where he is now?'

'No. He's usually out in the daytime. He often comes back quite late at night. Sometimes he doesn't have breakfast.'

Anne nodded as she scanned the room again. It all seemed very plausible. Maybe he was lying about his relationship with Marlow. They both worked in what could be a murky world of property dealing. Did Marlow double cross Hutchinson? Or outbid him for a property that he really wanted? Was there a nasty falling out? According to Anthea Marston, Marlow hadn't seemed to recognise the name Hutchinson, but maybe that was a false name. They would have to get the technical team on to this to see if there was any history between the two men.

'OK, thank you, Mrs Richardson.'

As they were getting into the car, Anne looked up at the tall Victorian house. They hadn't found any answers. This case was proving to be very elusive, but at least there hadn't been any further murders – so far.

~

That afternoon, Ailsa trudged back wearily with Sam and Rosie from the school. There was only one day left until the end of term. Rosie was not well. She'd been coughing all day and her cheeks were red. Ailsa hoped that she was not coming down with a virus. The little girl was not strong enough to deal with something like that. At least Sam was happy. He was full of enthusiasm for what he'd been doing at school, chatting away about his science project on magnets.

'Mum, did you know that the biggest magnet in the world can lift an aircraft carrier weighing a hundred thousand tons?' There was no reply. 'Mum, are you listening?' He tugged at her coat.

Unfortunately his mother was rather distracted by worrying about his sister.

'I'm sorry, Sam. Tell me again.'

Sam looked down, shook his head and went quiet.

When they got home, Ailsa put on the kettle and then leaned down to get Rosie out of the pushchair. She released the straps and picked up her daughter. At that moment, the girl was racked with a terrible coughing fit. Her eyes rolled and she was struggling to get her breath. Ailsa panicked; she had never seen Rosie as bad as this. She rushed to get the little girl's inhaler and a few breaths from this seemed to revive her a little, but then her head lolled back on the sofa. She looked exhausted.

Ailsa jabbed at her phone. Terry was at work, but answered via the car phone.

'Terry! She's bad! I don't know what to do. She's going to die!'

'Whoa! Slow down, love – what's going on?'

'She's not breathing properly and she's weak and floppy. I don't know what to do!' she repeated. 'I've not seen her like this before.'

'OK,' said Terry firmly, though he was shocked. 'Try to stay calm. I think you should call an ambulance.'

'Oh God, Terry!' Ailsa started to cry.

'Yes, love, call now. Explain what she's like and then you'll feel better. Tell me when the ambulance arrives and I'll meet you at the hospital. OK?'

'Yes,' she replied in a weak voice.

&

Luckily, the ambulance was quick to arrive and whisked the family to the hospital. Sam was very quiet, knowing that something was wrong. Ailsa stroked Rosie's hair and face all the way there, but the little girl was unresponsive. At the hospital, she was taken straight away into an emergency ward and Terry arrived not long afterwards. He sat down, put his arm round Sam, and held Ailsa's hand.

'What did they say?' he asked.

'Nothing yet. Oh, Terry, she looked awful. I don't know what's wrong with her. I hope it's not meningitis. I've heard people with that go weak like she did.'

'I don't think so, love, it's unlikely. Where would she have picked that up? Maybe—'

At that point a doctor came into the waiting area, and led them into a consulting room where they all sat down. Ailsa couldn't contain herself. 'She hasn't got meningitis, has she?' she said with a voice rising in panic.

The doctor smiled. 'No, it's not meningitis.' He looked at the notes. 'Rosie's breathing is badly compromised. She has a chest infection and I know she suffers from asthma. This is making her very weak, so we are assisting her breathing until we've stabilised her and treated the infection with antibiotics. She will be fine for now.' He looked at the worried parents. 'It's important when she goes home that she's kept in a dry and warm place so that nothing aggravates her breathing difficulties.'

Terry looked down and felt his anger rising. He explained their problems with the flat and the damp and mould.

'I see,' said the doctor. 'Those are not good conditions for Rosie.'

'We know that, but you try to get anything done about it. We've been on to our landlord and the council time after time.' Terry was close to tears of frustration.

The doctor was sympathetic, and said he had seen other families whose health had been affected by poor quality housing. 'I understand,' he said. 'I will write a letter to your GP emphasising that your housing situation is adversely affecting your daughter's health. You can show that to the local council. It might make a difference.'

'Thank you,' said Ailsa. 'Will Rosie be in hospital for a long time?'

'I don't think so, and we have arrangements so that a parent can stay here overnight with a young child like Rosie.' He got up. 'A nurse will come and talk to you about it. Try not to worry. We'll look after Rosie.'

Terry and Ailsa felt better after this, and even Sam, who seemed to understand quite a bit of what had been said, was smiling.

'We've got to get out of that place,' said Ailsa after the doctor had escorted them back to the waiting area.

Terry raised his hands in the air. 'I know, but we've tried, haven't we?'

'Yes, but this time it's different. Our daughter's life is at stake.'

Andy, carrying his shopping bags, met Oldroyd back at the station. Oldroyd was in the incident room, sitting back in his chair, deep in thought.

'I see you've been successful.'

'Yes, sir. It's amazing how sometimes you just seem to see the things you need.'

'Good. Now look, I've been thinking. You and I need to up the pace on this investigation if we want to see it resolved. It won't be long before DCS Walker will be telling us to return to Harrogate. I've been going through all the suspects, their motives and alibis, and none of them really stands out as a frontrunner so I think it's time to follow up on hunches and see where they take us.'

'OK, sir.' Andy was intrigued. Oldroyd's philosophy in detective work was always to rigorously follow the evidence, but also to listen to your instincts, especially after years of experience. They could lead you to uncover new aspects of a case. Andy's experience was that his boss's intuition about something was usually right.

'Let's go back to that Roman Museum. I want to speak to that curator again.'

'Philip Storey, sir? I thought we'd discounted him because his motive was weak and he had an alibi?'

'Yes, but I want to talk to him again – and have another look at the building.'

'The building, sir?'

'Yes. Come on, let's take a walk over there. I can't get enough of this Christmas atmosphere.'

It was mid-afternoon on a clear day and already the light was fading as they went through the streets. After a few perfunctory questions about what Andy and Steph were doing for Christmas, Oldroyd went quiet as he turned the case over in his mind again. When they reached the old centre, the narrow streets were more bustling than ever in these final days before Christmas. The huge minster came into view – the two towers on the west front already illuminated by floodlights. It was nearly the time for evensong in the minster, and this brought memories back to Oldroyd as they walked past the entrance.

'I remember my dad bringing me here to listen to the choir sing evensong. In those days, that was a choir school.' He pointed to a building across the road from the minster. 'And the choir boys – it was all boys at that time – used to walk across to the minster from the school. The singing was fabulous. It looks like the old school is a restaurant now.'

'It does, sir,' said Andy, wondering what on earth it must have been like to go to a school like that.

When they arrived at the museum, it was quiet and not very warm inside. Philip Storey was reading a book as he sat by the table at the entrance. He looked surprised to see the detectives. He closed the book.

'Chief Inspector,' he said with concern in his voice. 'I didn't expect to see you again. Is there anything else I can help you with? There's been another horrible murder since we last met, hasn't there? I do hope you find the culprit soon.'

Oldroyd looked at him. 'We're here just to check on things. I think an officer has been to ask you where you were on the nights of the other murders?'

'Yes, though I must say I found it very strange that anyone would think that I would go out killing homeless people.'

'And where were you on those occasions?'

Philip looked rather perplexed. 'I told the officer – I was in the pub again on the Sunday, and on Monday evening I was rehearsing in a pantomime.'

Oldroyd raised his eyebrows. 'I see. You must be getting near to the performance dates for that.'

'Yes, the first one is on Saturday.'

'Had you ever met either of the homeless men who were killed? They were wandering around the streets near here.'

'No, I don't even think I've heard their names. But I'm not familiar with anyone unfortunate enough to be living rough.'

'You know,' continued Oldroyd, changing tack, 'you were very kind to show me around. It was fascinating and I remember you saying that you had a lot more artifacts in storage – in your cellar, wasn't it? I was wondering if I could see some of those?'

'Well, Chief Inspector, it's very gratifying to have someone so interested in the museum. By all means, let's have a quick look. I have to warn you it's very dusty down there and there are many trip hazards, so please take extra care.'

'We will, don't worry.'

Philip asked Brian, his volunteer assistant, to cover for him at the entrance, and then he led the detectives to the cellar door, which creaked when he opened it. He switched on the lights and they saw a steep stone staircase going down into the depths.

'Be careful, it's quite narrow and it twists around.'

The detectives found the cellar very impressive. The term 'cellar' hardly did it justice. It was a large, surprisingly dry and airy underground room with very impressive vaulting, which must have been medieval. The lighting from a few bare bulbs was poor, and shadows were cast everywhere. The heavy stone walls glimmered, ghostly at the edges. Everywhere there were stacks of pieces of stone, boxes, empty glass exhibition cabinets and old bookshelves lined with box files.

'There's so much down here,' said Philip. 'It hasn't all been properly catalogued yet. I never seem to have the time to get on with it.'

Oldroyd wandered around, looking briefly at the statues and pottery. Then he saw that the furthest part of the room from the stairs was still in complete darkness.

'What's over there, then?' he asked.

'Oh, just more of the same, but I'm afraid the lighting system has failed in that section and it's far too dark and dangerous to go over there.' He flicked an old switch on and off, but no light came on. 'We can't afford to get it fixed at the moment. Look, Chief Inspector, I think you'll be interested in this.' He led Oldroyd to a piece of ancient, worn sculpture, which depicted the face of a man. 'By comparing this with other portrayals, there's some evidence this could be Constantine the Great. We certainly think it's from that period.' He led Oldroyd to a small display of coins and picked up a silver one damaged at the edges but still fundamentally intact. 'This is a denarius from the time of Constantinius 1 – Constantine the Great's father, who died here in York.' He put the coin back down.

'So you see, we've got a lot of stuff with connections to York. One day I'd like to have it all on display.'

Oldroyd thanked him and they climbed back up the steps to the museum level.

'Again, thank you for your interest, Chief Inspector,' said Philip as the detectives left.

Outside it was nearly dark as they made their way down the short passageway back to the streets.

'Was that useful, then, sir?' asked a sceptical Andy.

'Yes. He's concealing something in that cellar. I don't know what it is, but we need to find out – and quickly. I think it could be the key to the whole thing.' He stopped and faced Andy. 'My plan is to come back here and break in. We can't afford to let time pass following the correct procedures when someone else's life might be at stake. It's high stakes but I'm convinced the answer is there. Are you with me?'

Andy smiled and didn't have to think about it. He trusted his boss's judgement and enjoyed the thrill of doing something unorthodox and risky.

'Of course, sir.'

'Good man. Not a word to anyone else. We don't want to involve them. The responsibility is ours.'

Andy nodded.

Later that evening, Ailsa and Terry tried to distract themselves by watching television. Terry had not gone out to work, and Sam was in bed. They sat on the sofa, holding hands, trying not to think about Rosie. Ailsa's mother was visiting Rosie, and later on Terry was going to return to the hospital for the night.

There was an unexpected knock at the door. Terry opened it to reveal a woman he didn't know. She looked a little nervous.

'I'm sorry to disturb you,' she said. 'I'm Janice Marlow, your ex-landlord's wife.'

Terry frowned.

'I quite understand that you probably don't want to have anything to do with me,' Janice continued, 'but I'm here to tell you that things are going to be different from now on. I mean, much better for you. Can I please come in?'

'You're that cruel sod's wife? I feel sorry for you,' said Terry.

'I don't blame you for feeling that way, but I would like to come in and talk. I came now because I know you work as a taxi driver, and I wanted to try to find you and your wife at home together.'

Terry was still very suspicious but he said, 'OK, come in.'

Janice stepped tentatively into the flat. She saw immediately how stark it all was, but kept very clean. There were no carpets on the floors and the furniture was old and battered. Terry introduced Ailsa. She sat on the sofa and glared at Janice, who sat down in an armchair.

'How are your children?' asked Janice. 'You have a boy and a girl, don't you?'

'Sam's OK, but Rosie's in hospital,' said Terry, raising his voice. 'Respiratory problems, the doctor said.' He looked at Janice angrily. 'It's the fault of that bloody husband of yours. We shouldn't be living in a damp place like this.'

'Terry, calm down,' said Ailsa. 'It's not helping. See what she has to say.'

Janice had put her hand to her mouth. 'Oh my God, no!' she cried. 'My younger sister was very ill as a child. I remember how worried my parents were. And at least their house was dry and warm. Look, let me get straight to the point. I'm very, very sorry for the way that my husband treated you. And I'm also very sorry that I took so little interest in my husband's business and how he was conducting himself. I genuinely didn't know about the plight of people like you. But I should have done. It's no excuse.'

Terry nodded but didn't say anything.

'I'm going to inherit my husband's properties, and I promise you that this flat, and lots of others, will be properly repaired and refurbished, and your rent will be re-assessed so that it's not too high.'

Ailsa and Terry exchanged glances.

'Are you serious?' asked Terry.

'Yes. I'm absolutely ashamed of what you've had to put up with. My husband deserved to be arrested for putting your little girl's health at risk. The first thing I will do is send people round to make an assessment of this property, and if the repair work is going to be very disruptive, we will move you somewhere else temporarily.'

There was a stunned silence. Terry shook his head. 'I don't know what to say. It's hard to believe. We've tried so many times to get things done but it never happened.'

Janice smiled. 'Trust me. It will happen. I want you to accept it as a Christmas present from me. This is going to be a home where your daughter will be safe.'

The couple were still too amazed to say anything. Ailsa burst into tears, but this time they were tears of relief.

'OK,' said Anne at the final case meeting of the day. 'We've spent a lot of time interviewing today. Have we found anything useful?'

Oldroyd reported on the encounter with Craig Jordan. 'He's certainly an aggressive type who could lose his temper and strike out, but planning a murder is a different matter.' He glanced at

Andy. 'I think Andy and I disagree. He thinks that Jordan could have killed Marlow because he hated losing the battle with him. I don't think any motive he had was strong enough. At the end of the day, he could have changed the route of his ghost tour, however much it irked him to do it. Is that right, Andy?'

'Yes, sir. But he would hate to be bested by somebody like Marlow.'

'That's good to know. DC Jefferson and I visited the place where Hutchinson has been staying. He wasn't there but the owner was, and she gave a good report on him as a guest. We went into the room but there was nothing of significance we could find there.'

'Anyway, we're investigating him and his business dealings,' said Anne. 'I assume his company is registered in Scotland.'

'*If* he has a proper company, ma'am,' said Andy. 'He may well just operate under the radar with cash dealings. That would probably work well for the development companies he deals with, so it might be difficult to track him down.'

'True . . . Well, we're on it. And I think if you're right, and if he proves to be some kind of a rogue dealer, that would make it more likely that he and that other rogue, Marlow – two of a kind – fell out about something.'

'Ma'am, doesn't the account by the secretary – Marston, wasn't it? – suggest that Marlow didn't recognise the name of Hutchinson?' asked DC Warren.

'True, but he may well have operated under different names over the years.' She paused, wondering where to take the investigation now. Despite all their efforts, the precious breakthrough had still not appeared.

'None of our investigations into Marlow's affairs have uncovered anyone with a better motive and opportunity to kill him than the suspects we have, so we must keep exploring until we find more leads.' She frowned. She seemed to have said this, or something similar, a number of times before. It was beginning to sound weak, but she didn't know what else to do.

DC Liam Jefferson raised his hand. 'Ma'am, I don't know whether it's relevant, but we've had a tip-off that there is going to be a march in the city centre on Friday in support of homeless people. It's a spontaneous thing, and they won't have permission for it. How do you think we should handle it?'

'Well, somebody else will be responsible for that,' replied Anne. 'I'm too busy with this investigation to get involved, but, Liam, you can pass my views on. Even if it is an unofficial march, I think it would be wise to take a softly-softly approach, given that the homeless community must be feeling terrified at the moment. I imagine that they already feel rather let down by the police, so we don't want them to become even more hostile towards us.'

'OK, ma'am.'

Anthea Marston felt much better after her frank conversation with Janice Marlow. She knew she'd done the right thing in telling Janice about her sister, especially once she saw that Janice was sympathetic.

She left the office and walked along the lively streets to meet with some friends in a wine bar just inside the city walls. It was in an old building, dimly lit with a low ceiling and wood-panelled walls. A flickering candle on each table created a very cosy atmosphere. She couldn't stay late because her husband would need her, but now that she was alone in the office, these were social occasions that she valued.

The get-together was in full swing when she got there. Two bottles of wine and some sharing boards had been ordered, and there was much laughter and merriment. She sipped her wine and nibbled on the local cheeses, pieces of pork pie and small slices of sourdough bread. Burdens she had been carrying around with her for years now seemed to be resolved with Marlow's death and the truthful reckoning Janice was undertaking about her behaviour. Whether Anthea could actually continue working in the same office for the same company was a question that she hadn't yet decided about. It might be time for to her have a completely fresh start but at least she wouldn't feel compromised working for Janice. But whatever her decision on that was, she felt at last that she had achieved some justice and recognition for her sister, and could now let her rest in peace. She stopped thinking about it all, and relaxed into the evening.

Oldroyd and Andy turned into the snickelway leading to Roman Hall, making sure that no one was watching them. It was dark and quiet as they approached the museum stealthily. It had turned a little foggy again, which helped to conceal them. They could hear the noise of conversation and the occasional shriek of a happy partygoer in the nearby streets. There was a misty glow of light in the sky from the busy and well-lit areas, but the museum building was very dark; external security lighting was expensive.

'Let's go round the back,' whispered Oldroyd, who quite enjoyed these escapades into the daring and illicit. Maybe a bit of recklessness was a necessary corrective to his normal role as the respectable upholder of the law.

'OK, sir.'

The rear of the building was even darker, and the detectives switched on their phone torches. They discovered some leaded windows that seemed rather flimsy.

'Well, now,' said Oldroyd, putting his hand melodramatically to his ear. 'Did you hear that? I'm sure there's someone moving around inside. I bet someone has broken in, and as responsible officers we need to investigate right away.'

Andy grinned and took up his part in the little charade. 'Yes, sir – and, look, I think they got in through this window, which could be easily forced with a large screwdriver like this one I happen to have with me.'

Oldroyd could barely suppress his laughter as Andy opened the window. The gap was just big enough for them to get into the building, which they did as carefully and quietly as possible. Oldroyd had a brief look around before he followed his sergeant into the dark building.

Once inside, Oldroyd produced a much bigger torch. He avoided flashing the light across the exhibit room so that they would not be seen from outside. Instead, he made his way to the door leading down the steps into the underground vault. The torch produced a big pool of light, making it easy for them to descend the twisting stairs.

'OK,' said Oldroyd quietly. 'Let's look over there, where there was no light before.'

Oldroyd swung his torch across the ancient barrel vaulting and round stone pillars. It was all rather ghostly in this light, and reminded Andy again of the terrifying case in Knaresborough that had centred on an ancient church.

'Now then,' mumbled Oldroyd. 'Where shall we look?' He raked his torch from side to side. This section of the vault looked very similar to the section they had already seen with the curator – collections of bits of sculpture, boxes, another bookshelf containing dusty volumes. Oldroyd wandered around, picking things up and putting them down again.

'What are you looking for, sir?'

'I'm not entirely sure. But you'll notice that everything around here is very dusty. Let's see if we can find a spot that seems as if it has been disturbed recently.'

'Right, sir.'

Andy looked around carefully using his phone torch. It felt fairly aimless – but then he did notice an area of the floor that seemed to have been disturbed. It was less dusty and there were signs that things had recently been moved around with some fresh scratch marks on the floor.

'Sir – over here.'

Oldroyd joined him and looked at what he'd found. 'Yes, well done, Andy,' he said. 'Now, see those piles of what look like old picture frames? Let's lift them out of the way and see what's underneath.'

They set to work clearing an area of the floor. Underneath they found a three-metre-square area where the ground had been excavated to a depth of about half a metre. Oldroyd shone his torch on to the bottom and gasped.

'Oh, yes! It's what I half suspected. I—'

Suddenly there was a click, and the vault area was illuminated by lights.

'Well, you got there in the end, Chief Inspector. Or should I say that you got here? It's beautiful, isn't it?'

Oldroyd turned to see Philip Storey at the bottom of the stone stairs. He was holding a long knife and had a nasty smile on his face. 'I knew what was going through your mind the other day. You suspected I was hiding something down here, so I've been staying around after the museum has closed, watching out for your return. I heard a noise from where I was hiding. I went to the back of the building just in time to see you climbing through the window. You didn't have enough on me to get a search warrant, did you? I do admire a man who follows his instinct.' He moved slowly towards Oldroyd, who instinctively moved back.

Oldroyd's mind was racing as he tried to figure out how to de-escalate the situation. But he had registered that Philip had not mentioned Andy. Maybe he had not seen the younger officer breaking into the building? Could it be he thought Oldroyd was by himself?

But, Oldroyd wondered, where *was* Andy?

He struggled to remain calm, focussing only on the deadly blade in Philip's grip. As his heart rate increased, he could feel beads of sweat on his forehead.

Philip continued to walk over slowly to where Oldroyd was standing. He tried to move back again but there was a wall behind him. 'It's a great shame that I have to kill a man with such a lively and inquisitive mind – and such an interest in history. It was a great pleasure to show you round the museum. Unfortunately, as you can see, our greatest exhibit is not on display.' He smiled in a chilling manner, his eyes cold. 'I'm glad you've seen it before you go.'

Oldroyd looked down into the hole again, where a section of an ornate and colourful mosaic had been revealed. Key elements of his training were playing out in his mind as he tried to slow down his breathing. He looked at Philip, whose face was stern and implacable. The tactic in these circumstances was always to keep the person with the weapon talking to distract them from using it.

'Are you sure that it's Roman?' Oldroyd asked.

'Oh, yes, without a doubt. I've spent a long time researching it. This building is medieval but it is within the walls of Eboracum. I believe it was built on the site of a Roman villa, probably owned by a wealthy merchant. There weren't many civilians here – it was 'primarily a military base.' Suddenly he became intensely excited, a fanatical gleam in his eye. 'Just look at the quality of that work, and we're only seeing a fragment of it. It could extend over the whole of this room, and it's wonderfully well preserved.'

As Philip was talking, Oldroyd noticed that Andy was slowly creeping from behind a large piece of statuary, where he must have hidden as soon as the lights went on. Philip had clearly not seen him, and he was too absorbed in telling Oldroyd about the mosaic to be aware of anything else.

'It's buried beneath layers of earth and clay, which have protected it. It's the greatest find of a Roman antiquity in Britain probably for a hundred years or more. And it's here in my museum!' He giggled with fanatical enthusiasm.

Desperate to keep Philip talking, Oldroyd took up the point. 'Yes . . . I began to wonder about layers and strata down here when my daughter told me about her visit to the Viking centre.'

Philip nodded and looked at Oldroyd again. There seemed to be genuine sympathy in his expression. 'I'm really sorry about this, Chief Inspector. It's bad that you have to suffer the same fate as Marlow, that money-grabbing philistine, but I'm afraid it can't be helped.'

'I'm sorry too,' Oldroyd said. 'I was very interested in what you told me about the collections here. You're a very knowledgeable and cultured man.'

'Ah, flattery won't save you, I'm afraid. But I must say you were a very receptive audience, and I do appreciate that.'

'What will you do with my body?' asked Oldroyd, increasingly desperate, his heart beating even faster. Andy was creeping closer and Oldroyd willed him not make any noise. 'Inspector Hopkins knows that I'm here. You'll be caught – you're the only person who could possibly catch me entering this place. So what's the point?

You might as well give in without killing someone else. No one will damage this mosaic. I'll make sure it's kept safe and I think you know you can trust me on that.'

But Philip was unrelenting, and seemed to be enjoying the terrible drama of this moment. 'Things may have turned against me, "Yet I will try the last", as Macbeth said. I'll think of some way of disposing of you.'

He raised the knife, but Andy was now behind him and moved quickly to grasp Philip's arm. There was a struggle, the knife lurching perilously close to Andy's neck. Oldroyd rushed forward, and grabbed Philip's legs, bringing him to the ground.

Oldroyd held him in place while Andy applied the cuffs.

Once they were sure he was subdued, Andy called for back-up.

~

'Well, thanks for saving me there, Andy,' said Oldroyd as Storey was taken away by officers.

'It's OK, sir. I was standing further away from him when he came in, and I managed to hide before he saw me.'

'Well done. I was worried for a moment there when he nearly stabbed you in the neck. Steph would never have forgiven me if the father-to-be didn't come home.'

'No chance of that, sir – we easily subdued him.'

Oldroyd nodded, but he wasn't so sure he'd have been so lucky without Andy there. It had been a nasty-looking blade that the curator had threatened him with.

Oldroyd watched Philip Storey leave his beloved museum for the last time. 'It's a shame.'

'What is, sir?'

'Storey. He's such a bright man and so enthusiastic. It's a great loss to history and conservation.'

'I think he was more than enthusiastic, sir. He was a deranged maniac.'

'True, but it's a fine line sometimes between enthusiasm and obsession. I'm sad that he crossed it.'

Six

From the eighteenth century onwards, York became famous for chocolate and confectionery through the firms of Terrys, Rowntrees and Cravens. They introduced brands of toffees and humbugs and international favourites such as the Kit Kat, Aero, Smarties and Chocolate Orange. The Rowntrees were a Quaker family and concerned with improving the lives of the poor. Joseph Rowntree built the garden village of New Earswick, providing good quality affordable homes for poor people. His son, Seebohm Rowntree, conducted studies beginning in 1899 in York, which were some of the first sociological investigations into poverty and its causes. These studies influenced the construction of the welfare state in the 1940s. Four trusts still bear the Rowntree name. They engage in social action, research and campaigning for social justice.

The next day, Philip Storey and his solicitor faced Oldroyd and Anne Hopkins across a table in the interview room. Andy had returned to work at Harrogate now that the case was drawing to a conclusion. The knife Storey had tried to use against Oldroyd turned out to be the murder weapon used to kill his victims – ideal evidence in the case against him – but he also wasn't denying his guilt, and sat across the table from Oldroyd looking very equable.

'How did you find the mosaic?' began Oldroyd.

Philip's eyes lit up, clearly keen to talk about his great discovery.

'I stumbled on it by accident. The floor of the vault was crumbling, and I dug away some layers of loose earth to see if I could find out what was happening. You can imagine how completely flabbergasted I was when the small coloured tiles came into view. And I knew straight away what it was because I had already established that the museum was on the site of a Roman building. What an amazing thing for the museum to have!'

'I knew that you were concealing something down there,' continued Oldroyd. 'Your mistake was to invite us down into that vault. You couldn't resist the temptation to show us more of the collection, but I was suspicious of the so-called faulty light. I think you clicked on an old switch that was disconnected.'

Philip nodded.

'I began to wonder what you were hiding in that section. When my sergeant mentioned small coloured tiles, I began to think about the ancient foundations of the city, the location of the museum, and what you could have found there. I never imagined it would be something on that scale.'

'You're right, Chief Inspector. I was hiding something very wonderful. And when I found it I thought, in my naivety, that the right thing to do was to tell Marlow, the owner. To my surprise, he came straight over to look at it. I thought it was because he was pleased and interested.' Philip shook his head. 'How wrong I was about that. He instructed me not to tell anyone else, otherwise he would immediately eject the museum from the building.'

'Why was that?' asked Anne.

Philip looked down at the table, trying to contain his anger. 'Not only was he completely uninterested in the mosaic, he wanted to get rid of it – concrete it over.' Philip's face contorted with horror at the prospect. 'He said that once the mosaic became public knowledge, it would have a preservation order put on it, meaning he would lose control of the building. Someday, he hoped to sell it as a development opportunity. The mosaic would ruin that possibility – he didn't think anyone would want to take it on. He actually said that he wasn't prepared to lose money over a few old pieces of coloured tile.' Philip's face distorted with hatred. 'I told him that it would be a great thing for the museum and for the city, and that it might even make him money in other ways. He just laughed at me and said that even if he put our rent up it wouldn't compensate for the lost revenue, which could be worth millions for a building like that. But any company who bought it would want to completely rip out the interior and rebuild it. He wanted that mosaic to remain secret, buried . . . And probably seriously damaged – if not completely destroyed.'

'His response must have devastated you,' said Anne.

Philip stared ahead. 'Of course. I was stunned. It took me a long time to process the situation and decide what to do. I couldn't believe that anyone could have such an attitude to a marvellous treasure like that. I tried to mislead you when you asked if we would find it easy to move to a different venue if Marlow evicted us. The truth is that there isn't another suitable place in the centre of York, but what was much more important was that I was never going to leave that building with a Roman mosaic in the cellar. Just think of it: it could become one of the best museums of Roman artifacts in Britain, with a marvellous mosaic on site. It would be the fulfilment of my wildest dreams.'

'But if you revealed the mosaic, Marlow would have kicked you out?'

Philip nodded. 'Yes. And that would most probably have been the end of the museum, so I decided that the only way was to get rid of him.'

'And this is where Donald Hutchinson came in,' said Oldroyd. 'We know that you dressed up and played the part of Hutchinson to try to throw us off the trail. When I heard you did some acting, I began to wonder about Hutchinson's big beard and his Scottish accent. It was a very effective disguise, and you booked a B&B under a false name and paid cash.'

'Yes, Chief Inspector. I hoped that you would waste time investigating Hutchinson and his story about leaving Marlow alive, and believe that Marlow's death was as random as the homeless men.'

'Which is when your next strategy came in.' Oldroyd's hawkish eyes fixed on Philip and his voice became harsh. 'I understand how marvellous a Roman mosaic is to someone like you . . . but don't you think it's despicable to kill two homeless people in order to create the narrative that Marlow's death was part of a sequence of murders by a serial killer?'

Philip wilted under the glare. 'I'm sorry about that, but I hoped that if I succeeded it would take suspicion away from me.'

Oldroyd looked at him with contempt. 'You called Marlow a philistine. I think you are almost the opposite: a person who overvalues art and relics from the past and places them above human life.'

Philip looked down and said nothing.

'So, what were you going to do next?'

'When the whole thing had died down, I was going to announce that I had just discovered the mosaic. I was confident of getting a more positive reaction from whoever inherited Marlow's properties. Then the mosaic could be properly excavated and a world-famous, enhanced museum created.' He gazed into the far distance, savouring the dream that would never now come to fruition for him. 'Of course, I believe that will still happen, it's just that I will not be involved. But I'll be happy knowing that I facilitated it by stopping that man from destroying a wonderful treasure.' He looked at Oldroyd with defiance.

Oldroyd gave him one last searching and contemptuous look after this justification for murder. There was a fanaticism and a self-satisfaction in the eyes, but no warmth.

He turned to the officer on duty. 'Take him away.'

'Just before I go, Chief Inspector,' said Philip, a taunting smile on his face. 'I'm afraid you can't wrap all this up yet because I have to disappoint you. I didn't kill the second homeless man.'

Oldroyd looked up sharply. 'What?'

'I'm afraid not. I'm not a complete monster. Killing one man was enough to put you on to the wrong track together with Donald Hutchinson. It was just unfortunate that I came up against you. The third murder was helpful to me, but I didn't do it.'

'You're lying.'

'No. The knife I used was a replica of a Roman pugio dagger – long, but also wide. I doubt if the second homeless man had a wound exactly the same as Marlow and the first homeless man. Also, that evening I was rehearsing solidly for the pantomime. All evening. I never left the hall. Lots of witnesses will support me.' He stood up, ready to be escorted out. He was enjoying this moment. 'So I'm afraid the great detective has got that part wrong. You've a bit more work to do.'

When Philip had been led out, Oldroyd scowled and rubbed his chin. 'Have we had the report back on Fraser McLean yet?'

'I'm expecting it any time now, sir. Surely Storey was lying?'

'Well, I hope so, or we'll have to start all over again. But he sounded pretty clear about it. Let's go and see if there's any further news.'

Back in the incident room, Anne went to her computer and discovered there was a report from Dr Redgrave. It did indeed state that Fraser McLean's stab wound was different from those inflicted on Smith and Marlow – the knife was much narrower. She also confirmed that there had been a struggle before McLean had been killed, unlike in the first two murders.

Anne told Oldroyd all this and he sat down, breathed out, grimaced and shook his head.

'This is my fault,' Oldroyd said. 'I was rushing us into thinking that the murders of the two homeless men were a strategy to put us on to the wrong track. But, as Storey said, one murder was enough to confuse us, especially with his Hutchinson facade. It was laziness, and I'm sorry.'

'But you were right about Jeffrey Smith, sir. And anyway, we don't know if Storey is telling us the truth. He may just be messing with us in order to stay in control.'

'Well, we need to check his alibi for that night, but I have a feeling it will be sound. The knife wound, together with the struggle before the stabbing, suggests something different motivated McLean's death. If I'd only kept my mind on it: McLean probably knew his attacker, and I don't think he knew Storey.'

'We need to get in contact with that homeless young woman again – Samantha, wasn't it? She will be able to tell us more about McLean. I'll see to it. I'll get a team to look for her and I'll get it out on police radio.'

'Good.' Oldroyd put his elbow on the table and rested his head on his hand. It was a sickening blow to realise that they had not got to the end of the case. He had been too keen to wrap it all up before he and Andy were recalled by Walker.

Then he suddenly realised something. 'Anne, last night my daughter told me that there is going to be a march for the homeless tomorrow here in York. That woman at Roof, what's her name again?'

'Saskia Middleton.'

'Yes, she invited Louise to take part and told her that Samantha was organising it. So she's bound to be there.'

'That will be a big help if we can't find her before then.'

'What about the press and the public?' asked Oldroyd.

'I'm going to say that we have made an arrest, but there may be more than one perpetrator involved, so the danger has not passed.'

'That's good. Let's hope that we can catch the second murderer quickly. We deserve a bit of luck in this case.'

Unaware that she was being sought, Samantha was wandering through the streets and snickelways of the city centre trying to raise support for the march. Many of the people she spoke to were incapable of taking part: ill, exhausted or under the influence of alcohol or drugs, but some promised to be there. The two murders of homeless people had hit them hard.

She went down a narrow passage that led to a yard behind some shops. Here there was a dirty metal grating on the ground from which warm air rose, presumably from a kitchen. A number of homeless people were sitting around this, trying to keep warm. One was laid out, covered in blankets, and seemed asleep.

Here Samantha found Tracy – a woman in her forties with a lined face and missing several teeth. She was dressed in filthy jogging bottoms and a large, shapeless jumper full of holes. She wouldn't ever say anything about her past, although it was clear she'd suffered trauma. Her mental health was poor and she sometimes went into violent rages.

'I can't deal with these murders,' she said when she saw Samantha. 'Do they want to kill us all?'

Leaning against the wall was a man in his early thirties called Stevie. He had a skeletal frame, and wore a baseball cap. His right leg was twisted as the result of an accident, which meant he walked with a limp. 'If anyone comes for me, they'll get this,' he said and produced a glass bottle from the pocket of his long coat.

'Where did you get that?' asked Samantha.

'It was lying around in that waste area behind the garage.'

'Be careful with it,' said Samantha, who had gained respect amongst the homeless people. She seemed to be the most together person who was living on the streets. 'If the police find you trying to use that as a weapon, you'll be the one who gets arrested.'

'Yeah, you're right,' Stevie said, angry. 'They always think that we're the ones that cause trouble.' He slammed the bottle into his palm a few times before putting it back into his coat pocket.

'Well, don't give them any reason to think it. The best way we can defend ourselves is if we stay together.'

Tracy nodded. 'Too right. You won't catch me on my own on these streets any more after dark. But we shouldn't have to live in fear.'

Samantha told them all about the march.

'I'm with you,' said Tracy. 'We can't just let people get picked off like this. What about you, Stevie?'

He shrugged his shoulders. 'Yeah, why not? It's summat to do.'

'Aye, but what good will it do?' asked one man with a straggly beard and staring eyes, who was aimlessly poking about in a pile of rubbish with a stick. 'Shut up, Flo, yer stupid old bugger.' He said this to a woman who was sitting on the ground, wrapped in a blanket, muttering and occasionally singing to herself.

'We've got to try something to get their attention,' replied Samantha. 'Two people like us have been killed. We need protection.'

No one said anything. Distrust of the police was deep. Then a man with long hair, who was sitting with his back against the wall, called out.

'Are you that Samantha who knew Fraser?'

Samantha turned to him in surprise. 'Yeah, who are you?'

'Barry. He were a good bloke, Fraser. I saw who killed him, yer know.'

'Eh?'

'Yeah, but I'm not saying owt.'

'Why not?'

'Because t'bloody police'll think it was me and I'm trying to blame sumdy else. Ah don't trust 'em.'

'But we can't let the murderer go free, can we?'

The bearded man joined in. 'If you saw owt, Barry . . .'

'Ah did, I'm telling yer!'

'Then she's right. Think of the poor bastard who got killed.'

'Ah am doing. He was a mate of mine.'

'Then come to King's Square tomorrow morning at twelve. The police'll be there. I met some of them when Fraser was killed and they weren't bad.'

'I'll think about it,' was all he would say.

The rest of them were not listening any more, so Samantha decided to move on.

∼

By Friday, the news had filtered through most people that someone had been arrested. Anne reassured the public that significant progress was being made but that there was still a need to take care.

Oldroyd had told Patrick and Louise that he was also going to attend the march because there was a chance that Fraser Mclean's murderer could be identified. He drove them into York again. Louise and Patrick sat in the back of the Saab.

Louise was not too pleased with the situation. 'I hope the police aren't going to hijack this event, Dad. I know you have to follow up looking for this Samantha, but we don't want the message about the vulnerability of homeless people to get drowned out by police activity. You lot can be clumsy – and worse, sometimes. I've seen it on marches in London.'

'We'll stay in the background, don't worry. We just need to have a word with the young woman who organised this.'

'Well, don't intimidate her. Saskia said that she's got some issues, like most homeless people have.'

'I promise. I believe as strongly as you about highlighting the plight of homeless people. Anyway, you've got one big advantage now. No police officers will intervene in the conduct of the march while Anne and I are there. We won't speak to the woman until the end, so we don't frighten her off.'

'OK.'

'Hey, listen to you,' said Patrick, laughing. 'Telling the chief inspector of police how to conduct himself.'

'It's OK, Patrick, I'm used to it. She's always been a feisty character who wanted to defend the underdog. When she was a little girl she used to ask me if I was going to put anybody in jail that day and, if I was, to be kind to them because they were sorry for what they'd done and it wasn't nice to be locked up.'

Patrick laughed again. 'That sounds just like her.'

'And I was right,' said Louise with a smile. 'And also you have to remember he might be chief inspector, but he's also my dad, so I can say what I like to him.'

Oldroyd caught her eye in the rear mirror and she stuck her tongue out at him.

~

Luckily the weather was dry and not too cold. By twelve o'clock, a little over one hundred people had gathered in King's Square – a respectable number given there hadn't been much time to get information out. Saskia and Linda had done as much as they could in printing out flyers and distributing them to sympathetic charities and organisations.

Saskia and Linda were joined by Louise and Patrick. Louise explained about the police operation. Saskia's response was similar to her friend's, but she accepted Louise's assurances.

Anne and Oldroyd stood quietly at the edge of the square, almost invisible behind other pedestrians.

There was no sign of Samantha. 'Her breath often smells of alcohol,' Saskia said. 'I think she has a drink problem, but I hope she makes it. It won't be the same if we have to do this without her.'

'I don't know how anyone can live any kind of an ordered life when they're on the streets,' said Louise.

'I know. We'll just have to wait a bit longer. I'll make an announcement so that people know what's happening.' She raised her voice and asked people to gather around. 'Thank you all for coming today. We'll be starting the march in a few minutes' time. From here we're going up Low Petergate.' She pointed out the direction. 'Up to Stonegate, and then left; then left on to Davygate and Parliament Street; left on to Pavement, left again on to

Colliergate, and complete the circle back to here. OK? When we return, there will be a few brief speeches.'

'Oh good, she's here!' said Linda, pointing across the square to where Samantha had appeared. She was walking slowly, looking rather pale. Lucy was beside her on her lead.

'Hi, Samantha,' said Saskia, approaching the young woman and her dog. 'Nice to see you. I've just explained the route – shall we get going? If you're OK?'

'Yeah, that's fine,' replied Samantha. 'Has anybody got any water? I could do with a drink.' Louise gave her a bottle of mineral water. Samantha looked around as she drank, catching sight of a man on the edge of the group. She went over to him. 'Thanks for coming,' she said. 'Walk with me. We'll talk to the police later.'

The man shrugged and said nothing but he stayed by her side as she introduced him to Saskia. 'This is Barry.'

The march headed off with Samantha, Lucy, Barry, Saskia and Linda at the head. Many people were holding up banners with slogans such as, 'End Homelessness Now' and 'Safe Streets for Everyone'. As they walked down the busy shopping area of Parliament Street, some people clapped as they went past.

Saskia overheard Anne as they passed, speaking on a radio to plain clothes officers they had nearby. 'OK, the person we need to talk to has arrived. Late twenties, long dark hair. There is a small dog with her. She is walking with the main group. We do not want to disrupt this march. I repeat, do not disrupt the march. The task is to monitor her movements and make sure that she does not slip away before myself or Chief Inspector Oldroyd have had a chance to talk to her.'

A number of officers moved into position along the route.

The march proceeded peacefully. There was not much chanting apart from, 'What do we want?' 'Safe homes.' 'When do we want them?' 'Now!'

The people they passed as they wound their way through the streets and back to King's Square seemed to be supportive. They caught sight of some uniformed police officers but none of them intervened. When they arrived back at the square, Saskia produced a megaphone.

'Do you want to say a few words first, Samantha?' she asked.

'Yeah, OK. Will you hold on to Lucy?' Samantha gave the lead to Saskia and took the megaphone.

'Thanks for coming, everybody,' she began. 'It's been an awful time for those of us who are living on the streets here. Can you imagine how frightening it is when a killer is targeting people like you, but you have nowhere to go inside where it's safe? We need better hostel accommodation, and help to find something permanent. I know some people say that it's our choice, but who in their right mind would choose to be out on the streets in winter like this? So please write to your councillor, write to your MP about it. Finally, I want to dedicate this march to the memory of Jeffrey Smith and Fraser McLean, who were murdered in this city just days ago. Thank you.'

There were cheers and clapping as Samantha handed the megaphone to Saskia and took back Lucy's lead.

'Well done,' said Saskia, and then carried on herself. 'Thank you, Samantha, for those brave words. The truth is that none of us know what it's really like to be on the streets until it's happened to us. Now, everybody, I work for an organisation that helps people with housing problems, and I see the struggles of families living in substandard accommodation: damp, mould and so on. But even they are better off than the people with nowhere at all to live. It's ironic, is it not? That here we are in this ancient city where some of the earliest studies into poverty and bad housing were undertaken by Seebohm Rowntree over a hundred years ago, but this country is still unable to put a roof over the head of all its citizens . . .'

Saskia went on to talk about housing policy and strategies to end homelessness. A few questions were taken and then Louise spoke briefly about her work at the hostel in London. Then the march came to an end.

Samantha was sitting on the ground, cuddling Lucy. She was too weak to stand for very long, especially after the march. Saskia and Louise sat next to her.

'Well done for organising this. I think it went well, don't you?'

Samantha nodded. But despite the obvious success of this event she'd organised, she seemed detached.

'Can we help you?' asked Louise. 'I work in London with women who have problems, mostly because they've been badly treated by men. I think your problem is drinking, isn't it?'

Samantha sighed and nodded again. 'I can't hold a job. I was drinking vodka last night. I thought I wasn't gonna make it here. I keep meaning to do something about it, but I'm all over the place. Most of the hostels won't take her,' she said, looking at Lucy. 'And in some of them I don't feel safe.'

Saskia and Louise exchanged glances. 'OK,' said Saskia. 'I'm going to find out what's available for you, and when you've settled down a bit, we'll get you on to something that will help you dry out.'

Samantha clutched Lucy. 'With her, I'm not going anywhere without her.'

'No, I understand that, don't worry. I'm going back to the office to do a bit of research and make some phone calls. Louise is going to take you somewhere inside where it's warm, for a drink and something to eat. OK?'

Samantha nodded. 'Thanks,' she muttered.

'There's just one more thing,' said Saskia. 'Please will you have a brief word with the police who are looking for who murdered Fraser? I've spoken to them and they're nice people.'

'Oh,' replied Samantha. 'Yeah, OK.' She looked around. 'Where's Barry?'

'I'm here.' Barry was sitting on the ground behind her. 'Where are these cops?' he said to Saskia. 'I've got things to tell 'em.'

'Oh, I see,' replied Saskia, a bit confused. She turned to Louise. 'Are your father and the inspector around?'

Louise spotted Oldroyd still standing in the same spot as he was before the march began. She beckoned to him. He and Anne came over.

Louise had a brief word with them. 'Apparently this bloke wants to speak you. He seems to be a friend of Samantha's.'

Oldroyd nodded and then smiled at Barry, who stood up. 'I'm glad you were able to come to the march today. We're trying to find out who killed Fraser McLean. Do you have something you want to tell us?'

Barry glowered at Oldroyd and looked very uncertain.

'Go on, Barry, tell them,' said Samantha. 'It's what you've come for, isn't it?'

Barry took a deep breath and glanced from Oldroyd to Anne. 'I saw t'bastard that killed him,' he blurted out, shaking his head and looking agitated.

'OK,' said Oldroyd. 'Take it easy. Just tell us what you saw.'

Barry licked his lips. 'Ah'd been sheltering in a doorway but got moved on. Ah went dahn near to t'river and saw t'two of 'em. There were noise coming from a club on t'corner so I couldn't hear what they were saying. It looked as if they were arguing. Then they started fighting, punching each other. I recognised Fraser; t'other bloke had his back to me. Fraser got hold of this metal bar he keeps to defend himself and then t'other bloke took out a knife and stabbed Fraser before Fraser could hit him. Fraser fell down; t'other bloke looked round to see if anybody wa' watching but I hid in a doorway.' Barry paused. 'When he turned round, I recognised his face but I couldn't place him till later. It was that bloke who leads them ghost tours. Ah don't know what he's called; walks round wi' a cape on, long hair, tall chap and a bloody big black hat.'

Oldroyd's heart leaped: the description fitted Gary Owen perfectly. 'So what happened next?' he asked.

'He didn't see me. He had a last look at Fraser and then walked off down t'street.'

'That's very helpful,' said Anne. 'Would you recognise him again? There are a few people who lead ghost tours and we want to make sure we get the right person.'

'Yeah.'

'Can I ask you why you didn't raise the alarm at that point?'

Barry looked at her with suspicion. 'I went down to look at Fraser. He wa' dead, no doubt about it, but I wan't gonna do nothing. You lot might've accused me of killing him.'

'But you changed your mind?'

Barry looked a bit uncomfortable. 'Yeah, well, it was Samantha and that bloke Dave – they said I should tell you, so I have. Hope you catch the bastard. Fraser were a good bloke.'

'Thanks a lot. With your help, we'll get justice for him. Can you just stick around for a while?'

Barry nodded.

Anne turned to Oldroyd. 'This seems to confirm, sir, that Fraser McLean's murder was unplanned. It seems like a fight that went too far. Luckily Barry here saw it.'

'Yes,' replied Oldroyd, 'but what were they fighting about? Where's Samantha?'

Samantha was sitting on the ground, stroking Lucy and looking tired. Anne approached her. 'You knew the victim Fraser McLean, didn't you, Samantha?'

'Yeah.'

'Can you tell us anything about him?'

Samantha shrugged and carried on stroking Lucy. 'He was a nice bloke. Scottish. Said he'd been in the army and couldn't get a job when he left, got into drugs and stuff like some of us. Never talked about any family or anything. That's all I know – sorry.'

Oldroyd was listening. 'That's very important. Thanks.' He took Anne on one side. 'I think we've got the break we were hoping for. His description of the murderer matches that of the guy who conducted the ghost tour when we found the body. I think we should move quickly and bring him in.'

'You don't think he had anything to do with that first murder, sir?'

'No, and I'm more and more certain that the last one was not connected to the first two.'

～

It didn't take the police long to locate Gary Owen, who was arrested later that day. At first he protested his innocence, but when a knife was found in a search of his address and he was informed that there was a witness, his resistance collapsed and he confessed.

Oldroyd and Anne went to question Gary in the interview room. His long hair was lank and he sat with his elbows on the table, his hands supporting his head. He had an air of defeat about him, but he was defiant that he had not intended murder. He sat up when the detectives arrived.

'Look, I didn't mean to kill him. It was an argument that got out of control.'

'About what?' asked Oldroyd.

Owen sighed and shook his head. 'We were in the army together, stationed up in Scotland. McLean and I never got on. He and his cronies were hard drinkers. I wasn't and they used to taunt me. I didn't fit in the army. My father basically forced me to join up. He refused to support me when I left school and didn't have a job.

'So I started to rebel. I was only in my late teens. I was pulled up a few times for going AWOL. Then, one night, one of McLean's friends just went too far and we got into a fight. We were really slugging each other before it was broken up. McLean and the others lied and testified that I had started it and, because of my other offences, I ended up being dismissed from the army.

'My father wouldn't have me back home in Manchester, so I came over here to York.'

'And you got on with Craig Jordan?'

'Yeah. I did a bit of acting at school. Not many people wanted the tour job, 'cause it was funny hours. Then I got fed up with it. The pay was rubbish. Jordan was a mean sod.'

'So you decided to blackmail him?'

Gary looked sheepish. 'I deserved more than he was paying me.'

Oldroyd looked at Gary with his sharp grey eyes. The man was a rogue but would he plan a murder?

'So, what happened with Fraser McLean?'

'I was waiting to go into a club at the top of the road when I heard this sing-song Scottish voice calling out, "Ga-ry Ow-en". I looked down the road and I could make out this figure waving his arms at me and staggering a bit, as if he was drunk. I walked down towards him to see who it was that knew my name. In the light of a street lamp, I just about recognised him. Obviously his drinking had got much worse. He was thin faced, dirty, unshaven and dressed in not much more than rags. I realised that he must be homeless.

'I felt sorry for him and was willing to talk to him as an old army comrade, but he was as hostile to me as ever: taunting, abusive. I told him to shut up and he said he would tell people that I'd been kicked out of the army.'

235

'Do you think many people would have listened to him?' asked Anne.

Gary frowned. 'Maybe not. But the idea of him spreading stuff about me was too much. I lost it. I grabbed him by his filthy old jacket and warned him not to say anything about me. To my surprise he swung out and punched me in the face. I hit him back, and he fumbled on the ground where he had his stuff. He picked up this bloody iron bar. I could see that he was going to come at me with it, so I pulled out my knife. I always carry a knife for protection. I should have just turned round and run, but I lunged at him with the knife and it went in deep. He crashed to the ground and lay still. I examined him – no sign of life and blood all over the place. I realised what I'd done.

'I looked round but there was nobody about so I walked off, cursing my luck – why the hell had he sprung up from nowhere? Later I thought that you would assume that he'd been killed by the same person who'd killed the other homeless man.'

'Unfortunately for you, you were seen. The account by this person of what he saw tallies with your version,' said Oldroyd. 'Which is actually in your favour.'

Gary put his head in his hands again. 'I didn't intend to kill him, believe me. He got me angry and then he was going to hit me with this bar. I had to defend myself.'

'OK,' continued Oldroyd. 'It's for you and your legal team to consider what your plea is going to be and for the jury to make their decision.'

～

After Owen had been processed, the two detectives returned to the office and sank into chairs. It was an enormous relief that the whole thing was now over.

'Well done, sir,' said Anne 'What did you make of him?'

'He's a dodgy character, isn't he? But I think I believe his story. There's no evidence that he planned to kill McLean or even that he knew he was in York until that night. He'll probably get done with manslaughter.'

Anne nodded; she was feeling very relieved now that they'd got to the end of the case. She looked at Oldroyd with the same mischievous smile as she had on the first morning of the investigation. 'Well, sir, it's a good thing that you and Andy investigated that break-in at the museum, otherwise we might never have got to the bottom of it all.' Oldroyd grinned rather sheepishly. 'I'll bet everyone at the Harrogate station enjoys working with you; never a dull moment.'

'We do have some fun,' said Oldroyd, laughing. 'And we get results.'

Anne shook her head. 'I'm so pleased that we've solved the case before Christmas. It was casting a pall over the city. Chief Superintendent Hainsworth is delighted and asked me to pass on his thanks to you. I'm sure he was under pressure from higher up to get results. He's always very loyal to those of us who work for him and he would never replace us on a case unless he had to.'

'It's the same with Chief Superintendent Walker at Harrogate. I'm still waiting to hear from him, but I know he was on the brink of having to recall us back to service because of staffing issues.'

As they got up to leave the interview room, Anne turned to Oldroyd. 'I suppose this is goodbye for now, sir. It's been great working with you and Andy. We couldn't have solved this one without you.'

Oldroyd laughed. 'I'm sure you would have – you've got the ability. A lot is down to experience. After a while you start to sense things and to trust your hunches. We seemed to be getting nowhere with the people who had the best motives for killing Marlow, so I decided to have a rethink. Maybe the killer's motive was concealed. This turned out to be literally true – that mosaic was hidden in that dark vault at the museum, after all! Now you know why I wanted to see a map of Roman York and some details of the history of that museum building. I wanted to establish that it was on land that had been part of the Roman fort. I had the idea that he'd found something from antiquity but I didn't know what or how it might relate to the murders.'

'I see, sir.'

'The other thing I was suspicious of was that the murders of those two homeless men struck me as too much of a coincidence coming after Marlow's death. I got the feeling that we were being lured on to the wrong path, and so it turned out.'

Anne nodded. 'I could kick myself for being taken in by "Donald Hutchinson", sir.'

'Well, look at me. I jumped to the conclusion that the third murder was committed by the same person, and I was wrong. Sometimes we get so desperate to get things sorted out that we start ignoring or twisting evidence, and taking what I call mental shortcuts. The different knife wound and the evidence of a fight should have told me to slow down, that something wasn't right.

'I think you were well on the way to discovering the truth about Hutchinson. Storey was very careful. That day he came to the police station as Hutchinson, he waited until myself and Sergeant Carter were not there because we had previously interviewed him. If either of us had encountered him pretending to be Donald Hutchinson, we might have seen through the disguise. It was another attempt to distract us. I think, on reflection, that Storey was trying too hard to confuse us, and that's why his machinations didn't ring true.' Oldroyd stood up, smiling. 'Anyway, we got there in the end.'

The two detectives shook hands. 'We did, sir. And thanks again. I hope you have a good Christmas. I've learned a lot just in this short time working with you.'

'I've enjoyed it, Anne. And a happy Christmas to you too.'

~

Oldroyd was getting ready to leave the station when he received the expected call from Tom Walker, who usually called him at the end of a case.

'Well done again, Jim, and just in the nick of time. I would have had to recall you at the end of this week – tomorrow, in fact. They're going down like flies here with flu and bad colds. So, who did the killer turn out to be?'

Oldroyd explained about Philip Storey, the museum, the Roman mosaic and the second killer.

'Two killers? Good Lord. Well done tracking all that down. And Roman mosaic underneath the building, you say. Well, you can understand how this chap felt about it, can't you? And that miserable skinflint wanted to concrete it over? Disgusting! Some people can't think about anything but money, can they? It will be great for Yorkshire to have a thing like that in its ancient capital.'

Oldroyd was somewhat surprised. Walker was a proud Yorkshireman like himself, but he was not noted for his interest in the arts or history. There were obviously sides to the old boy with which he was unfamiliar.

'Andy Carter has been brilliant again, Tom.' He explained how Andy had tackled the murderer in a dangerous situation.

'Excellent! It's good for our prestige here in Harrogate for you both to have played an important part in solving such a prominent case. I shall lose no time in telling Watkins all about it. He'll probably just say something like, "What were they doing in York?"

I think Carter should be put forward for some kind of award. That's not the first time he's risked serious injury in a case of yours, is it?'

'No, Tom. That's a good idea.' Oldroyd moved on swiftly before the conversation could take an ominous turn. 'I have to say that Inspector Anne Hopkins did an excellent job running the investigation. We could do with her in Harrogate, if she's ever looking for promotion.'

'Good, I'll remember that. Anyway, I won't keep you. There's a lot to do here, I'm afraid, but we'll have to push some of the less urgent stuff on until after Christmas. I'll see you back here soon.' He rang off, and Oldroyd smiled at his success in preventing another rant from Tom against Watkins.

∼

Anne Hopkins was tired but relieved when she finally got home. She was a little earlier than normal, and the house was empty and dark. She remembered that Paul and Amy were going to some friends' for tea, and Peter was still at work. She put the lights on, including those on the Christmas tree, and sat down on the sofa.

The house was warm and jolly with its festive decorations and quiet apart from the gentle thrum of the central heating. She sank down more deeply into the cushions and closed her eyes.

The next thing she was aware of was the sound of song. She opened her eyes to see Peter sitting in an armchair. He was smiling at her, holding a glass of wine and singing, 'O Come All Ye Faithful'.

She yawned. 'Bloody hell! How long have I been asleep?'

'Probably about three quarters of an hour. You were asleep when I came in and I hadn't the heart to wake you up. I know it's been a tough, high-profile case, and I'm proud of what you've done.'

'Oh, that's a nice thing to say.'

'Well, I mean it. There's been a lot of pressure on you leading the investigation. I know you had DCI Oldroyd helping but don't you think that was a bit of a pressure as well? You know, having to be in charge of a famous detective?'

'It's not really like that with him. He's so informal, never pulls rank or makes you feel inferior. He's a brilliant man. We couldn't have solved it without him. I told him so too.' She looked at Peter sipping his wine. 'Pour me a glass, then, and come and sit next to me.' He obliged, they put their glasses on the coffee table and snuggled up to each other.

'What did you learn from the great man?' he asked.

'Oh, things like being prepared to think creatively if you're not making progress, listening to your instincts, and the overall power and importance of experience. He was very flattering about me, actually, but I don't see myself as ever being able to attain his level.'

'Well, who knows? I can certainly see you getting up to his rank. I think you're a good leader and a tough character.'

'Maybe. I'm just glad it's over and we can enjoy Christmas. Which reminds me – I've done virtually no Christmas shopping and there're only days to go.'

'Don't worry about it. We'll go together tomorrow and get it all done. No doubt Paul and Amy will be doing things with their friends.'

'Good. It will be a bit spooky going around those streets. I'm not going down any of those snickelways for a while. I'll be seeing bodies all over the place, never mind sinister figures crouched in the dark shadows.'

Peter laughed. 'I'll keep you on the main streets where it's crowded.'

'Good. I'll need your help. It will have to be the fastest Christmas shop I've ever done.' She looked at him and smiled.

'But I'm going to enjoy it now that I can relax and spend some time with you.'

~

Andy arrived home in Leeds that evening to find Steph resting on the sofa and reading a magazine. The doctor had signed her off until after Christmas.

'Hi, how are you? Can I get you anything? Drink of tea?' he asked as he entered the room.

'No, thanks, I'm fine.' Steph smiled to herself, wondering if Andy would keep this level of attentiveness up for another eight months. And maybe even longer. 'Come here, sit down and talk to me. I haven't seen anyone all day to speak to, though I've had a successful shopping trip in Briggate. I managed to get a few presents in the Corn Exchange too, including a vintage necklace for your mum.'

'Excellent,' said Andy as he sat down heavily. 'Isn't vintage a word for expensive second-hand stuff?' Steph punched him lightly and he put his arm around her, laughing. The last couple of days had been hectic and exhausting. 'My shopping has ground to a halt with what's been going on.'

Steph smiled at him. 'I'm glad to see you home at a reasonable time, not like the other night. No more nocturnal adventures, then?'

Andy had arrived home in the early hours of Thursday morning after he and Oldroyd had completed the arrest of Philip Storey. Things had been very tame by comparison in Harrogate since his return.

'No, I'm glad to say. It's all over, the boss triumphed again. His antennae are amazing; he seems to sense where the answer lies and then the evidence follows. Although he did make a mistake regarding the third murder, which turned out to have been

242

committed by somebody else. He told me on the phone that he jumped to conclusions about all three murders being the work of the same person. It's almost a relief to know that he's fallible.'

'Yes, but that's another of his strengths: he's not arrogant enough to think he can never make a mistake, so he questions himself as much as anyone else.' She sat back and sighed. 'It's nearly Christmas now. Hopefully things will wind down a bit.' She paused and looked at him. 'You know, when you said you had to disarm the murderer who was holding a knife, it made me think – being in danger has a whole new dimension to it when you're about to become a parent.'

'I know. I thought of that at the time. It went through my mind – I could get stabbed here – and then I'd never see my son or daughter.'

'Oh, Andy, that's awful!'

'I know, but we're not going to be the first police officers to have a family, are we? In fact, most of the police people we know have children. We can deal with it.' He took her hand and smiled at her. 'Let's not get gloomy. After Christmas it will be New Year, and what a year it's going to be! I still can't get my head around it.'

'I know. I'm really excited!' said Steph.

'Me too. I've been wondering what this means for career progression – you know, getting promoted to inspector.' Both Andy and Steph had been looking out for inspector jobs in forces accessible from Leeds, but nothing had come up. They didn't want to move out of the area.

'What do you mean?'

'Oh, I don't know. It's going to be a big life change, isn't it? I'm not sure whether I want to start work as an inspector somewhere at the same time as becoming a father.'

She held his hand tighter. 'You're so thoughtful. It's one of the things I love about you. You're a big, hunky bloke and you look like a tough police officer – which you are . . . but you're also soft hearted and tender.'

'Oh, thanks. Especially the hunky bit! But what do you think, about the jobs?'

Steph thought for a moment. 'To be honest, I find it difficult too. Sometimes it seems as if I ought to put everything to one side and concentrate on the pregnancy, but then I think – why? That's just pressure from society making a woman think she can't pursue her career if she's a mother. So, I'm going to go on as normal, and if any jobs come up that I really fancy, I'm going to go for them.'

'Good for you and why not?'

'We're a good team and we'll cope.'

'Of course we will. We'll have a great Christmas. Oh, you won't be able to drink, though, will you?'

'It doesn't bother me as much as it would bother you, Andy. Thank goodness you don't have to go teetotal for another eight months. Actually, it'll be longer because I'll be breastfeeding.'

'You're right, that would be hard! By the way, being in a daze about it all I forgot to ask you: what do your mum and Lisa think?'

'Delighted both of them. Lisa's cool about the issues because she's got two kids of her own already. She says not to worry about anything. Mum wants to cosset me by doing everything for Christmas, but I won't let her.'

Andy smiled. 'That's just like her.'

'Anyway,' said Steph, giving him an arch look, 'what about your mum and the rest of the family?'

Andy slapped his hand on his forehead. 'Oh God! With everything that's been happening, I completely forgot.'

Steph laughed. 'I knew it. What a terrible son you are! You'd better call her now before she finds out from somebody else! Don't leave it to when we go down for New Year because she'll ask you how long you've known and why didn't you tell her straight away.'

'She will, you're right.'

Andy got up and went to look for his phone. Steph had a thoughtful smile on her face. She remembered how she and Andy had met when he first came up to Yorkshire. She was very uncertain about herself in those days, after growing up with an alcoholic father who had abused her mother. Her relationship with Andy had given her stability and confidence. And now they were going to have a family together. For all his faults, overall he was very good – for a man!

~

Henry Marlow's will was read out by his solicitor a few days later. It confirmed that Janice inherited most of his estate, including Marlow Holdings. The only unexpected and curious thing was that Marlow had left a number of artifacts to his cleaner, Melanie Jackson: a small painting, a silver candlestick, silver cutlery, and a few items of jewellery.

Janice was surprised at this generosity, which was atypical of her husband, and she correctly suspected that her husband's cleaner had provided other services besides those related to the cleaning of floors and windows.

Unfortunately, Melanie was unable to fully benefit from this legacy for the simple reason that she had already taken most of the items that Henry had bequeathed her, and they were now scattered around the country.

The police officers who investigated the disappearance of this treasure suspected what might have happened but nothing could be proved. Melanie took open possession of the items that remained and was able to sell them through more legitimate channels for a higher price, much to the chagrin of Craig Jordan.

～

That evening, Janice cooked a meal for Justin. They'd been shopping in the city centre later in the day after hearing the will. And were now having a quiet, romantic meal by candlelight sitting at the table and watching the lights by the river and the traffic going across the bridge.

Justin held up his glass and grinned at Janice. 'Cheers! To us.' They clinked glasses. 'We're going to have a lovely Christmas now that we've sorted things out and been honest with each other. I think it's great that you've been round to that poor family and reassured them that things are going to be better.'

'I know. It wasn't easy. In fact, it was very embarrassing, and I had to be really sincere in what I said to them because they've had very little help from other people and, not surprisingly, they don't trust anybody. I've decided that straight after Christmas I'm going to move them out of that place. There's a vacant property Henry had that is far better.'

'That's great, and you still did it despite it being hard.'

'I did, Justin, but it was because you confronted me with things and made me realise what kind of a person I'd become.'

'Well, you were beginning to work it out for yourself. This casserole is wonderful, by the way.'

'I'm glad you're enjoying it. It's one of my specialties, and this is a special occasion.' They smiled at each other. 'You know, when I'd been to the Braithwaites', I felt so much better afterwards. When I saw their faces after I promised that the flat would be repaired and that their daughter will be safe there, it was so moving I could have cried. I popped back yesterday with a few things and they seemed genuinely pleased to see me. And then I realised: what better to spend your money on than improving life for people who are not as lucky as you?'

Justin reached over and put his hand on hers. 'That's wonderful. And I love you.'

~

In the last days before Christmas, the weather turned colder and the streets of York were covered with a thin dusting of snow. Partly spurred on by the terrible things that had happened to homeless people recently, a big effort was made in the city to make sure that homeless people did not have to be on the streets in such severe conditions. Samantha and some of her friends were admitted to hostel accommodation, which was guaranteed for at least the Christmas period. Lucy was allowed in too.

It was Christmas Eve and a fine day. The weak December sun shone through the leafless branches of the trees outside York Minster as Oldroyd looked up once again at the Great West Window. On a day and an occasion like this, he found it hard to look at this impressive piece of architecture without feeling emotional. Here was the great minster at the centre of the city: the Cathedral and Metropolitical Church of St Peter in York. It was here the boundaries of the three ancient ridings of Yorkshire joined. The magnificent tracery in this window was symbolic of the minster's identity as the Heart of Yorkshire. Inserted in the 1330s by master mason Ivo de Raghton, it had undergone massive restoration, but was no less moving for that.

Oldroyd continued to gaze and to meditate on the wonderful sight. He was here in York for the carol service after many years of absence. His recent time in the Christmassy atmosphere of York had made him want to attend the service again and the others had joined him.

Deborah, Louise and Patrick had gone to do some last-minute shopping. Shortly before four o'clock, they would all enter the packed minster and take their seats. He was looking forward to it.

'Jim? Jim Oldroyd, isn't it?'

The Yorkshire accent was broad. Oldroyd turned to see a man of about his age smiling at him. He had a greying moustache and receding hair and was wearing an overcoat and scarf.

'Good Lord! Sam! Sam Armitage.'

'Aye. It's been a long time, Jim.' The two men shook hands vigorously.

'I haven't seen you since that business with the violins over in Halifax. Do you remember all that?'

'How could I ever forget it? It was one of the most astonishing cases I've ever been involved in. You were brilliant, as ever.'

'Thanks, but it was a team effort. It always is.' Oldroyd had known DCI Sam Armitage for many years, since they started out together as junior detectives in Leeds. Armitage had risen up the ranks at the Halifax station while Oldroyd had moved to Harrogate. But there was something about him today that was different.

'How are you? You seem to have lost weight, Sam. Have you been on a diet?'

Armitage's expression turned serious. 'Aye, Jim, I had no choice. I had a heart attack a couple of years ago. I thought I was going to snuff it. I've had to cut down on the beer and pork pies, you know.' He laughed. Sam's diet had been famously unhealthy.

'Well, you look better for it.'

'I've got rid of all the stress as well. I've retired.'

'Have you now? That's interesting.'

'It was the health scare that pushed me into it, but it's the best thing I ever did, Jim. I feel much more relaxed and in much better health. Thought I'd miss it all, but I don't. Stella and I do a lot of walking around the Calder Valley and I've taken up golf. I didn't realise how unfit I was until I started doing things, but I feel a lot better now.' He looked at Oldroyd. 'Anyway, you look well, if a bit tired. I take it you're still at it?'

'Oh, yes.'

'I expect you're looking forward to having a break at Christmas, then.'

Oldroyd nodded, and explained about the case in York.

'Well,' replied Armitage, 'I can see it's exciting stuff, but it's also a lot of stress and pressure, isn't it? You know, if I were you, I would seriously think about stepping down. You don't realise the effect the work is having on you until you stop. And none of us are getting any younger, Jim.' He looked at his watch. 'Sorry, I'll have to dash off. I'm meeting Stella back at the hotel and I'm already late. We've been staying here in York for a few days – you can do things spontaneously like that when you're retired. It's been great, and we're off back home now. The family are coming round. You should come over to Calderdale, Jim, and we'll do a walk. Nice to see you – and give it some thought, won't you? None of us are indispensable, you know, and we can't go on forever. Have a good Christmas!'

'And you!' replied Oldroyd as he watched Armitage walk away in a sprightly manner over Minster Yard towards High Petergate.

Oldroyd did give it some thought as he continued to gaze up at the minster. It felt like Armitage had popped up out of nowhere with a message for him. Should he be taking heed of it? Was it a warning? He'd discussed retiring with Deborah but had not come to a conclusion about it. She would never force him to do what he didn't want though, and she knew how important the work was to him.

When Patrick, Louise and Deborah arrived at the minster, Oldroyd was still contemplating the building, but he sprang out of his reverie. This was not the time to talk about the issues that Armitage had raised.

'Did you get everything?' he asked.

'Yes,' replied Deborah, looking up at the minster herself. 'Doesn't it look magnificent in this winter sun?'

'Yes, but it's time to go in, I think.'

They entered through the west door and took their seats in the glorious long high nave with its decorated Gothic lierne ceiling. Soon the choir and assorted clerics and dignitaries assembled at the back of the nave. Everything went quiet until the lone, unaccompanied voice of a young member of the choir was heard singing the first verse of 'Once in Royal David's City', the traditional start to the Festival of Nine Lessons and Carols. It was always a very moving moment. As the carol progressed, the choir and the others, including the bishop with his mitre and cope, processed around the nave and took their places by the altar.

Oldroyd had very little religious faith, unlike his sister Alison who was a retired vicar in the Church of England, but he still enjoyed a musical experience like this in a beautiful setting where the glorious sound drifted up into the majestic heights of the nave, as if rising to heaven. It certainly made you think about life and he found himself pondering on what Sam Armitage had said.

Did he want to retire? Should he? Sam had made it sound a very attractive proposition. He would certainly not take up golf, in which he had no interest, but he would welcome the opportunity to do more pottering about in places like this. He could do more walking and spend more time on his other hobbies: bird watching, writing and listening to music. And he and Deborah could go away on holiday whenever they wanted, if she decided to retire too. He knew she would like that.

But deep down he wasn't sure that it was for him, at least not yet. He thought about the case just completed in this very city. Of course it was stressful but it was also exhilarating and fantastically rewarding when you solved the problem, arrested a dangerous person and saved people's lives. What could replace that in terms of satisfaction? Surely it was more than just vanity? More than just getting high on success and victory over the perpetrator?

'Jim.' He looked up to see Deborah beckoning him. Abruptly he stood up for 'O Come All Ye Faithful'. The sound of the choir and the congregation singing together resonated in the nave.

No. While he had the physical energy and the mental agility, he wanted to continue making his contribution; in fact, he felt a duty to do so. He also wanted to stay and help Steph and Andy move forward. He would be very proud if they both became detective inspectors.

He'd once heard a professional footballer say that he'd asked a former player about how to decide when to retire. The older man's answer was, 'You'll know when the time comes.' Oldroyd didn't feel he could say that about himself at the moment. Like Walker, he'd lost none of his enthusiasm for his work and he didn't think he'd lost any of his abilities either.

At the end of the service, the door under the Great West Window was opened and people filed out slowly, gazing back along the whole length of the nave to the fifteenth-century choir screen and its famous carvings of English kings from William the Conqueror to Henry VI. Louise and Patrick went down to have a closer look, as Deborah walked up beside Oldroyd.

'It's breathtaking, isn't it?' she said.

'Absolutely. I think it's my favourite building in the whole world.'

Deborah laughed. 'That doesn't surprise me. It's one of the greatest cathedrals in northern Europe and it's in Yorkshire. It's the perfect candidate for that honour!'

Oldroyd smiled. 'Indeed.' Then he turned away from the minster and rubbed his hands together, his face beaming. 'Anyway, it's Christmas Eve! Hurrah! Let's go and get a drink and something to eat. I'm starving!'

～

The Braithwaites were having a better Christmas than they had expected. Rosie seemed much improved. Janice Marlow had brought an electric heater for the little girl's bedroom, some money to help with the electricity bill, and presents for the children.

Terry wasn't working on Christmas Eve so the family were all together watching *The Snowman* on television. Light snow was falling outside. On the mantelpiece was the card that Sam had made at school. The front had a drawing of an angel with big wings coloured in gold. Inside, Sam had written as neatly as he could:

To Mummy, Daddy and Rosie

Merry Christmas

God Bless Us Every One

ACKNOWLEDGEMENTS

As ever, I would like to thank my family, friends and members of the Otley Writers' Group for their help and support, and the many people around the world who buy my books.

There are a number of ghost tours in York, which is one of the most haunted cities in Britain. They take place all year round, but there is a special spookiness about them in the dark days of December!

The work of the Rowntree Trusts goes on after over one hundred years of investigating poverty in Britain and its causes. Their reports regularly hold governments to account.

As Oldroyd explained to Andy, the term 'snickelway' was invented by Mark Jones in his wonderful book 'A Walk Around the Snickelways of York', 1983. The book became a bestseller and has gone through many editions.

The Heart of Yorkshire tracery in the Great West Window of York Minster is a potent symbol of York as the capital of the county and the place where the ancient ridings of Yorkshire join. Ivo de Raghton's original early fourteenth-century stonework became badly eroded and was replaced by an exact copy in the 1980s. The old stone was laid out in the original pattern and buried under the grass near to the minster.

Did you spot all the references to Dickens' *A Christmas Carol*? The messages in this famous story about caring for the poor and the dangers of worshipping money are as relevant as ever.

If you couldn't stop turning the pages as DCI Jim Oldroyd and his team solved the twisty mystery in York, then you'll absolutely love *The Body in the Dales* by J. R. Ellis.

An unpopular victim. An impossible crime. A murderer on the loose.

A body is discovered deep in a cave beneath the Yorkshire Dales. The deceased is Dave Atkins, well known throughout the village but not well liked. While there is no shortage of suspects, the details of the crime leave DCI Oldroyd and DS Carter stumped. How did Atkins' body end up in such a remote section of the cave? When someone with vital information turns up dead, it becomes clear that whoever is behind the murders will stop at nothing to conceal their tracks.

Oldroyd and his team try to uncover the truth, but every answer unearths a new set of questions. And as secrets and lies are exposed within the close-knit community, the mystery becomes deeper, darker and more complex than the caves below.

Don't miss this incredibly gripping bestselling crime thriller! **Available now or read on for an exclusive extract.**

Prologue

Unless tha's careful on thi ways, Providence Pot will end thi days.

Deep under the Yorkshire Dales, cavers were scrambling along dark passageways. Apart from the eerie echoing of their voices, the only sounds came from water dripping on to their heads and gurgling down the shallow streams. There was the distant roar of an underground river. The dancing lights from their helmets illuminated the rocky walls and cast huge shadows into the heights above them.

They were walking through a strange underground world of rock, mud and slime where the temperature remained at the same chilly level throughout the year and intricate systems of interconnecting tunnels plunged hundreds of feet below the surface. The slow action of water dissolving limestone over thousands of years had sculpted shapes like the cave art of a strange subterranean civilisation: long fingers of stalactites hung from the cavern roofs and stalagmites thrust in opposition from the floor.

The cavers were still only halfway through the system. They were entering a long and fairly straight passage with a shallow stream in the bottom, about twenty feet high with rocky, uneven walls.

The leader called back, 'Easy bit here. We'll stop for a rest soon.'

Echoing replies reached him in his forward position. As he splashed down the tunnel, he calculated the time and distance. Two and a half hours to get here, stop for food, another two and a half hours to get through to the end. It was a big responsibility, leading an inexperienced party like this. So many things could go wrong. People fell and broke limbs and it was hours before Cave Rescue could reach them. Reckless amateurs got lost in the labyrinth of passages and sometimes died of exhaustion and hypothermia.

Suddenly his foot struck something and he tripped forward. His first thought was how stupid *he'd* been to allow himself to get distracted. He'd be the one who broke his ankle, and then they'd all be in serious difficulties. Whatever he'd stumbled against had moved and seemed soft. He looked down to illuminate the object and staggered back in shock. His lamp was shining on to a human head. The body of a man lay across the floor of the passage. Congealed blood covered the matted hair and the skull was smashed at the back. Two facts immediately struck the caver.

First: the dead man was not wearing any caving gear.

Second: he knew who it was.

One

Watch out when striding over th'ill, Especially near to Gaping Ghyll.

Detective Sergeant Andrew Carter would never forget his first day with the Harrogate Division of West Riding Police. It was a sunny day after heavy rains and he arrived early, smartly dressed in an Italian designer suit and his favourite Armani shoes. He was tall with a handsome face and a dazzling smile. He had short blond hair and was powerfully built, with a slight tendency to be overweight.

Carter hesitated outside for a while, fiddling with his tie before finally going through the door. Inside, everything seemed quiet compared to the bustle of the Met. There was a reception desk with a middle-aged female officer, who smiled at him in welcome.

He was filling in a form for his security pass when he heard a voice call out in a strident northern tone.

'Ah, the lad from the Great Smoke!'

Carter turned to see a figure walking purposefully towards him down the corridor. It was a man wearing what looked to Carter like a battered old anorak and heavy boots. He stopped and looked the new boy up and down with grey eyes that were both warm and penetrating.

'Come on, then, no time to lose, do your form-filling later. And we're going over rough ground; I'm afraid that smart suit could get crumpled.' With that, he walked off towards the door, calling back, 'As for those shoes!' He laughed as he disappeared out of the building.

Carter gave the receptionist a bemused look. She laughed too.

'You'd better follow him; that's Chief Inspector Oldroyd. Here, take this.' She handed him a temporary pass. 'Just fill in your name.'

Carter's eyes widened. Detective Chief Inspector Oldroyd was his new boss. Hastily he put the pen down, apologised, stuffed the temporary pass in his pocket and rushed out of the door.

Oldroyd was already starting the engine of a shabby old Saab saloon. Carter got in and they drove off through the gated entrance.

'DCI Oldroyd, lad; pleased to meet you. We'll shake hands later. It's Andrew Carter, isn't it? Do you go by Andy?'

'Yes, sir.'

'Good. Well, Andy, this is going to be a very interesting first case for you. I've just had a call from Inspector Craven from the Skipton station; a body has been found down Jingling Pot.'

'In a pot, sir?'

'A pot *'ole.*'

Carter looked bemused. Oldroyd shook his head. 'Come on, lad, frame thisen.'

'I beg your pardon, sir?'

'Tha's come to t'county o' t'broad acres, so don tha thinking cap and get thisen ackled.'

Carter had a strange feeling of dislocation: was his hearing scrambled or was his new boss a lunatic? He opened his mouth to reply when Oldroyd burst out laughing.

'Sorry, it's my little joke, just a bit of Yorkshire dialect. They call me "Yorkshire" Oldroyd round here but don't worry, people don't speak like that much any more. More's the pity.'

Carter was still confused. 'Right, sir, but, er, what were you saying?'

'Just teasing. The important thing is that the body was discovered in a pothole; that's an underground cave system. That's not a very common occurrence, even round here where there're hundreds of caves. I've got a feeling we might have something unusual on our hands.'

Carter hadn't thought of Yorkshire as a place full of caves. He looked out of the window on to the landscape. After a while, the picturesque countryside around Harrogate, which reminded him of some parts of Surrey or Kent, started to change into something much more unusual. The hedgerows were replaced by rough stone walls that criss-crossed intensely green fields full of cows and sheep. Dotted in the fields were squat rectangular stone buildings. Oldroyd slowed as the road narrowed between walls at either side. Carter saw a sign with the words 'Yorkshire Dales National Park' and a sheep's head.

'This is Wharfedale, Andy, and we're now in the Dales National Park – oops, better slow down.'

A flock of sheep filled the road ahead. A farmer sauntered along behind them and two black-and-white sheepdogs darted backwards and forwards on either side of the flock. Carter thought of Streatham High Road, clogged with traffic throughout the day.

'They can be a nuisance if you're in a hurry but we all love them, really. They keep the landscape looking the way it is.'

The sheep started to disappear through a gate. Oldroyd waved to the farmer as the car sped on past one of the collie dogs, crouched in the road blocking the path of any sheep considering escape.

The road undulated up the fellside and then down.

'I'll slow down here so you can see the view.'

A spectacular landscape spread out before Carter's gaze. Grey stone cottages clustered around a village green. There was an old church by a bridge. In the distance, the landscape looked even wilder. The river was still very swollen after the recent rains and some of the low-lying fields were flooded.

'That's Burnthwaite and Upper Wharfedale in the distance.'

'Not bad that, sir.'

Oldroyd laughed.

'You'd better watch it, lad, or you'll fall in love with it. Alf Wight was hooked the first day he saw this landscape.'

'Alf Wight, sir?'

'James Herriot to you. He lived way over those fells in the town of Thirsk.'

'He wrote those vet books, didn't he?'

'That's right.'

Carter had never spent much time in the countryside and he had a clichéd view of it: just a lot of fields stinking of cow muck and 'local yokels' grunting 'oo-aa' as they downed their cider. But there was something about this that was different, something grand and sweeping in the landscape.

The car went through the village and past two police cars, the first sign that something was happening. After about a mile up a steep road, Carter could see more police cars squashed by the wall, and a van that had 'Wharfedale Cave Rescue' on the side. He noted that the police cars here were Range Rovers, a model more suited to rough terrain than fast pursuits through the city. As they stopped, a police officer came over.

'This is the local inspector, Bob Craven. We pull his leg about this area being called the Craven District.' He opened the window and mimicked an upper-class English accent. 'Ah, Lord Craven of Craven. I hear nasty things are happening in your patch today?'

Craven grinned. He had a large red face and looked like a weather-beaten farmer.

'Hello, Jim, good to see you. You're right there and I'll tell you something, I'll bet even you've never seen one like this; it's a real puzzler.'

'We'd better get out and have a look at it then.'

He introduced Carter and the three men climbed over a stile and walked along a path across the field, Craven looking rather quizzically at Carter's expensive suit and shoes.

'So fill me in then, Bob.'

Craven consulted his notes.

'The victim was male, late thirties; found by the leader of a party of potholers, a Geoffrey Whitaker.'

'A party of what?' asked Carter.

'Potholers are cavers. This lad's from the south, Bob; don't assume anything. Carry on.'

'The body was lying across the passage with the water flowing around it.'

'Couldn't it have been an accident? A fall?'

'Very unlikely, Jim. The deceased wasn't wearing any caving gear and he'd no equipment. The wounds suggest he was hit on the back of the head with something fairly small and sharp, like a hammer. Not the kind of wound you get from a fall.'

'So someone murdered him and dumped the body in the pothole?'

'So it seems, but the point is, the cavers found the body when they were about halfway through. It takes over two hours from either end of the system to reach that point. Why would anybody take a body down so far and then just leave it where the next time anybody passes through they're going to walk straight into it? It doesn't make sense.'

Oldroyd frowned; it was an unlikely scenario.

'But that's not all, Jim. Listen to this. Two of the blokes who went down to help to retrieve the body swear they went through the same place only three days ago and saw nothing.'

'So?'

'But when you see the body I think you'll agree that it's been in the cave much longer than that.'

'I see what you mean. Well,' he rubbed his hands together, 'this sounds like the kind of case I like: plenty to think about. What do you say, Andy?'

Carter had been looking around at the grassy fells rising up; he felt the breeze on his face and saw the white clouds moving across the blue sky. The earth was so firm; it was difficult to believe that beneath their feet was a dark underworld. Now he was thinking fast, eager to make a good impression on his first day.

'I know this sounds obvious, sir, but couldn't he have been murdered down there? Why are we assuming he was killed elsewhere and the body taken down the pot?'

'Pothole,' corrected Oldroyd.

'That's extremely unlikely,' said Craven, consulting his notes again. 'The victim's already been identified as David Atkins of Burnthwaite, apparently a very experienced caver, so the chances of him going so far down a cave system without any equipment are nil, I would say.'

'So that rules out him being murdered on a descent with someone else?'

'I'd say so, yes.'

'But he could have been forced down the cave by somebody at knife point or something and then killed,' continued Carter, 'and he could have had all his gear removed after he was murdered.'

'That's not impossible,' conceded Oldroyd, 'but it's very unlikely. You'd be struggling for a long time, forcing somebody along narrow passages. Then you kill them, then you remove all their climbing gear and carry it all out again. Why bother?'

The path entered a steep and gloomy valley. Carter shook his head. 'No,' he concluded. 'I agree; it doesn't make sense.'

They turned a sharp corner and suddenly Carter could see their destination. About halfway up the fellside was the dark opening of a cave.

'That cave is the entrance to the Jingling Pot system,' said Oldroyd, 'and I see the body. Come on.'

In front of the cave was a collection of boulders of various sizes and piles of scree tumbling down to a stream in the valley bottom. Carter imagined this was normally a lonely place but today a large group of people had gathered at the mouth of the cave, some wearing helmets and waterproof clothing. Attention seemed to be focussed on a stretcher laid on the ground covered with a plastic sheet.

The narrow path drifted up the fellside and Oldroyd walked at a surprising pace, obviously eager to see the evidence for himself. Carter began to see why Oldroyd was wearing his boots. The path was wet and muddy. His shoes were already caked with mud and he kept skidding off the path.

At the mouth of the cave, a group of men dressed in caving gear were sitting on the grass or the rocks looking exhausted. Some had removed their helmets and one was drinking hot tea from a thermos flask.

'I could do with something a bit stronger after that,' he remarked to the others.

'Aye,' a few mumbled in reply. Their faces were filthy with mud, their gear wet and grimy. They looked dazed.

Two police constables were standing by the stretcher and Craven went over to them.

'OK, you've met Chief Inspector Oldroyd before and this is Detective Sergeant Carter.'

The constables nodded and acknowledged Oldroyd with a brief 'Sir'.

'Let's have a look then,' said Oldroyd. He put on plastic gloves and gave a pair to Carter, then pulled back the sheet covering the stretcher.

The body of a medium-sized but powerfully built man with dark hair and beard was revealed. He was dressed only in a blood-splattered T-shirt, jeans and trainers. His skull had been crushed at the back and his hair was clotted with a blackened mass of blood. The wetness was the most striking thing about the body. Everything, from the head to the clothes, was damp and when Oldroyd touched the skin it had an unusual texture. It was not icy but clammy. In many ways it was like bodies dragged out of lakes and yet not quite. It had not been cleaned by submersion in water, but was as grimy and muddy as the Cave Rescue men who'd brought it out. Oldroyd covered it up again and frowned.

'Found two hours into a cave system in jeans and T-shirt and he's been down there a while if I'm not mistaken. Any more ideas, Andy?'

Carter was perplexed. Just my luck, he thought, to come up against a case like this on my first day. The whole thing was bizarre. He decided rightly that there was no point trying to pretend to the chief inspector. 'I don't know, sir; it's right outside my experience. We don't have caves and potholes in London.'

'Come on then, you'll have to use your imagination. Anyway, don't bodies occasionally turn up in the sewer systems down there?'

'I'm sure they do, sir, but I haven't seen one.'

'No.' Oldroyd's brief and distracted reply seemed more to himself. He looked down at the stretcher again and shook his head. There was a pause as all three men went quiet, reflecting on the puzzle.

Craven went over to the rescuers; Oldroyd and Carter followed. 'Thanks for your help. We couldn't have done this so quickly without you. A bit of a nasty job though. Who's been leading?'

'That's me. Williams, Alan Williams,' one of the group replied, wiping drops of tea from his grimy beard, 'and you're right; we're used to bringing people out on stretchers and sometimes they're dead, but not murdered. But it's only to be expected, Inspector; these caves are always likely to spring a nasty surprise on you.'

He turned to look at the black mouth of the entrance and his face took on an expression of reverence. 'They've been feared for centuries, well before they were explored. People thought there were creatures from hell down there; if you went too far in you'd be caught in their lair and never get out again.' He looked down at the body. 'If you don't show respect, well . . .'

It all sounded a bit fanciful to Carter and he dived in rather recklessly.

'What do you mean exactly? He was killed by the cave itself? By a goblin or something? What're you talking about?'

Williams shot Carter a hostile look, taking in his accent and dress. 'No, I mean that, where these caves are concerned, death is never far away if you're not careful. What's happened here is weird, but weird things happen down there.'

Carter still had no idea what the man was talking about but decided not to pursue it.

'I don't know how those two found it all.' Williams gestured to two of the group who looked more exhausted than the others. One was carrying a case that looked as if it contained photographic equipment. 'They're used to bodies but not the caves.'

'Those are the crime scene officers who went down with the cavers,' Craven informed Oldroyd. 'As you can imagine, it's a highly unusual crime scene.'

'Even so, it's a pity we couldn't see the body where it was found,' said Oldroyd, 'though I appreciate the difficulties.'

'Impossible to seal off the scene, Jim; you couldn't be sure that there aren't any other cavers around who could interfere with things. We couldn't leave any officers down there; they'd get exposure if they stayed too long.'

'I understand. I assume you got plenty of pictures?' He addressed this to the CSI with the camera.

'Yes, sir. Good job I had a powerful flash. It's pitch black down there. There was really nothing except a dark muddy passage with a stream passing through.'

'Did you search around thoroughly?'

'Yes, sir,' replied the other officer. 'There was just mud and stones. The only thing we found was this.'

He produced a plastic bag containing a small hooked piece of metal, rusty and ancient-looking.

'Good man,' said Oldroyd, examining the find. Carter looked on curiously.

'What do you think it is, sir?'

Oldroyd twisted and turned the object around.

'I don't know; maybe we'd better ask these gentlemen.'

Oldroyd walked back over to the cavers, now in conversation with each other.

'Sorry to interrupt. I'm Detective Chief Inspector Oldroyd and I'm in charge of the investigation. Any of you know what this might be? It was found at the crime scene.'

Williams took the bag and they all examined it closely. They shook their heads and he handed it back.

'It looks like a hook or something.'

'Is it anything you would use?'

'No. All of our stuff is made of steel or alloy. This looks like a piece of old iron, a bit primitive.'

Carter looked very sceptically at the bit of metal. 'I can't see how this is relevant, sir.'

'Bits of metal don't generally find their way deep into cave systems without a reason. This isn't just a piece of litter.' Oldroyd continued to look at it closely.

'Inspector?'

Oldroyd and Carter turned to see that the Cave Rescue team were on their feet.

'Is it all right if we go now?' asked Williams.

'Have a word with Inspector Craven; he's organised the recovery and he'll be taking statements.'

'We all knew him, you know.' Williams pointed to the stretcher.

'Yes, I understand he's a local man; must be a shock to you all. Did he have any enemies?'

Williams grunted and frowned. 'His death's a shock but no great surprise. Dave Atkins wasn't exactly popular.'

The two detectives were instantly on the alert.

'Why was that?' asked Carter.

'He was what my dad would have called a dead wrong 'un. Always up to something dodgy to make money and messin' about with other people's wives and girlfriends,' said another of the rescue team.

'I see.'

'I don't think you'd have to look far to find people who had a motive for doing him in.'

'Was it you then?' Oldroyd was suddenly direct and serious. The caver looked taken aback, until Oldroyd smiled.

'Don't worry, I've no evidence against you – yet,' he added with another smile. 'It sounds like we might have ourselves a lot of suspects.'

Another of the team called out, 'He was an absolute bastard.'

'I get the message,' said Oldroyd, 'but wasn't he one of you lot? I mean, a caver?'

'Yes, he was in the Wharfedale Club but he wasn't in the rescue team. He wouldn't put himself out for anybody else even if they were trapped down a system,' replied Williams.

'Not everyone who's in the club is also in the rescue team then?'

'No, but most are. We think it right that we should use our skill and knowledge to save other people's lives, even if they are a bunch of idiots who go down without the proper equipment and get lost. Like I said, people who don't show respect to these ancient caves.'

'Very noble.'

'Atkins just laughed at the idea, of course; thought we were the idiots. He would have just left them to die.'

'Ironic that he ended up dead down there himself then.'

Williams shook his head. 'Did I hear you say he's been down there a while?'

'Well, I'm not sure, we'll have to wait for forensics, but from my experience I would say he must have been down there for several days at least.'

'You see, Chief Inspector, that doesn't make sense.'

'Why?'

Williams glanced at his companion.

'Today is Monday. We went through this system following the same route on Friday, wasn't it?' The other caver nodded.

'So I understand from Inspector Craven. And you didn't see anything?'

'No, there was no body in Sump Passage at that point, I can assure you.'

'Are you absolutely certain about that?' Carter was fed up with all this 'mystery of the caves' stuff. 'I understand there are lots of holes and passages down there, so how can you be sure that you were in the same one?'

It was immediately obvious that Carter had said the wrong thing again. For the second time Williams's bearded face looked with contempt at the young detective.

'Look . . . officer, we know these systems better than anyone else. Jingling Pot is a pretty straightforward one. We know where we were – Sump Passage – and I'm telling you, there was no body.' He stabbed his finger at Carter to emphasise the point.

'Why is it called Sump Passage?'

'You've never been down a cave system, have you?'

'No,' admitted Carter.

'The sump is the name for the deepest part of the system where water collects. Am I right?' Oldroyd joined the conversation.

'Yes,' replied the caver. 'Sump Passage is right at the bottom of the Jingling Pot system, one of the reasons why the stream in the passage constantly flows strongly. At the end of the passage, the stream goes off down a fairly narrow hole into an underground lake and there's no way through.'

'How do you know?'

'It's been explored with diving equipment.'

'Diving?' said Carter. 'You mean people go underwater down there?'

'Yes.'

'That must be very dangerous.'

'Yes, underwater and completely dark. We've lost a lot of cavers in the flooded systems.'

Carter was struggling to make sense of this and he wasn't sure how relevant it was, but Oldroyd was listening intently.

'So no passages have been found out of the lake?' he asked.

'Only small ones, not large enough for anyone to get through. That lake has been well explored and it's a dead end.'

'What about the route through the system?'

'After Sump Passage it starts to go up again; fairly easy route until you come out at Mossy Bottom Cave.'

'So you're absolutely sure you were in that, er, Sump Passage three days ago and there was no body?' Carter still sounded sceptical.

'Yes.'

Oldroyd was looking thoughtful.

'Are there any other ways to get into that system?' he asked.

'Only one. There's a branch on the Wether Ridge Hole system that comes into Jingling Pot before Sump Passage, but that won't help you. It takes just as long to get to Sump Passage if you go that way.'

'And no other routes?'

'No. Jingling Pot's a well-known system and it's been thoroughly explored in the last fifty years. We would know if there were any other ways to get down there.'

'Was there anything different about Sump Passage today from when you went through on Friday – apart from the body, of course?'

'Nothing apart from a bit of a rock fall, but they're happening all the time.'

'So there were some rocks and stones in the passage today which you didn't see on Friday?'

'Yes, but nothing major.'

Oldroyd drifted off into a reverie for a few moments, then he turned to Williams again.

'Is there anyone around here who you'd say was an expert in the history of caving? You know, someone who might know just a bit more about the systems and how they've been explored over the years?'

Williams bridled a little at the implication.

'You could try Simon Hardiman up at the hall. He's quite well up on things like that, but I'm telling you, Chief Inspector, there are no other ways into that system and Simon won't be able to tell you about any.'

'I'm sure you're right, but we have to explore all the possibilities, of course. When you say "hall" do you mean Garthwaite Hall?'

'That's right, him and his wife run an outdoor-pursuits centre there.'

'I know it, and I know someone else who may be able to help too.' He turned to Carter. 'Come on, we can't do any more here now. We'll have to wait for the forensics report to confirm what I think. Let's go back to Burnthwaite and I'll buy you a spot of lunch at the Red Horse.

ABOUT THE AUTHOR

John R. Ellis has lived in Yorkshire for most of his life and has spent many years exploring Yorkshire's diverse landscapes, history, language and communities. He recently retired after a career in teaching, mostly in further education in the Leeds area. In addition to the Yorkshire Murder Mystery series, he writes poetry, ghost stories and biography. He has completed a screenplay about the last years of the poet Edward Thomas and a work of faction about the extraordinary life of his Irish mother-in-law. He is currently working (slowly!) on his memoirs of growing up in a working-class area of Huddersfield in the 1950s and 1960s.

Follow the Author on Amazon

If you enjoyed this book, follow J. R. Ellis on Amazon to be notified when the author releases a new book!
To do this, please follow these instructions:

Desktop:

1) Search for the author's name on Amazon or in the Amazon App.
2) Click on the author's name to arrive on their Amazon page.
3) Click the 'Follow' button.

Mobile and Tablet:

1) Search for the author's name on Amazon or in the Amazon App.
2) Click on one of the author's books.
3) Click on the author's name to arrive on their Amazon page.
4) Click the 'Follow' button.

Kindle eReader and Kindle App:

If you enjoyed this book on a Kindle eReader or in the Kindle App, you will find the author 'Follow' button after the last page.

Printed in Dunstable, United Kingdom